THE
DARK
WATER

ALSO BY SETH FISHMAN

The Well's End

SETH FISHMAN

THE DARK WATER

G. P. PUTNAM'S SONS

AN IMPRINT OF PENGUIN GROUP (USA)

G. P. PUTNAM'S SONS
Published by the Penguin Group
Penguin Group (USA) LLC
375 Hudson Street
New York, NY 10014

USA | Canada | UK | Ireland | Australia
New Zealand | India | South Africa | China
penguin.com
A Penguin Random House Company

Library of Congress Cataloging-in-Publication Data is availible upon request.
Printed in the United States of America.
ISBN 978-0-399-15991-6
1 3 5 7 9 10 8 6 4 2
Text set in Warnock Pro.
The publisher does not have any control over and does not assume
any responsibility for third-party websites or their content.

Weston, one day I hope to write something else for you, but that doesn't change the fact that you are on every page of this book.

THE
DARK
WATER

1

THE WATER FEELS THICK, SILKY ALONG MY SKIN. I TREAD easily, the way a bird might fly, lazily pushing down against the current. Even with Odessa's ski jacket on, the water's welcoming. It's buoyant and warm and massages me softly.

Rob and Jo float nearby, and every few moments one of their hands brushes against mine as we tread, like we need to remind one another that we're really here. I open my mouth to let some water in and swallow, tasting copper, like the earth, like our blood. My body shivers, craving more.

We've been in the water for a while now. Ten minutes maybe. We haven't said a thing. It's so quiet, like we're drifting in a vacuum. The shore isn't so far away, but I'm reluctant to move. I think I could stay here for days.

The basin we swim in is large, about the size of the lake that borders my prep school. I can't believe that only two days ago I swam across that lake—under three inches of ice—and nearly froze to death. That feels like a lifetime ago now, though not a good lifetime. This place is something new and impossible and it makes everything I've ever seen or believed seem smaller. On the shore, some hundred yards away, there's a haze of light, as if the ground itself is glowing. There are trees, plants, a full vibrant green forest leaning as far over the water as possible, as if the water itself were the sun. I peek above me, and can only see black. The darkness is complete and presses down on us. There's no ceiling, no stalactites dripping over our heads. No stars twinkling through the haze.

Then there are the gates. Giant, beautiful, unreal. They jut from the foliage like Roman ruins. They must be two hundred feet high, suspended between massive gold pillars, the opening in a wall that I can now see stretches off in either direction and curves away from us, seemingly endless. The gates are open, beckoning, and between them are hulking shapes I can't make out, the light is so weak here. A city, maybe? What else could it be? My mind is having a hard time processing the shapes, the gates, the endless room. It's just too unreal, this whole thing. But what my mind believes doesn't really matter because right now the light from the gates *is* real, and it shines brighter than the brightest building in my hometown of Fenton, Colorado, or the world.

"What is this place?" Rob says, finally breaking the quiet. A small part of me was enjoying that silence, that pause we were having. His voice floats along the water and disappears. It awakes the memory of why we're here, of the lunatic we're running from.

"I'm not sure," I say, looking at my two best friends. They're watching me, trusting. And why not? I guess I'm the one who brought them here. They actually dove into the well, following me, risking their lives on a hunch of mine that we should swim down and down and down through the water; now we've ended up floating in this underground cavern. I sort of can't believe how amazing they are, how lucky I am to have them.

"How did you know what to do?" Jo asks. "You knew we'd show up here?"

I shake my head and picture the map, the wall of stone covered in paintings that my dad found all those years ago, with its vibrant colors and images and hints. The diving figure, the flowing well, the gates. "Not here specifically. Somewhere, yes. There were a few clues on the map."

"What, clues to get *here*?" Jo replies.

"Remember that pale-skinned figure on the map? The one that was upside down and near the well?"

Jo laughs incredulously. "You jumped into the well because of *that*?"

I make a face. "We're here, aren't we?"

"You realize that we swam down, right?" Rob points at the blackness above. "When you swim deeper into water, you shouldn't break the surface. This isn't natural."

I look once more at the endless space above us, like a vacuum of light.

"Yeah, this shouldn't be possible," I reply. We were being chased by Sutton and his men, running through the Cave and now I don't know if we're better off at all, or if we can even get back. "Come on," I say, and begin swimming toward the shore. The winter gear I wear is bulkier than the drag suit I have to use in practice, but I'm soon far ahead of the others. I can't help but swim fast, years of training refuse to go to waste. So it's me who steps on the shore first, lifesaving water gushing from my pockets and squishing out of my boots. There's no sand, only a very fine moss that carpets the earth. I kneel and rub my hand gently on the surface, and it's so soft I almost want to take off my boots and go barefoot.

"I wish Odessa were here," Rob says, splashing up from the water and grabbing at an overhanging leaf. It's wide and thick, like a giant piece of iceberg lettuce. Almost as pale too. "She'd know what all this plant life was." I try not to think of how Odessa and Jimmy might be captured already. Prep school townies, they escaped Westbrook with us, and now they're stuck back in the Cave with soldiers-for-hire. Maybe they stand a chance; they're fully grown adults now that they've contracted the virus and it's aged them some. Weird how just one drop of water was enough to kill the virus in them. One drop was enough to halt their premature aging, saving them from dementia and a wrinkled death, like what happened to our teachers. To Jo's dad. Weird to think that there's probably enough water in this lake to eradicate all illness in the world.

"I doubt anyone would know the plant life down here," Jo says, taking off her jacket to wring it out. The nylon doesn't make it easy, but she has the right idea. My jacket weighs a waterlogged ton.

I remember the story Dad told us about finding the well as a student some thirty-four years ago, spelunking on a class excursion. He tripped into the water, the same water that we just dove through, and he found out that it that heals everything it touches.

"Do we get to name everything we see?" Rob asks, wiping his face. His jet-black hair is plastered to his forehead, as if he gelled it to look that way. He blinks water away from his eyelashes, then pulls out his Warbys from an inner pocket and tries to put them on. Of course, with the water coursing through his body, his vision is perfect now and he doesn't need them. He gives a goofish smile and puts them away.

We all stop and look into the underbrush. There's a hum to the air, and the branches sway; something, maybe a bird, flits. I'm suddenly aware of the sound of nature, as if I hadn't been hearing it before. Rustling underbrush, quiet chirps. A bug flies slowly by, its butterfly wings familiar but its cicada-like body an odd fit. There's an entire ecosystem deep in the earth, one that's never been seen before. It's thick and impenetrable, like a rain forest, dense enough that standing here below the trees makes it difficult to see the wall and the gates.

"Check this out," Jo calls, squatting near the base of a tree. She's tied up her hair already, looking at ease even in her scrubs. It's like she's back in our dorm, pointing out some mistake on my calculus homework. If my dad had died two days ago, I'd be a mess. She's not even fidgeting her fingers the way she does when she's nervous or distracted. I know she has to be feeling it, that she's purposefully pushing it away, but I don't see it at all. Man, she's impressive.

She's hovering by a patch of tall flowers with long, shivering petals, their stems no thicker than a millimeter each. Almost like spaghetti, like tiny Medusa heads. The petals are white, incredibly white, enough so that they actually shine. Looking around, farther into the trees, I can make out another dozen clumps, some flowers even dangling like vines from the branches, illuminating the woods. They make their own sun down here.

Jo reaches out and gently plucks one from the ground, and immediately the remaining flowers in the patch go dark, shockingly fast, as if hurt. But the one Jo holds keeps its light. On a hunch, I squeeze my wet hair and put my moist fingertip to the broken stem she's holding, and as the flower shines brighter, I can't help but smile. I'm suddenly ridiculously grateful for these flowers and the light they bring. How awful it would have been to arrive here completely blind.

"What now?" Jo says, waving her flower around her head in fascination. She's gone a few days without makeup, and she looks like a softer version of herself. Her lips are a pale pink and fade into her skin, her eyes still intensely blue, but without mascara, they seem more dominant.

They both look at me like I've got the answer. Sure, the map gave me clues, but I wouldn't have had the guts to jump into the well if not for Sutton and his men chasing me. They're probably up there right now, searching for us. My stomach churns, thinking of Brayden, how he might be there with them. What if he had found me, if he'd looked me right in the eyes and then shouted for Sutton? I don't like the feeling, the churning, because it betrays me as much as he betrayed us. Brayden, new to Westbrook, the boy who escaped with us, who helped us. Brayden, with his scarred chin and his sly smile. I blink away the thought. He's back in the Cave, helping Sutton get his supply of the lifesaving water. I wonder if they'll leave Dad alone when they catch him. Does Sutton hate my father that much, to hurt him even now? Will he care enough to try to contain the outbreak at Westbrook, to distribute water to all of my classmates and heal them if it isn't already too late? Does that fall into his game plan at all? He doesn't know them. He doesn't care about them. I think of the party where I met Brayden, how everyone there's probably dead. I remember the infirmary, where the first infected went. Where our teachers died, their bodies piled on top of one another, their hair turned gray, their faces so wrinkled they were hard to recognize.

I bite my lip and pull my jacket closer, and I realize I'm not cold. The water keeps me warm as my blood paces through my body. I pull my own flower and it shines enough so that I can see through the webbing of my fingers.

I take a breath. They're waiting for me. Even if I don't have the answer, it still falls on me. "I saw the well in the map, and I've seen the gates there too—"

"Look," Rob shouts, interrupting me to point down the shore. My instinct is to jump back into the water, where I'm safe and confident I can outswim anything, but I force myself to get a grip and follow his finger. There's a lump of something out of place on the beach, something blue and familiar.

My stomach sinks, knowing what I'm seeing before my mind does. I hurry over, maybe twenty, thirty yards, and realize halfway there that those are scrubs, like the ones we're wearing. The only person I can think of who could have had those on and made it here is my dad. I pick them up, as if I might find him underneath, maybe a smaller version of himself—maybe the water shrunk him, maybe I'm going crazy. The shirt is wet from the lake, but it's also stained red, a smear of blood.

"Whoa," Rob says. I flare up inside. *Whoa* doesn't really cut it. Apparently, my dad came before us, and now he's gone. Hurt too. I can't see any blood on the beach, though. What exactly happened here? Did he know about this place all along? Why didn't he tell us? Why didn't he tell me?

I look toward the gates, wondering whether I can see him, whether he's only a few hundred yards ahead of us, limping in pain. But he's not there. The forest has broken, and there's a clear path from the lake to the gates, which are gaping and bright, but no naked Dad. Tall shadows loom beyond the gates, like burnt-out skyscrapers. I don't know what Dad's doing here, but I know where he's gone. If we hurry, maybe we can catch him.

"We should go back," Jo says.

"What?" I have to stop myself from shouting. "You're kidding, right?"

She's taken a few steps toward the lake, and stares out over its black surface. "We should wait a halfhour for Sutton and his men to clear the room, and then dive back down and swim wherever the hell we need to go to get back out." She turns and looks at us. "We have to save Fenton, and Odessa and Jimmy and Todd and my mother and Rob's family and everyone, if we can." I fight down a sense of panic. I never expected this from Jo.

"What about the map?" Rob says, digging into his pocket. "It's a gigantic golden gate, Jo. We can't *not* go check it out."

"Forget the gates, what about my dad?" I say, still incredulous, holding up the bloodstained shirt for them to see.

"There's no blood on the ground, Mia," Jo says, trying to sound soothing. "That's an old stain."

I rub my fingers against the fabric, unsure.

Rob, meanwhile, pulls out his OtterBoxed phone and starts messing with it.

"You won't get a signal here," I say, clenching my teeth.

"Duh," he replies in a way that I know doesn't mean any harm.

To Rob, everyone's a step behind. He flicks his screen a few times and then holds it up for us to see, his face smug. I remember now, in the Map Room, when he was taking pictures. His obsessiveness pays dividends, because he's holding up an image of the map. Even from here, on the tiny screen, I can see the painted gates. He points to them. "The gates are here, so all these other things must come after." He waves at the remaining images: a city, a waterfall, a cup, a prone figure in white, a spear-like thing sticking right through another pale figure, the strange objects we'd have to decipher if we don't turn back. I can't help but notice that he's at 23 percent power.

"The well. This lake. Dad clearly figured out the map like I did, so he's probably just following the clues. The same ones that led us here."

"To what?" Rob asks. "I mean, I understand that this place is crazy. It's a miracle. Yay. But there's a virus outbreak and you were in the Cave. Why would he come here right now, especially if he knew Sutton was about to break in?"

"I don't know," I say uncertainly. "But he wouldn't come here for no reason."

"That's not good enough, Mia," Jo says, insistent. "We *have* to go back."

I can't believe this. I know she's mourning her father, but that doesn't mean we should abandon mine. "You know I can't do that. He's my dad." I hold up his scrubs and wave them at her. "Why'd he strip? What if he's really hurt?"

She turns to me, her face anguished. "Don't you think I know that, Mia? Of course I do. I want to find your dad too, but you aren't looking at the big picture." She pauses, gathers herself. I can see

9

how hard this is for her, and an ounce of my disbelief fades. "The virus broke out two days ago. It's already infected our friends. We know that the quarantine didn't work. That the virus managed to infect soldiers in *hazmat suits*. It's spreading, Mia. And the only thing that can stop it is this water." She rubs her thumb and forefinger together, still slick from our swim. "Even if this place is like Narnia, even if there's a magical talking bird that spits water from its mouth and teaches you the secrets of the universe, we don't have time. We have to get back and figure out a way to get past Sutton and bring the water to Westbrook and Fenton. If we don't, the whole town dies. Maybe more."

"Jimmy and Odessa can handle him." Even as I say the words, I know I don't believe them at all.

"Are you serious? Jimmy and Odessa? They'll stop Sutton all by themselves?" she asks, eyebrows raised. "Mia, do the math. Every second we're here, the greater the odds that we won't have a home to go back to. Not only that, you said yourself Mr. Kish came here on purpose. He came here for a reason, *without you*. He knows what he's doing and he knows how to get back. The town doesn't have the luxury of seventeen years of planning."

We're quiet, all of us. Breathing deeply. My skin tingles I'm so angry. I'm angry because she's right. Dad came on purpose. He's fine, with or without clothes.

Rob seems to agree; after a moment, he looks at me apologetically and I've lost. "She's right, Mia."

His parents live in Fenton too, and he must be just as concerned for their safety, but it doesn't make his siding with Jo sting any less.

I take a shuddering breath. "I mean, what's down here? What's

10

he walking into?" I say out loud, but Rob and Jo have the sense not to answer. *He'll come back, of course he will.* I stare at the giant wall spreading out before me, and feel sorry for myself. Until I see something move.

"Mia, I'm sorry," Jo says, but I cut her off, grabbing her arm and squeezing hard.

"What's that?"

There's something bobbing up ahead—many somethings—coming through the gates. Rob puts a hand over his eyes, as if to shade them from an imaginary sun.

"There are six of them," he says.

"Six of what?" I reply.

"Mia, we should go," Jo pleads.

Suddenly, the shapes become tall pale figures moving at incredible speed. I remember the images from the map. The white characters, the brilliant blue eyes. I take a step backward, my foot sloshing in the water. They're only fifty feet away, and it may be a trick of the light from the gates, but their eyes seem enormous, too big to be real. They each have something in their hands, knives or spears or something.

"Oh shit, hurry," I shout, and turn to the water. The others follow and we dive in. The skiwear is problematic, but I don't want to waste any time shrugging it off. I buzz across the surface, letting my adrenaline push me. I hear sounds, one two three six splashes behind us as they follow us into the water. I swim possessed, the water guiding me, until suddenly I'm there. I can *feel* a suction below me, as if there were a drain. I stop, look around for my friends, but I'm alone.

"Rob, Jo!" I shout, treading water.

"Mia, go!" This from Jo, who I can see now, being dragged out of the water. I couldn't tell how tall they were before, but her captor's gotta be seven feet. Rob's there too, held by another one. I feel the tingling beneath me. I could get away. I *should.* Jo's right, I need to save Fenton.

But then I hear it, too late. A swish in the water. I spin around and he's there, eyes like softballs, blinking wet and curious in front of me. I scream, and don't stop until he's dragged me all the way back to shore.

2

THEY TIE OUR HANDS WITH ROPE, LOOPING THE ENDS together and then around our waists so that we're connected, and we're forced to walk single file. They're giants, my head only reaching their chests, and they walk on either side of us, sometimes staring at us but not saying a word.

After I was dragged out of the water, thrown together with Rob and Jo in a pile on the shore, I finally got a good look at them. They're human, I think. Some sort of long-divergent relation. Their bodies are built the same as ours, with their disproportionately enormous eyes and stature the noticeable difference. Their eyes probably adapted for the dark long ago. I wonder if they can see the end of the blackness above our heads. These beings are unreal, but then no figment of my imagination has ever picked me up like a rag doll and tossed me onto shore.

"I guess we're not going home," Rob says.

A part of me is relieved. Now I can find my dad. The rest of me is in shock.

"Do not speak, little one," says the guard at my shoulder, looking back at Rob.

"You know English?" I blurt out, unable to help myself. The

guard lifts a hand as if to strike me but a different guard shouts him down in another language, his voice so sharp it echoes.

This guard has high cheekbones and curious eyes. He reaches out his hand and I flinch, but he tsks at me and uses the sleeve of his shirt to wipe the water of the lake from my face, like my dad used to do at the pool when I was young. "I am only trying to be of assistance," he says, his voice softer than the other one's, almost bashful. "I have never seen one of you. A Topsider. He should not have threatened you." The fabric is cashmere-soft and form-fitting. They all wear the same thing, this red long-sleeve shirt that hugs the body and tight pants. They look like they're ready for a slumber party. My guard has short black hair that curls tight on his head, like a Roman emperor. On the bridge of his nose there's a smear of paint, also red.

I have to bite my tongue, afraid to speak but now filled to the brim with questions. How'd they know we'd be here, especially if they've never seen one of us before? They're calling us Topsiders, they've given us a name. They know *of* us but they haven't *seen* us.

Turns out that the gates are kind of far away, which means I totally miscalculated the size of these things. They're as tall as skyscrapers, and as we approach them, I have to crane my neck to get a better look. There's an odd buzz in the air and it takes me a second to realize that it's coming from the gigantic columns the gates are hinged to. As if they're plugged in somewhere.

"Stop there, friends." The voice isn't from one of our guards. Another pale man, dressed in the same tight-fitting night wear— except his sleeves are bright yellow and his pants and the chest of his shirt are blue—stands by one of the columns. His arms are crossed and his pale head is shaved. Across his face, covering his eyes, is a band of blue paint. I wonder if the paint indicates rank. Jo shoots me a look. Something's going on here.

"What is this, Keeper Straoc?" my guard asks, hand reaching up to take hold of the thin spear he has strapped to his back.

"I am to take the Topsiders from you."

My guard shakes his massive head, his ringlets shivering. He says something in their native tongue and the bald new guy, Straoc, interrupts. "No, keep to the Topsider language. I want them to know what you are ordered to do, so that they might better understand who are their friends."

My guard glances our way, and when he continues, it's back in their hesitant English.

"It matters not, because we were instructed by Keeper Arcos to search for other Topsiders and to escort them to the Lock. We have searched and we have found. They will join the other, they will stand and be judged."

That was English, maybe, but I understood almost none of what he said. Either way, it didn't sound good.

Straoc looks me up and down, then smiles, flashing brilliant white teeth, as polished as a movie star's. "Of course, friend, but it is from Keeper Randt himself that I have orders to take these. We must separate the Topsiders. They cannot be kept in the same place."

My guard hesitates. He looks to his friends for help. One of them shrugs.

"Friend Keepers," says Straoc, "I will not have Randt waiting. Thank you for your service and please return to your normal duties."

"We cannot," my guard says, almost apologetically. "Our Keeper Arcos tasks us to bring them to him."

"Do I mishear you?" Straoc replies, in mock confusion. "I believe you were tasked to escort them to the Lock. Now you say Keeper Arcos asks for them himself?"

My guard stays quiet, chastised.

"Arcos and Randt rule the city now," Straoc says, speaking confidently. "Keeper Randt requests the Topsiders and will send them to the Lock in due time where Arcos may have his personal interview, so leave them and go back to your side of Capian, where you and Arcos belong." Straoc pulls a long yellow ribbon from his belt and lets it drop, hanging from his hand like a whip. The guards surrounding us immediately draw their weapons and tighten their grips on our arms. Jo even squeaks in pain. I can hear the creak of leather against skin. This guy's either crazy or that ribbon isn't used to decorate birthday presents.

No one moves for several moments. I hear the sounds of rustling in the forest, of birdcall. Finally, my guard clears his throat. "You make idle threats," he says, openly reluctant. "There are six of us. You cannot take the Topsiders."

Straoc sways the ribbon back and forth. What is that thing that they're so scared of? He smiles, a strangely gracious smile. "It is not you, friend, or your men that I would worry on. I have my own orders, and if I cannot take them to my Keeper Randt, then neither shall you."

"Did he just say he'll kill us if they don't let us go?" Rob asks.

No one answers. My guard rocks forward and back. Another dips his fingers into a small pouch at his belt and leaves them there, like he's ready to pull something out and throw it.

"I don't want to die here," Jo says, her voice soft but carrying.

"My clan leader does not want you to either, Topsider," my guard says, and apparently this means he's given in, because hands release weapons, fingers slip out of pouches. "Keeper Straoc, take them as you will. Keeper Arcos will be looking forward to seeing them placed in the Lock soonest."

"Of course," Straoc agrees.

The guards separate from us and hurry through the gates at a sprint, their long legs moving them ridiculously fast. The nearby columns hum and we're left alone, still bound, with the new guy who just threatened to kill us.

"I am sorry about the confrontation. Keeper Arcos and my Keeper Randt have not been entirely friendly of late. And I am sorry for the rope." Straoc smiles sadly. "But until I take you to Keeper Randt's tower, it would do well for you to have the appearance of having been captured."

I catch Rob frowning at what he just said. There's clearly something bad going on between the leaders of these people. Why would we need to only "appear" to be captured?

He moves toward Jo, and I can see that it's taking all her willpower not to pull away. He's not just a strange man approaching her, he's a *strange* man. He doesn't touch her, but it's clear that he's checking out every inch of her body—it makes me feel sick just watching. He walks in a circle and finally crouches, looking at her feet.

"Leave her alone," I say, trying to make my voice as intimidating as possible. I strain in my bindings, as if I could stop him.

He stands in a hurry, hands up in apology. "I am very, very sorry. It is just that I have never seen a Topsider before. So delicate. You do not have the water, and yet you somehow survive. You are different from me, but the same." He pokes Rob's arm, and Rob flinches. "I am interested in how you are so small. I just wanted to see. I do not mean any harm."

"Who are you?" Jo says, scrambling back as far away from him as physically possible, which, with the rope, isn't very far.

"I am Straoc, a friend. And you are lucky I was ordered to come. You would be otherwise on your way to the Lock. Nothing good would come of it."

"Right," Jo says. "And we're lucky we're not dead now either."

"Yes, that is true," he replies earnestly. My skin crawls.

"Is that where my dad is, the Lock?"

He raises an eyebrow. "Dad? Yes, the Topsider who came earlier." Straoc whistles. "He is your father?"

"Yeah, is he okay? Is he hurt?" My mind flashes to the blood on Dad's scrubs.

"He is perfectly healthy at the moment."

"What do you mean, 'at the moment'?" I say, panic rising in my throat. It's like talking to a puzzle.

"I am sorry—did I say that wrong?" Straoc asks, "We believe we know your language, but without a Topsider to teach us, it is hard to be sure. You have a father, and he is alive and well at this exact moment. Come now, we must go." He pulls on the rope, forcing us ahead. I let myself get pulled, almost exhausted with relief. The blood must have come from something else. He's okay.

We move quietly, each mulling our own fate, moving closer to the towering columns and gate.

"Look at that," Rob says, talking half to me, half to himself. He's pointing at a massive hinge—six feet high, just the hinge. The gate is completely open and lined with long, cylindrical bars that reach to the sky. They're on such a scale that Straoc seems puny. Where are the lumbering giants who built this?

"It's moving," Rob says, his voice unsure.

"What do you mean?" I ask. Straoc gives me some slack on the rope, apparently carrying an insatiable curiosity regarding his new prisoners and how they'll react to his world. "I don't see that."

"Feel this," he says, placing my hand on the giant hinge.

"Is this gold?" I ask Straoc, trying to imagine its value. Gold is, what, twelve hundred an *ounce*? This hinge alone must be worth a few million dollars.

Straoc doesn't say anything. He's looking beyond the gates now. Scanning the horizon.

"Isn't gold too soft to be functional?" Rob asks.

"Shh," Jo says. "Mia, you have to *feel* it."

I try to shove Fort Knox from my mind and focus. I close my eyes and almost instantly I know Jo's right. There's a tug, a very gentle tug, like the sway of a boat on a still lake. The gates aren't just moving.

"That's why the water stops," I say, alarmed. "They're closing."

"Of course they are, little Mia," Straoc says over his shoulder. I don't like that he uses my name so familiarly. "It is the cycle, though the water will always run on this side of the gates after they close. The source provides. Now we must hurry onward. I would like to allow you more time to discover us, but I cannot wait any longer."

"When do the gates close?" Jo asks.

"Ten days," I say grimly. Ten days is how long my dad said the water flowed. Then the gates will shut, and cut off the water. Cut off our way back.

"Days, Mia," Straoc says, taking the rope in his hand and pulling us along. "We do not have those down here."

3

JIMMY

JIMMY WAKES THIRSTY. HE SLAPS HIS HAND AGAINST the dresser, trying to find a cup of water, but nothing's there. He always keeps a cup of water near the bed; the dorms at Westbrook are just so damn dry and he isn't about to get a humidifier for the room; he'd never live it down.

It's dark, Jimmy can barely see a thing, but he can see enough to know this isn't his dorm room. He's dazed. Where is he? Not at home either. He's on a couch, must have fallen asleep. But there's someone here, snuggled up behind him. Jimmy blinks, and remembers.

"Odessa," he whispers, and she wiggles a little, down for the count too. Jimmy cranes his neck backward to look at her, but it's too dark.

"Odessa," he says again, louder this time.

"What?" she says groggily.

"I feel weird." It's true, he realizes. He *does* feel weird. He tries to move his arm and it's clumsy, as if it's not fully listening to him. He takes a breath, and even that feels strange, the air sifting into his lungs in an unfamiliar way.

"That's because you're an old man, remember?" Her lips are

near his neck, and her breath is warm and comforting. Her arms give a reassuring squeeze around his waist; they feel good.

The squeeze releases the last gasps of his selective amnesia. He remembers it all. He had the virus, the one that's killing everyone. The one that ages you to death, wrinkles you up and takes you down. But Jimmy had it for just a short while, so that he only aged up into an adult, not a decrepit old man. Odessa's joking about that. He's older looking, sure, but fit as can be. He wiggles his arm and it buzzes with a familiar pain; the arm's just asleep. Jimmy's still finding it hard to remember that his big body is now even bigger. He takes another breath, deeper this time, and lets the air settle in his lungs.

"Not sure I'm gonna get used to this."

"What about me?" Odessa replies, fully awake now. There's an undertone of a grin in her voice. "I'm, like, thirty-two. Guys just get sexy. Me, I'm already going downhill."

Jimmy rolls over to face Odessa. She's definitely aged, but even in the dark he can tell she looks amazing. Her freckles, something he had teased her about just a few days ago, feel new and exciting. Her chin has sharpened, her eyes too. Her curly red hair floats around her in the dark like seaweed, but Jimmy loves that.

He touches her cheek. "I don't think so. I think you look better than ever."

He hears her smile as much as he sees it. And then he hears something else. A *crack*, muffled. Then another. Like a string of Black Cats going off.

"What's that?" Odessa whispers.

Jimmy sits up, bringing her with him. "You hear that?" he asks the others. But no one says anything. "Guys?" he says, speaking louder.

It's too dark to know, but he knows. His stomach sinks. They left him and Odessa. They're out there right now, and they left him. Jimmy hops up and runs to the wall, tripping over a chair. He gets to the light, and in the brief moment before he flips the switch, he wonders if he shouldn't. If he should crawl over to the couch and snuggle up with Odessa and forget everything.

There's another *crack*. Jimmy flinches, turns the light on, and reality sticks. He's in the rec room, a bomb-shelter lookalike that is really just part of the Cave, Mia's dad's fortress that he and his Westbrook alumni friends built in order to protect and research the water. Odessa's still on the couch, but she's got deer eyes at the noise. There are four sleeping bags, empty on the floor. Mia, Jo, Rob, Brayden.

"Where'd they go?" Odessa asks. "Why didn't they wake us?"

Jimmy's not sure he wants to know, but they've come this far, thanks to Mia, and if she's out there and those are gunshots, then she might need help.

"Come on," Jimmy says, slipping on his fluffy booties, the ones Mr. Kish gave him to replace his winter boots. He feels ridiculous.

Odessa opens her mouth to argue, but thinks better of it. She's changed in more ways than her looks since they left Westbrook, Jimmy realizes. Normally she'd be sulking right now, or hiding in a closet. Now her eyes are set and she's tying back her hair. Maybe getting shot in the leg will do that to you.

"You do realize those are gunshots, right?" she asks, joining him at the door.

"Yeah," he replies unhappily.

She stands on her tiptoes and kisses him lightly, with his dry lips, bad breath, and all. He's so surprised he forgets to kiss back. It's over in a second, broken by another gunshot, but it happened.

"What was that for?" Jimmy asks, distracted in the best of ways.

She shrugs. "I like that you care about them." She frowns. "What are we gonna do?"

"I have no idea," he replies, and opens the door.

The hallways are empty, just like earlier, but this time it reminds Jimmy of an abandoned spaceship, one Kirk might run through before self-destructing the *Enterprise*. Jimmy doesn't remember where anything is; that was always Mia or Brayden's job. And he's not about to look to Odessa for help—she's awful with directions.

There's a short but sustained push of gunfire, but the sound echoes from either direction and doesn't help guide them at all. So he just runs, pausing near corners, checking open doors, seriously considering calling out for help but not wanting to draw the wrong kind of attention.

They turn a corner and see a T junction up ahead. Maybe fifty yards away. And then someone in scrubs like theirs runs by, from the left to the right, disappearing as fast as they materialized.

Odessa yelps, as much from surprise as fear, and Jimmy doesn't blame her. He almost did the same.

"Who was that?"

"I didn't see," he confesses, but he pulls Odessa along after the fleeing figure. That someone was in scrubs, so she or he wasn't one of Sutton's men. Good enough for Jimmy.

They hit the intersection and turn, but after another twenty yards or so there's already another junction. A maze. Jimmy stops and listens.

He hears footsteps, clomping fast, up and to the left. But he hears something else too. Very faint, coming from the walls, the floors, everywhere. Creeping into his skin.

Miaaaaaa. Miaaaaaaaaaaaaaa.

"What the fuck?" Odessa says, squeezing his hand.

"Come on!"

They keep running, and Jimmy catches a glimpse of someone up ahead, but then whoever it is takes a turn and is gone. No more footsteps, nothing. There are doors on either side, just like in most of the hallways. He assumes they're locked. Maybe from the inside.

"Hey," he ventures, risking a semiloud voice. "It's Jimmy and Odessa. We need your help!"

Nothing.

"Please—we don't know where we are."

A door on the right pops open, and a woman pokes her head out, looking both ways. Her dark hair is in a frayed bun and her pale skin is somehow paler, like she's just got out of a frigid lake. It's Veronica, one of the Westbrook alumni who run the Cave. She always seemed to be Mr. Kish's number two. She helped Odessa, fed her some of the last of their special life-water. She was poised and calm and sure of herself. But now there's nothing in her twitchy, red-rimmed eyes that inspires the least bit of confidence.

"I thought you were them," she says, and she hops back into the hallway and takes off running. Jimmy and Odessa hurry after her, sprinting through the gray halls. He hears the thunking of footsteps somewhere far away. Jimmy hates not knowing what's going on.

And then Veronica stops so quickly that she slides past the door she wants. She enters a code into a keypad and motions them in.

It's a control room. Monitors everywhere. On one of them there's a tank, an actual real-life cannon-wielding tank, aiming at the Cave doors. It's not firing, though. And there are some soldiers in hazmat suits, but they're facing the other way, toward the road, where Jimmy can see three sheriff cars have pulled up, men standing behind their doors, talking, waving. The deputy who gave him a ticket for riding his bike on the sidewalk. Prick. Guess the secret's out. Fenton knows about the quarantine by now. Jimmy's veins freeze. Maybe it's spread farther. Maybe his parents are sick.

"What's going on?" Jimmy asks. Veronica has tossed herself into a seat and is flipping through channels like his roomie on a rainy day.

"I'm not sure," she says. "But it isn't good."

"Where is everyone?"

"Don't know. Don't know anything."

She stops at a still image of an open vault, the map shining bright in the center of its domed room. Chuck, the other Westbrook alum, lying on the floor. Veronica curses, but keeps going. "Where are you where are you where are you?"

Then she pauses again, at a feed from the greenhouses, where Jimmy and the others had snuck in. The back entrance to the Cave. The door's open. How'd that happen? The greenhouses filled with hybrid creations are a tattered mess of broken glass and steam. Odessa—the botanist—lets out a moan. She, more than he, understands exactly what's being lost. Veronica keeps flipping, slower now, almost resigned, like she knows what's coming.

Maybe she does.

There's Sutton and a group of heavily armed men, crouch-running with their rifles up. They must've entered the Cave through the back door, even though Mia blew up the Aqueduct to try to stop them. Jimmy tries to imagine a bucket brigade of soldiers in hazmat suits passing rocks down the hill until they've cleared enough space to enter the tunnels. On the monitor, they've hit the elevator doors to the well. Veronica patches in another monitor, simultaneously showing the cavern where the well is. There's Mia, Rob, Jo. They're standing on the catwalk, yelling at one another, their mouths moving even if their voices don't come through.

"Run! He's almost there!" Jimmy shouts at the screen.

"They can't hear you," Veronica says.

"But can't you speak to them through the loudspeakers or something? Like you did to us back at the greenhouses?" Odessa asks.

Veronica flips a switch, but before she gets a chance to speak, Mia jumps. It's as if the switch was for Mia, as if Veronica just made her do it. Mia *dives* into the well. Rob and Jo look at each other and then do it too, one after the other, disappearing below the surface. It's only when the water settles that Jimmy realizes there's *actually water in the well,* while before, it was empty, and that whole story Mia's dad had told them about the water coming every seventeen years was really real. The virus is real, the water is real. Jimmy's an adult now. Everything's real.

"She can't do that. That's impossible," Veronica says, shaking her head at the screen.

"What just happened?" Odessa murmurs.

Veronica flips the switch again, turning off the intercom. Just in time, because there's a flash, blinding the screen, and soon after, Sutton's there, at the water, with his guys. He makes a motion and they fan out, running to search all the nooks and crannies in the Cave—fat luck there. A number of other soldiers hurry to activate the pumps and suck water into the fifty-five-gallon blue plastic barrels Mr. Kish had set up for storing the water. Sutton bends over and takes a mouthful of the water. Jimmy can see him relax as he sits down and drinks more. He motions to someone. Odessa grabs Jimmy's arm and squeezes, like they're watching a thriller, like she can't bear to see what's coming next.

Brayden steps forward. There's no one else in the room, the other soldiers are out of the frame, searching the small tunnels nearby. Brayden, the new kid Jimmy finally got around to liking. He's shaking his head, he's saying no to something.

"Turn on the sound," Jimmy says.

Veronica looks at him, then back at the screen. "Okay, but no talking. They'll hear us."

She flips the switch.

. . . no way.

That's the deal we made.

It's so strange hearing their voices in surround sound.

You want me to jump into the well? Are you insane?

Sutton draws his gun and holds it out to his side, the threat clear.

Fine, say I don't drown. Then what? What am I even looking for?

Greg always called it the source, so it's probably a stream or brook or whatever—I don't know. But I bet you my life your friends

28

are already there. I bet you Greg told them where to go. Find them, they'll lead you to it.

But why do you even care? What could be more "special" than this? Brayden kicks the water with his foot.

Jimmy wonders the same. Why not just be happy with the water? It *heals* people. What more is Sutton looking for?

You think I wanted all this death, you think I wanted to create the virus? Not at all. I saw a way to take the water to the next level, to make it do more than just heal an injury or the flu. I wanted it to keep on healing, to make the body immune to everything.

You mean make you immortal?

Of course, immortal. The virus is just the other side of the coin. It is death, and I want to find life. If the crap that Greg's been babbling about for years turns out to be true and there really is something down there, something I can use to make the water make me . . . Just find Kish's daughter and tag along with them. Got it?

Watching, Jimmy feels a rage building inside him that's hard to fathom. He's felt something like this at football games, before storming the field or after taking a big hit. He's felt it the one time he got in a fight, when he almost killed Trent Bishop for calling him a townie. He feels it building from his gut and pushing through his skin, making his gum up and his ears burn. And when Brayden speaks next, it's just too much for him.

Okay, whatever. Just . . . just this is it. After this, I'm done.

"Brayden!" Jimmy screams, his voice a roar, something unfamiliar and animal, his aged vocal cords tearing up his throat. On the screen, the two figures freeze, then look around. Sutton picks up his gun and aims it at the elevator.

"Brayden, you fucking traitor. I'm going to rip your face off. Do you hear me? Do you *hear me?*" He's screaming so hard he's spitting. Veronica slams down the switch and pushes Jimmy back against the wall. For an instant, she's about to get punched. But then Odessa's there, calming him down, taking his arm. He breathes, big gulps of air, so angry he's blind. So angry he hurts.

"You idiot!" Veronica says. No need to explain why. On the screen, Brayden disappears into the water. And Sutton's men return. He points at the camera, right at them, and then his men rush offscreen.

"I'm going to kill him," Jimmy says.

"Yeah," Veronica replies. "We heard."

"Hey, it's not his fault," Odessa chimes in. She looks at Jimmy, her forehead wrinkled in concern. "That guy was our friend."

"No one's your friend," Veronica says. She takes a deep breath. "Okay, the front is guarded by a tank, but the back looks clear for now. You need to get out of here. Get to safety."

Jimmy shakes his head. "I'm not leaving them."

Veronica points at the screen. "Do you see that guy? He created a *virus.* You think he'd suffer any compunction about shooting you in the head?"

"Jimmy," Odessa says quietly, "maybe she's right. If we can get out of here, we can help people. We can save our families. My little sister. She doesn't know anything about anything. We can't let her die."

Jimmy thinks about it. "But if we don't stop Sutton from taking over this place, then we're no good to anyone. Not our family, not our friends." He turns to Veronica. "You don't have any guns, do you?"

She shakes her head. "Just lots of syringes."

"Do you have anything? Anything that can stop them?"

"You really should go. With these cameras, I can guide you safely out of here. Listen to Odessa."

Jimmy's face is set in stone. "I did. I'm sorry, Dess, but this comes first. We need the water to help people, which means we need to stop Sutton." He turns back to Veronica. "Now, again, *think,* what can we use? What do you have?"

Veronica takes a deep breath and seems to steel herself. Suddenly she looks more like the woman they saw yesterday, the one who could handle herself. Handle anything.

She takes a walkie-talkie off a wall charger and hands it to Jimmy. "Okay, you two—go. Sutton knows this place, he heard you, so he'll come here first. That should take another two or three minutes. Enough time to get moving."

"But where are we going? What's the plan?" Odessa says.

"You asked what we have if not guns," Veronica says, opening the door for them and motioning them out. Odessa moves reluctantly, not sure she's ready to leave the relative safety of the room. "You asked me to think?"

"Yeah . . ." Jimmy replies, wary.

"I'll tell you what we have. We have monkeys."

4

THE GATES ARE SO LARGE THAT IT TAKES A GOOD TEN minutes of walking to get past their wide arms. The trees behind us have faded away into a soft glow, but there's another light coming up ahead, down a slope. The moss has given way to a road, paved in flat smooth stones, black and white at regular intervals, like a flowing chessboard.

Below us, spread out in stunning beauty, a city opens like a sunrise. Tall buildings, towers and spheres and geometrically pleasing triangles jut high into view, filling the air with spires. I can make out balconies, large windows, rooftop terraces with gardens and trees. Big and small birds fly across the streets, their wings shimmering softly. It seems as if every inch of space has been accounted for, jammed together. The city's bursting at the seams. It's unlike anything I've ever seen.

"This is incredible," I say, unable to help myself.

"This is Capian, my home. Your cities are like this, yes?" Straoc asks.

"New York, maybe," Rob says. "But not really. Nothing like this."

"Not many of us venture to the gates, as they are usually closed," Straoc says, taking it all in. "Not many of us ever see how beautiful it is from this same perspective, how perfect." He pauses, takes a breath. "But soon that will change."

I think of the lake behind us, the portal back to the Cave. It sounds to me like Straoc's planning on bringing up some friends soon. Not sure that's a good thing.

"How many people live here?" Jo asks, rubbing at her wrists. The rope's burning my skin too.

"Several tens of thousands," Straoc replies, pride in his voice.

"What's that?" Rob says, pointing with his bound hands beyond the city. Capian sits in more of a bowl than a valley, a crater almost, with the massive wall snug against the surrounding hill, like a crown. It's divided in half by a wide boulevard, the only open space in the entire city. At the far end of the boulevard, above the city, is a mountain, lit brightly by the shine of the buildings below. It shoots straight up, as steep as one of the towers, but is jagged and glistening, shimmering in the light.

Straoc grunts. "That is the source, young Rob. You will not be going there. Only the Three can enter." He tugs the rope, and we start to descend toward the city, down stairs built into the rock. I'm buzzing off of what he just said, about a source. There *is* somewhere special here, somewhere the water originates. Dad will have figured that out before he came. I'm sure that's why he's here. He wants whatever the source is.

I'm so distracted I almost trip, taking the others with me. We move slowly, and far below us I can make out the shapes of the Keepers who captured us, just arriving into the city streets.

"But who are the Three and why do they get to go?" Rob presses.

"The Three are the oldest of us, our forefathers. Who were granted the source and who guide us. They are the true Keepers."

Suddenly this place makes more sense to me. These people are guardians of the water. Maybe that's why we're tied up; we were breaking and entering. Considering that Dad is probably here to steal some of whatever the source is, they're not exactly out of order.

"So where did they take Mr. Kish?" Rob asks.

"Mr. Kish?"

"My dad," I clarify.

"Your father, he was taken to the Lock. We do not have many problems here, nor many places to put those problems. The Lock is where they go."

"Why aren't we going with him?" I say, helplessness beginning to overwhelm me. "Why can't I see my dad?"

"You will, I am sure," Straoc assures us. "But Keeper Randt asks to see you first. He asked to see your father first too, but I did not get to him in time. Keeper Arcos and Keeper Randt have been at odds for some time now; it is deliberate that they rushed to find him. You will see him later."

"Wait, how did you know we were here?" Jo asks.

"Keeper Randt could see you, the water showed him." Straoc replies, as if it were the most natural thing in the world.

"What do you mean?" I say. Suddenly I'm hyperaware of my wet hair. How can the water spy on us? What's going on?

"You are not of the Three, so you cannot fully understand. But those granted the source can see through the water. They can do many things." Straoc makes an impatient noise. "It matters none for now. Randt will explain and we must hurry to him."

"So we're following you while Dad's stuck in a holding cell?" I ask. The stairs are starting to tire me out. They're steep enough to give me vertigo if I look straight down, so I stare at the city. It's distracting enough, anyway. Like walking into a dream. Or falling down the rabbit hole.

"Why should we follow you? Why should we do anything?" Jo asks, pausing on the stairs, looking defiant. Her mouth is set in a thin line and my heart leaps in pride just seeing that. Ever since her dad died of rapid aging caused by the virus, I've felt like Jo's needed me to prop her up. She's shown flashes, but rarely her real self, and it's almost like this place is dragging her back, forcing her to deal with reality. To be the alpha chick I've always looked up to. "You stared down those other guys. Why not just let us go, then? If you want to help us so much, take us back home."

In front of us, Straoc slows, his body lumbering a step or two more before it can be fully controlled. He tilts his head and I see the pupils in his huge eyes opening and closing, as if he were zooming in and out. There's a dismissive curl to his lip. A tightening of the jaw. "You do not understand yourself, or the world you have stepped into, young Jo." He speaks with a heavy weight, a threat rumbling in his throat. Straoc suddenly embodies the full seven-foot frame he possesses, his pale skin and eyes and voice so starkly unfamiliar and daunting that I try to take a step backward, only I can't move because he's gripping the rope too tight. "We are not sitting idly waiting for your arrival. We are our own people, and one of our leaders, one of the Three, has been killed just this past night. The minds of the Keepers tremble in anger and *you* walk in. Never has a life been taken so, her heart cut out from her chest, and at the exact same moment as the gates open and the water flows and you arrive. Do you not see? My sisters and brothers believe you are connected to the death of a Keeper!"

Jo shakes her head. "But that means that you holding us here is putting us in danger. You can still let us go!"

Straoc tsks. "Maybe if I had gotten to you first, I could have let you go. I want to know the Topside. Maybe this cycle I will get to see your sun. Yes, I am a friend. The source only told Arcos and Randt that Topsiders had come, not how many, and now that you have been seen by my brethren, all has changed. If I do not present you to Keeper Randt, as I promised, I will myself be taken. They believe you were connected with the assassination of our sister. They will believe I helped you escape."

"But we *didn't* kill anyone," Rob complains. "We didn't cut out some Keeper's heart. We just got here."

"No," Straoc agrees, the corners of his lips twitching upward into a smile. "No, you did not kill one of the Three. This I know. I know for many reasons. How could you? But the others will ask how it is that one of our most cherished leaders was assassinated on the very day Topsiders appear for the first time ever. Dead by no weapon a Keeper would use. The others will believe you know."

My mind's running through the facts. We're in this crazy secret underground world, with a clearly intelligent society, standing beyond a lake filled with magic healing water and looking out over the most beautiful city I have ever seen and instead of being able to marvel, we're being set up like scapegoats for the offing of some Keeper woman we know nothing about. Rob's dazed, but Jo looks like she's about to make a run for it, rope be damned. I wonder if we could make it if Rob weren't here. Jo and I are fit; swimming and diving might be different sports, but we both have trained nonstop. An image flashes through my mind of Rob tripping immediately, sending us bounding down the steps, one over the other and back to Straoc's feet. We don't seem to have many options.

Straoc gives a gentle tug on the rope, pulling my arms forward. "Come now, do not be afraid. You may be safe yet. Let us see what Keeper Randt says. He is also of the Three, a very powerful Keeper. The source will show him the truth in your mind."

Jo's tensing, but I can't help thinking of Dad, of how he's down there and alone. I don't know the politics of this place, but what Straoc claims about protecting us seems to ring true enough. He *did* save us from those guards, who already know about my dad and had him imprisoned. I don't get how he knew we had arrived, but it's good he did. If this Randt guy is one of the two most important Keepers in Capian, then maybe he's our only hope of getting out of here with Dad. Maybe it's my only chance. I begin to walk, the rope tightening around my wrists, tightening around Jo's too, forcing both my friends to follow, and we trudge reluctantly into the outskirts of the city.

Quickly, something becomes apparent: no one's around. The stairs exit right into the same wide boulevard we saw above that cuts Capian in two, a street lined with high buildings running straight through the city to the mountain on the far side. A mini-aqueduct stands about chest-high in the center, made of stone and filled with running water that sounds like a forest stream. Straoc moves us fast—but there's so much to see, so much to wonder about, that it's hard not to want to yank on the rope and ask for a moment. There are lilies and tall mossy trees that hang over the boulevard. I swear I see a white cat sitting in an alley, but it doesn't move and soon we're past it. Glowflowers are everywhere, placed on the walls to provide a hazy light, but spaced evenly along the boulevard are also these enormous torches flickering on tall iron rods.

"How do they keep those going?" Jo asks about the rods, despite herself.

"Gas," Rob responds quickly, and looks to Straoc for support, who nods, apparently impressed. Rob sniffs the air. I do too, but don't smell anything. "See how the flame burns clean? How it doesn't end in black puffs of smoke? That probably means natural gas, and refined too."

"What do you mean, 'refined'?" I say. "We harvest the water from them, they sneak up and steal natural gas from us?"

"We do not steal anything from you. Not at all. We have all the resources we need. The water and the earth provide. Do you not have these?" Straoc says, pointing at the lamps.

"We do," Rob replies, "but not much anymore. We have electricity now."

"Ah, yes," Straoc says, spreading his arms wide. "The Three have long decreed a ban. The water is connected, and we are to the water. Electricity is dangerous." His voice turns defensive, prideful. "Still, Keeper Randt tells us that we have many other things that you find Topside, like gastrains and gardens and medicine and stores to cut hair." He wipes his hand on his bald head proudly. I look around; there's no sign of any of this stuff.

"Why don't you come up top?" I imagine this uneasily—thousands of Straoc-like men and women streaming through Fenton, buying Slurpees at 7-Eleven, skiing on the weekend.

"It is forbidden," Straoc says, his voice soft. "And we are here, behind these walls, *keeping* ourselves forever. But as I said, that might change soon." We stay quiet, waiting for him to say more, but he doesn't, and keeps us moving at a steady pace through the city. He turns, from time to time, down other roads; Straoc always unerring, the roads always empty.

"This place feels fake," Rob says. "Where's the wind? Why isn't anyone in the streets?"

"Maybe they're Morlocks," Jo suggests.

"That's a me joke," Rob says.

As we keep walking, a few other details become clear. The gas lamps are everywhere, and on most buildings we can see glow-flowers set into the walls like shining tattoos layered into the skin of the stone. Balconies and windows are extremely high up, and with none of the usual signs of life you might see, like curtains or chairs or laundry. Only buildings with two stories or fewer have noticeable entrances. The big ones, the towers, have no doors or windows or any other means of access below thirty or forty feet.

There are side streets, and along each street is what might be a drainage ditch, maybe three feet wide, filled with flowing water.

"Straoc," I call out, but he doesn't stop. "Is this the same water that's in the lake?"

He looks over his shoulder. "What other type of water is there?"

"What about the source?" I ask, unable to help myself. If Dad's here for it, he'd want to know.

"I have not seen the source. Only Randt and Arcos, now, have drunk of it." He pauses, hesitant, as if he's about to speak blasphemy. "I do not know what the difference is."

"What does that mean?" I ask, wondering again what Dad thinks he's getting into here. What does he know that he hasn't told us already?

"Keeper Randt, Keeper Arcos, they can do things we cannot." He's reverent now, speaking of his leader.

I try to go through a list of what I already know: it helps you see things, maybe the future, it helps with languages. What else?

"Check this out," Jo says, pointing up ahead. We're reaching an intersection that reminds me of a roundabout, except that in the center of the circle there's a stairway down. A fountain is positioned over the stairwell, a single round structure that rises about fifteen feet in the air, and the water drips over its edge into three pools that fill the roundabout.

"That is where we are going," Straoc says, moving ahead.

"There's an underground to the underground?" Rob asks.

"I do not understand why there is a difference," Straoc says, pointing down the dark entranceway and past the cool air that's siphoning up off the stairs. "We are underground both ways."

As we descend, I think back to the Cave, which my father built and the other Westbrook alums funded. All of those tunnels, created entirely to research the water, constructed in the hope that the water would come back again. It's crazy that they poured millions of dollars and years of their lives into speculation about the water that's just lying around in this world. This tunnel would put my Dad & Co. to shame; compared to down here, the Cave seems like it was built by a toddler in a sandpit. This tunnel's wide, maybe twenty feet across, and has something like track lighting made of small gas flames on both the floor and ceiling. The walls are polished and look like travertine, Dad's favorite, alternating, like the road, between white and black, and the floor is tiled in onyx inlaid with long, looping designs of gold and silver. I see Rob scuff his boot at the gold in curiosity, then glance up at me with an *oops* after he leaves a mark.

The walkway splits. Down one of the hallways I can make out some Keepers strolling along a series of stalls that run the length of my view, like a grand bazaar. It's grandly illuminated and full of voices and sounds. It's the first sign of real *life* here. As if aboveground were just for show.

I see clothing on display, dangling on lines, in the brightest of colors. There are several dozen pale men and women here, hawking or scrutinizing merchandise, and when we pass, they stop and stare. The women are almost as tall as the men, thinner, willowy. Their eyes are smaller, but similarly strange. Both men and women wear dresses or pants or sleeveless toga-like garb. They have sandals and shoes that remind me of Sperrys—trendy boater shoes lots of the richies at Westbrook wore. Everyone has different hair, braided or dyed, short or long. There are necklaces and ear-rings and once, I swear, I see a nose ring. I might as well be walking down a street in Turkey or India or Germany or East Timor. It's oddly comforting to feel the familiarity, even if I've only seen those places on TV.

"This is all part of the Exchange," Straoc says, motioning toward that pathway. It's hard to ignore the frowns and the palpable tension of our presence. "And that was the garment district. You will find food and engineering and plants and game and medicine and all things in other districts farther along the Exchange."

A couple Keepers break off from the crowd, and I realize that I don't know how to gauge their age. Everyone seems to look the same. These two might as well be twins: both female, both with high cheekbones and black hair parted in the middle, both in pearly white tops with black skirts that splay wide around them. Their eyes are sharp and angry. I take an instinctive step back.

One of them pulls a long piece of red silk from out of a pouch she carries and waves it languidly back and forth before me. The same sort of ribbon that Straoc whipped out earlier. The other spits on the ground and says something to Rob in their native tongue, something quick and nasty.

Straoc snaps right back at them, then points to the ribbon. The Keeper reluctantly puts it away but then gets right up in Rob's face, her smile wide and vicious.

"Hey, hey," he says, putting his hands up. "I didn't do anything."

"Word of your descent spreads quickly. You are here, and Keeper Feileen is gone."

"I didn't have anything to do with that."

The woman's slender hands shake and her lip trembles. It takes me a second to realize she's crying, her eyes filling with tears. "We spend cycles dreaming of meeting our first Topsider," she says in a harsh whisper, breathing raggedly through a stuffed nose. "And Keeper Feileen warned us. She said you were nothing but rot. That we should never go Topside. That we exist to stop you from coming here. We are Keepers." She wipes her tears from her face and her friend pulls her back by the arm. "You come, she dies. You come, and my clan leader's heart is ripped from her chest."

Rob opens his mouth but doesn't say anything. What is there to say?

"And you," she wheels on Straoc, who doesn't bat an eye. "Tell your Keeper Randt that we will maintain our place at the Three."

"Yes," says the twin, "Randt and Arcos cannot divide Capian in two. Clan Feileen will not have it."

"Please," Straoc says reassuringly. "Your clan cannot but be a member of the Three, yes? But to expect me to share your message after you threaten my charges? Absurd."

"We know you, Straoc. We speak and Randt hears."

She controls herself, runs her hands over her face and through her hair. Her cheeks are flushed and I can see how painful it is for her, thinking of her dead leader. Death here hits hard. If they really think we had something to do with it, for sure they must hate us.

The twins loop arms and leave, looking back over their shoulders, their faces full of hate. I realize that no one is moving. All of the other Keepers in sight are watching, faces set in stone. Word *did* travel fast. I wonder if Feileen told her followers we'd come. Could the source tell her that?

"What just happened?" Jo asks. "And that ribbon she had?"

Straoc doesn't speak until they're gone, and it's only then that I see one of his hands tight on the hilt of a dagger at his belt. He looks at Jo and smiles reassuringly. "Nothing at all, friend. But do not touch those 'ribbons,' as you call them. They are very sharp. Remember, not everyone is happy you are here. Please, hurry with me. We must be on time."

He keeps quiet after that and so do we. It just feels safer. The Keepers around us continue to stare and those enormous eyes bore into us with every step. I lower my head and follow Straoc's feet, and we go for a while until we hit a platform that curves gently around a corner.

"A subway?" Rob asks.

"A gastrain," Straoc replies. "And we only barely arrived for it." In front of us is a silver pod shaped like a football with a gaping door that opens as we near. Inside, things get tight, but there's a bench that's just big enough for all of us. I realize, as Straoc slides the door into place, that I've never ridden a subway before. I wonder how close this will feel to New York. I bet Brayden knows. We sit and stare and Straoc closes his enormous eyes and leans his head back. Resting, he seems gigantic, and I'm struck with a sense of helplessness. I want to say something, I want to be in control, but that's not possible and a growing sense of claustrophobia finally locks in. I try to control my breathing, but even the exercises I've learned over the years swimming don't help. Straoc's relaxed pose is in such contradiction to my fear, exhilaration and exhaustion that I finally get how reliant we are on him; if he wanted,

44

we'd never leave this city, or even this little box again. He's got our lives completely in his hands.

We begin to move, but there are no bounces, no jolts, just momentum. Maybe two minutes later, even that fades. Jo takes my hand and I close my eyes but am still here, stuck. "What is this thing?" Rob asks, rapping his knuckles on the wall. There's no *clang*, it's too thick.

Straoc smiles, pleased again to show off. "It's a wheel, built flat underneath the city. This gastrain is one of many around Capian, all attached to the wheel at different junctions, all sitting on top of it."

"So what, it spins in a circle and every gastrain in the city has to move at the same time because they are all attached to the same wheel?" Rob asks. "I guess if they have a strict schedule . . ."

"They do," Straoc assures us. "There is no need to wait as we know when the wheel turns."

"Like a record player," I find myself saying, the idea somehow helping me feel better. "This is like having a record player underneath the city and little cars glued to the record and they all go around when the player's turned on."

"It's also a clock, too," Rob adds. "No sun, regular intervals."

"I do not know exactly what you mean, but I am eager to find your gastrain record player Topside when I can." I feel a tug, and we've stopped. Straoc opens the door, his thick muscles bulging, and looks back at us. "This is the tower of Randt of the Three, a ruler here in Capian. Behave, and we will all see Topside soon enough."

5

BEYOND THE GASTRAIN, DOWN A FEW STEPS, I SEE A door, circular and sparkling, covered in jewels the size of tennis balls. Diamonds, emeralds, rubies, sapphires are the easy ones to pick out. Opals and amethyst, and more and more, each one big enough to adorn Queen Elizabeth's crown. It feels like there's a pattern here, and I wonder if this is like those Magic Eye tricks in books, where if you cross your eyes you can suddenly see in 3-D.

Before I have a chance to step closer, though, the door lifts like a portcullis. No *scrape* or *rumble*. Quieter by far than our garage door. But I don't linger on the mechanics because beyond the door, in a bright profusion of scent and color, is an enormous garden. We're in the middle of one of the towers we saw from the higher level and I'm reminded immediately of concept art for gardens in outer space. Around me is the perfectly manicured greenery culti-vated to support life in an alien environment. It feels like we're in one of those space stations right now. I'm not sure I can prove that we aren't.

"Impressive," Rob says, craning his neck in awe, his mouth hang-ing open. He takes a distracted step forward, almost bumping into Jo. I have to suppress the childish urge to knock him off balance. I can't help it. A small part of my mind hasn't changed after all I've been through.

"This is the home of my clan." Straoc seems smug, if I'm reading him correctly. He's hard to pin down, I realize. He seems important, entrusted as he is with bringing us back, and yet still as eager as a kid to amaze us. Here he is, bragging about his people. "We are one of the most ancient lines, traced back to the birthing waters of our universe. And this is a First Tower, one of the homes of a Keeper of the Three."

I'm guessing that Arcos has another First Tower. And Feileen did too, before she was killed. Seats of power for the Keepers, I suppose. Something to be proud of.

There are Keepers here, walking, sitting, enjoying the day, just like you might see students doing on campus in April between classes. Birds with glimmering feathers zip above us and I think I see a four-legged something lounging in the grass, more dog*gish* than dog. I almost expect to see red plastic cups filled with beer or Frisbees lofting through the air. The Keepers all look our way, casting furtive glances, though there's a younger-looking Keeper, with a shock of blue hair, sitting in a circle and full-on staring. The Keeper to her left covers her eyes with his hands, blocking her view of us. As if our looks could kill.

I want to ask Straoc about her but a couple of men, both in blue billowy shirts and mustard-yellow jackets over blue jean–like pants, approach carrying bowls of water. They're smiling, something we haven't really seen much of down here. They're the opposite of the Keepers we saw at the Exchange. "Welcome and drink," they say in unison. One has black hair in a bowl cut with narrow eyes, and the other has blond curls with wide cheekbones.

Straoc nods, and we drink. The water gives me a buzz of energy and a pulse of warmth that goes right through my head.

"Wow," Rob says, apparently feeling the same thing. "Like a bump of caffeine."

One of the Keepers—the one with dark hair—reaches out tentatively and touches Jo's blond hair. Jo manages not only to not cringe, but even to smile. The perfect diplomat.

"You have very small eyes," the hair toucher says.

"Breacha," Straoc warns.

"Is it true that for half of every cycle you must hide?" the other asks, looking at me for answers. He's got an earring—a thin chain that snakes in and out of the lobe.

"Hide from what?" I ask.

"From the burning."

"The sun?" Rob asks.

"That is not the way of it," Straoc admonishes, and the two cower back, as if in trouble. "Keeper Randt speaks better than that. You take your moments to speak to Topsiders and you ply them with questions of superstition?" Straoc had untied us while we drank, and now he hooks my arm and pulls us along. "Enough, you two. Go tell your friends of your speaking with Topsiders and leave us."

We keep walking through the grass, no other Keeper brave enough to approach.

"So each building has its own clan?" Jo asks after a while, stroking her hair absentmindedly.

"Yes, that is correct," Straoc says. "Come now," he continues. "I am sure you are exhausted. Let us go to your chambers, where you can rest."

I catch Rob's and Jo's eyes. Taking a nap is the last thing I can imagine doing right now.

Straoc guides us down a lovely path toward a gazebo-like structure and invites us to sit. There's a Keeper standing in the corner, a reedy man who refuses to meet my eyes, but peeks at our feet. "These are our chambers?" Rob asks. Straoc doesn't respond, and so, reluctantly, we take a seat. As soon as we do, the gazebo shoots into the air, surprising me but terrifying Rob, who was never the best with heights. He yelps. I fear the dark; Rob fears heights; Jo stepping immediately to look over the edge, fears nothing.

The reedy Keeper pushes a few buttons, kind of like an elevator operator. Maybe exactly like that.

"Mia," Jo says, practically dangling from the side. *Oh, it's great to be a high diver.* "Come see!"

Battling my own beating heart, I stick my head out and take it all in. I can't see the actual mechanism of the elevator, so there must be a cable or something pulling us up. We ride smoothly, quickly, passing balcony after balcony catching glimpses of Keepers through open windows going about their daily business, whatever that means here. Jo points to one woman who is hanging glowflowers upside down from a line, as if to dry them. They shiver and sparkle and remind me of Christmas.

I look down, and shouldn't have. We're *high* up. Thirty, fifty stories, I don't know. I grab Jo's hand.

"Aww," she says, making a funny face. "You should go sit with Rob and be scared."

"Watch it," Rob says, his eyes closed. "I know where you live."

"I do not know where you live," Straoc says eagerly. "Tell me more, please. Are you of separate clans?"

"We have clans, just small ones," I say. "Our families. We live in a small city, on campus at a school." Only now that I'm taking time to think about it do I realize how strange it is that the Keepers not only understand English, but that they clearly developed in a similar way to us. Being stuck down here for as long as they have, the chances are crazy small they'd be *anything* like us.

"How small are families?" he asks.

"Oh, they can be big, but usually only a few kids and a mom and a dad." I pause. Next to me, I can feel Jo take a deep breath, no doubt thinking of her father.

"Isn't it beautiful?" Jo says, obviously resigned to being here. "A whole world, like Atlantis." She's quiet for a moment, and because I'm staring at her, I catch the quiver of her lip. "It's like all of this has happened for a reason."

All of this, for her, has to mean the death of her dad. But Mr. Banner didn't die in some freak accident. It was an avoidable tragedy, it was Sutton's *fault,* but now we're here, witnessing the impossible. She can finally have a *why* for his death. Jo sniffs, tucks her knees to her chin. The floors whiz by; none of us say a thing.

And then we stop. It's so sudden and soft that I don't realize we're not moving until Straoc steps off onto a colorful mosaic of tiles. We're at the penthouse, so close to the golden domed ceiling that I could touch the curve. The balcony is large, enclosed like a sultan's foyer, with two trees on either side and a couple of bronze gas lamps. I take Jo's hand and help Rob up. It's only when I get to the edge that I realize the mosaic on the floor is of a familiar image. It's like a bridge made of stone, held up by two rows of evenly spaced arches rising higher and higher into the air. But it's too thin to be a bridge, and there's water pouring off the end.

"What's going on?" Rob says in disbelief.

"No way that's the aqueduct," Jo adds, but it sure looks like the aqueduct, the one we broke into and blew up to keep Sutton off our trail. In fact, the image shows what I'd expect the aqueduct to be now, *after* I blew it up. My mind flashes to the woods, and I wonder where all the water's draining now, if we've flooded the whole forest. Or if it's frozen into a mini-pond, an iced waterfall.

"Who made this?" I demand.

"Made what?" Straoc asks, confused. He's moved past the mosaic and is standing near a great wooden door, the entrance to the floor.

"The tiles, that image," Jo exclaims, flustered. "How do you know what the aqueduct looks like? How is it here? What the heck is going on?"

Straoc frowns, then answers very slowly. "I have paid no notice to this before." And with that, he beckons us through the door.

6

JIMMY

JIMMY'S RUNNING. HE'S HOLDING A WALKIE-TALKIE IN one hand and Odessa's hand with the other. The corridors are gray and long and with lights on the floors. Runway lights. Now that he's moving fast enough, he feels like a plane about to take off.

"Turn left," Veronica crackles through the walkie-talkie.

It all looks the same.

There are no more gunshots, but in some ways, that's scarier. With gunshots, Jimmy reasons, he at least can hear where Sutton and his people are. Without gunshots, they could be anywhere. Even Veronica can't track all their movements, and according to her, they've split up. Some are using the pump to get as much water out of the well as possible. Others are moving down the hallways, methodically kicking in doors, looking. And Sutton, with two armed cronies, is marching straight to Veronica's station. That's what she said anyway.

"Okay, now enter the code into the second door on the right," she says, and spits out a number. Repeats it so he can get it right. It beeps green, and Odessa opens the door. She's been quiet since they left, but there's not much to talk about. Still, it's a little unlike her.

"Close the door!" Veronica screams, oddly insistent, and he backpedals and slams it. He can hear the lock engaging.

"Great," she says. Jimmy hears a muffled *thud* in the background. Not a gunshot. Something else.

"What's that?" he asks.

"Sutton. He's outside my door, but never mind. Just hurry. Now you're going to go through a pair of sliding doors and I want you to head to the left, *not the right*. The right will take you to somewhere you don't want to be. Once you're through the door, put on the suits as quick as you can. But be thorough, check each other's seals."

Jimmy looks around, and sees that they're in a lab. There are microscopes and emergency showers and sinks. There are lab coats on the wall. Jimmy goes through a pair of sliding doors and hits a T junction hallway, except instead of a dead-end wall in front of them, it's windowed, and through the windows he sees cages upon cages. Dogs and cats and mice in aquariums. Some are bouncing around, others aren't moving at all. He's too far away to see if they are sick, or covered in sores, or bleeding.

"I don't like this," Odessa says. The dogs, as if they heard her, begin to howl.

"Me neither," he admits. He knows that this is what happens in a lab, but he has a German shepherd and a Siamese back home and he loves them and now he can only think of them aging to death and dying.

To the right, another door, one with a big bright red *4* painted on it.

To the left, a door with a *2*, painted blue. They go that way, press a big red button and the door lifts up, like for a garage. And inside, sure enough, suits. Not hazmats, but clunkier, made of a thick blue plastic that seems sturdier than those the soldiers wore at Westbrook.

Odessa hesitates, so he takes a suit down for her and helps her in, piece by piece. Veronica's been quiet, which means either she's being very patient or she's in trouble. Either way, they take their time, right foot, left foot, zip and seal. The helmet is part of the suit, so all you have to do is zip, Velcro, zip, Velcro. Two layers of suit, three layers of gloves, all built in together.

"If this is for level two, what do you think the suits look like in level four?" Jimmy says, and is gratified to see Odessa smile.

"Probably Michelin Man costumes."

"And why do they even bother? They have the water around. They can heal themselves from any virus or whatever they get."

"They'd need too much," she replies, her voice muffled, her breath leaving a small cloud of fog. "If they had to use it every time they left the room, they'd have run out years ago. They were almost out when we showed up, remember?"

They stand looking at each other, Odessa in her new body, locked away in a mobile plastic kit like an action figure still in its case. There's a lock of her red curly hair covering one of her eyes, and Jimmy has to fight the urge to reach out and try to move it, even with her helmet on.

"You ready?" he asks.

She snorts. "For what? I have no idea what we're doing."

He makes a face. "Veronica?" he says. The walkie-talkie is awkward in his clunky hands. She doesn't respond. He tries again. Nothing.

"No way," Odessa says.

"Maybe she's doing something." Jimmy lifts the walkie-talkie to try again, but Odessa bats his hand down.

"No," she hisses. "If someone got to her, then you're just telling them where we are."

"But we'll be on the monitors."

Odessa shrugs, a barely noticeable gesture in the suit. "If I were Veronica and Sutton was trying to get in, the last thing I'd do is keep the monitor focused on places I didn't want him to see."

"But we don't know that!" Jimmy says.

"What do we know?" she asks. "We know she sent us here. We know to put on these suits. And we know that she mentioned monkeys. So let's go with what we know, okay?"

Jimmy takes a few breaths to calm down. The suit isn't helping. But Odessa's right. He glances up at a camera along the wall, then jumps and knocks it to the right. He smiles at her, proud of himself, and she smiles back, which is all the reason he needs to keep going.

They leave the door open and quickly discover that this part of the lab is better equipped. Bigger rooms, crazier machines. Electron microscopes are nothing when compared to the MRI room. Mr. Kish wasn't joking; the Westbrook alums *funded* this place. It's better than a hospital. They open doors and check out each room, not sure what they'll find or where they'll find it.

At the far end of the hallway, past a number of small white rooms, some with dentist-style chairs, others with silver tables, and one with a colorful carpet and kid's toys, there's a thick, heavy-set door. A crosshatched window is fixed three-quarters of the way up, and through that Jimmy can see more cages, bigger ones. Small hands poke through the cages and hold on to the bars.

"This must be it," he says to Odessa.

"Now what?" she replies.

"I have no idea. That's what Veronica's for."

"So, are the monkeys, like, really sick or something? Is that why we have to wear these suits? Are we supposed to hope they find and bite and infect Sutton and his men?"

Jimmy cranes his neck, trying to see more of the monkeys. He realizes that he doesn't recognize the type, that aside from apes like chimpanzees, gorillas, and orangutans, and monkeys like um, baboons, he's pretty clueless.

"Dess," he says, trying to work out the logic while he speaks, "if these monkeys are testing water that's supposed to stop killer viruses, then it makes sense that they would have killer viruses here too, right? Like Ebola and Marburg. Maybe they have *the* virus somewhere in here, the one that made us like this . . ."

"Yeah," she replies, opening the door, apparently ready to get this over with. "But this is minimum security. I bet these ones are safe and the infected ones are past the door marked with the big four."

"Then what are we supposed to do with them?"

"Just trust Veronica, okay?" Odessa replies, looking over her shoulder. "She got us this far."

Jimmy clamps up, annoyed. He's never liked following orders.

Inside, the room's bright and the noise is loud. The monkeys, agitated, move back and forth in their cages, which are bigger than he thought—they're set back into the wall a good ten feet. They're smaller than chimps, but still a decent size. Long hair on the head and neck, a light brown that turns gray as it moves down the body and toward the belly. Several of them are screaming, baring their teeth. A few of the bigger ones stare, wide-eyed, mouths open. Like angry stoners.

"This is intense," Odessa says, looking at the cages.

Jimmy thinks that's code for her not wanting to be here. He's always been good at reading Odessa. "Why don't you go back out into the hallway and close all the doors down the corridor? We don't want the monkeys getting lost. Go ahead of me and make sure their path is going to be straight, cool?"

"I can do that," she says, grateful.

"But remember," he replies, smiling at her, "they might come running, so go hide in the corner, okay?"

"See you soon," she says, gently touching the clear glass in front of his face.

And then she's gone.

Jimmy takes stock. There's a walk-in fridge. More steel tables. Even through his filtered mask, it smells like a vet's waiting room. Jimmy walks to the far end of the cages, which are set atop each other, ten by five. Fifty monkeys. What did Veronica send them here for? To just wreak havoc? Jimmy supposes it will help, though he hates the idea of a monkey getting shot. Look at these guys, he thinks. Even screaming they don't deserve that.

He stands in front of a cell marked HENRY, where a bigger guy is staring Jimmy down. He puts his hand on the lock and begins to count down from ten, giving Odessa a little more time to get ready.

At three, though, an alarm goes off. It's loud and blaring and a spinning red light, like on a cop car, twirls above the door. It scares the crap out of him. All along the cages an additional lock springs into place, sealing the monkeys in. Jimmy looks at Henry, but the monkey just goes apeshit.

Odessa, he thinks. And runs.

She's at the end of the hallway, her body splayed on the floor. The thick metal door at the entrance is almost down the wall, only a few feet above her, held in place by a cart. On the cart, crushed, is a microscope. The wheels on the bottom are bent off, and Jimmy can see the whole thing trembling beside her. If it gives, the door will drop and cut her in half.

"*Dess!*" Jimmy screams, hurrying down the hall, cursing his clunky suit.

She rolls over, waves for him to come, seemingly okay. Jimmy doesn't even have time to feel relieved. He plunges onto the ground next to her, where she's peering out underneath the door. The cart groans next to them.

"What happened?" he says.

"I don't know," she replies, checking whether something's coming. "One minute I'm standing in the hallway, the next, this door is closing by itself. I put the cart under, but it's not going to hold long."

"I didn't get the monkeys," Jimmy says.

"I don't think it's about the monkeys, Jimmy," Odessa says, pointing at the BIOHAZARD LEVEL 4 door across the hall. It's been sealed by a mean-looking steel wall. Above the door is another spinning light, flashing in their eyes. "I think Veronica sent us here to save us. To lock the doors behind us. The monkeys were a stupid trick to get us here."

"What, why?"

"To protect us, obviously. I caught the door because I didn't want to be locked in, but maybe she's right. Maybe we should ride this out."

Jimmy looks at her. Her eyes are wide and blue behind her mask. She wants this all to end. The cart, next to them, groans against the weight. There's still a few feet free beneath the door. If they want to leave, they have to go now.

"That's not how it works, Dess. Mia needs our *help*. If we don't help, then she's going to come back from wherever the hell she is and find ten guns pointing at her face."

"We need to take care of ourselves," Odessa says, having a fit that surprises him. The door groans.

"Dess," he says gently, "we have to help them. We have to get out of here."

She's crying. He can hear it.

"You know that if Sutton wins, we aren't going to be safe here. How long can we stay? What do we eat? It's just as dangerous here as it is out there, only the danger will take longer to get to us. You need to trust me, Dess. We have to go." Jimmy feels something in his voice, a conviction stronger than anything he's ever felt in the huddle at a football game. Odessa sees this. She stares into his eyes, and finally she takes his hand and he knows she's with him. She's always been with him. He realizes then that she didn't object to save herself. She wanted to save him.

He grins, about to help her through the opening when he hears something. A soldier walks into the junction and immediately checks out the closed BIOHAZARD door across the way. Jimmy pulls Odessa back frantically, and they slide behind the cart, out of the gunman's view.

Jimmy's breathing too hard, his suit's fogging up. He wishes he had a needle or scalpel or something useful he could actually expect to find in a lab.

The soldier comes closer; Jimmy can see his black combat boots peeking underneath the door. The soldier crouches, the tip of his machine gun coming into view, and with no other plan in place, Jimmy lunges past the cart, grabs the barrel of the gun and pulls as hard as he can.

Maybe it's the surprise, maybe it's leverage, or maybe it's his newfound strength, but Jimmy hears the soldier's face smash into the other side of the door, and watches him fall flat on the floor, gun glittering with him. Jimmy takes a fistful of the man's shirt and tugs him under, then, with his enormous padded fist, slams him once, twice in the face until the soldier's nose bursts bloody and his eyes roll back.

"Did you kill him?" Odessa asks. Jimmy blinks. Of course he didn't, but he's surprised he knocked him out so easily.

"Get under the door, Dess. Be careful. Make sure there's no one else out there."

Jimmy unstraps the machine gun from the unconscious body and searches him. He finds a canteen. Flashlight. A handgun. A knife. A radio. He takes the handgun, and then slides under the door. Jimmy gives the trembling cart a kick and the door slams down, locking the soldier inside.

And them out.

Jimmy doesn't say a thing while Odessa unzips him from the suit. Soon she's free too. She holds his cheek for a moment, her palm against his newly grown scruff.

He smiles. Then hands her a gun.

7

WE STEP INTO A BANQUET HALL. THE ROOM STRETCHES out fifty yards straight from the door, with banquet tables, two of them, that run almost that entire length. The tables themselves are made of a swirling pattern of rock and crystal, and under them, there's a wide carpet of blue and yellow; every ten feet gas chandeliers hang from the ceiling. Keepers stand against the wall like Praetorian guards, silent and statuesque. They guard doorways that lead elsewhere in the tower.

And on the far side of the room, in an engulfing chair, sits a tall and regal Keeper. In front of him there's a small desk, which he's writing away at, dipping his pen in ink as he goes.

The Keeper looks up and beckons eagerly with his pen. Closer, I can see that the chair is a deep blue and shining. If I thought it were possible, I'd say it was a solid carved sapphire. The Keeper sits on what resembles a draped white down comforter. What do I know? Maybe it's stuffed with goose feathers. It looks remarkably comfortable, something you'd need on your sapphire throne. The desk, too, is not a desk but a clever contraption that swivels aside when the Keeper pushes a button. The Keeper's hair is long and dark, and falls gently down his back, over a formfitting shirt of glittery silver that reminds me of chain mail. He's wearing blue leathery pants adorned with patterns of gold, starbursts and circles. He looks like a rich raver.

It seems wrong to speak. Behind him is a glass window, stretching across the entire back of the room, but it's too dark and hard to make anything out to call it a view.

"Do we bow?" Rob whispers.

"No way," Jo replies, her voice fierce.

The Keeper smiles, his teeth a dazzling white. His lips, though, are pale and thin and his mouth opens up almost too much when he smiles. I can easily see the gums surrounding his teeth. It's not the most welcoming of expressions.

"Long have we known of the Topside, and our sisters and brothers who live there. It is an honor to see you, after all these years."

He seems to expect a response, but what do you say to that?

"I am Randt," he says, indicating himself and speaking slower, louder, as if our silence has made him distrust his English. "The water spoke of your arrival."

"The water told you," I repeat, dubious. "But I drank the water. It didn't tell me about *you*."

He shakes his head, looking at Straoc in amusement. "You are right to think as you do, young Mia, but the source speaks only to the Three, we who the source has chosen."

"So if you knew we were coming, and you knew our names," Rob says, "why did your man Straoc here have to be all sneaky to get us away from those other guys?"

Randt looks at Straoc questioningly.

"Little Rob tells true," Straoc replies reluctantly. "Arcos's men were there first. They came back after they took the other one."

"My dad!" I burst out, unable to help myself.

"Disappointing," Randt says, looking at me thoughtfully. His pupils go wide. I feel strange, my skin tingling. Like he's doing something more than staring. When he smiles, I can't help but think it's about something he's learned from me, something I didn't want to share. "You are the daughter of the Topsider who came this morning? I saw of him this morning and so did Arcos, but you three were not so clear. You were merely a haze, a *feeling*. Three, four shapes and words and newness coming. The water speaks in riddles as often as it speaks in color and I sent Straoc to the gates just in the case others came, but apparently so did Arcos. For such a hefty one, he moved quite fast to secure your father."

"And Feileen's people approached us at the Exchange," Straoc says. "They are becoming angry. They want a member of her clan to take her place at the Three."

"Of course they do," Randt says. "They have been holding quorums in their towers, attempting to choose a successor from their clans. Though no Keeper comes to mind. There has never been a succession, and there are no rules or traditions to stand by, so they move with confusion." He taps his cheek with a slender finger, thinking. "You see, young Topsiders, we three used to rule Capian quite effectively. Keeper Arcos, who took your father, he has long been the voice of balance, with Feileen on one side and me another. But Feileen is gone in such a tragic manner and the axis is tilted; how far will Arcos go to preserve that familiar order? Will he attempt to shift the dynamics after all these cycles? He wonders the same of me, which is why he moved so quickly to take your father. Having a Topsider as a pawn is important. He can play the judge, gather Feileen's clan to his side and then, I'm sure, he will install a puppet on the Three that he can control. Capian will be his."

I'm tempted to ask about my father but Randt stands up and heads to the glass wall behind him. He's even taller than I thought. Seven four, seven five, I don't know. He's a basketball giant. He's not as big as Straoc, but his movement is so sinuous, so graceful that it's way more intimidating.

"Come with me," he beckons, and then presses his palm against the glass, which swivels open along a near-invisible crack, creating an exit.

Randt leads us out and the first thing I notice is that there's no real change in air temperature; it's like we're in a bubble. There's a railing, and room for twenty or thirty people. Above and behind us arcs the dome of this building, glistening in the gaslight. We're in one of the tallest buildings in Capian, high enough that it's surprising to find only darkness when I look up—I'd expect the rocky ceiling to be close; instead, it's like looking into a completely cloud-covered sky on the night of a new moon. We're high enough that we're level with the mountain we saw on the way in. I can even make out the glow of the gates beyond the lip of the crater the city nestles in.

From here, I'm reminded that Capian's cramped and crowded. Other buildings have similar domes, and looking down on them makes the city appear like a collection of sparkling kaleidoscopes.

"This is our world," Randt says, waving his hand. "You must be wondering how we are here, and why. Just as we sometimes wonder the same. And why not? It is our nature to question existence."

He sounds like Rob, when Rob's stoned. And Rob, stoned, can go on and on. I don't have time for that. I want to know about this place, about everything, but I also want to find my dad, save Fenton from the virus, and stop Sutton from taking over the Cave.

"I'm sorry, Randt?" I say his name, stumbling over the pronunciation. "I appreciate how beautiful this all is. But right now we need help. I need to find my dad and to get back home."

"Yes, of course, young one. There is a terrible disease rotting away the Topside and you feel the need to hurry."

My skin crawls.

"You know about the virus?" Rob asks.

"Of course," Randt replies. He closes his eyes, as if contemplating something far away. "I can *feel* it."

"What are you talking about?" Jo asks, skepticism written across the lines on her forehead.

Randt glances at Straoc, who shrugs. "I had always thought that when the first Topsider came, he would come for the source, but not you three." Randt muses. "Now your father—I sense the desire in his heart like a beacon, the want of the source, of its gifts."

"Like knowing about the virus, reading minds?" Rob asks.

Randt laughs, an oddly musical sound. "I cannot read minds, young Rob. I can only *feel* what's going on in that head of yours. I admit, with practice, it becomes a similar thing. But were you to pick a number, could I guess it? Probably not. The source is different to each who have taken of it. I, for instance, *feel* further than Arcos can. But his visions are clearer. When Arcos, Feileen and I combined our gifts, we could know most of what anyone was thinking in Capian. But long ago are the days when the Three worked together."

"But you know we have to get back to help," I say, my voice rising.

"And you will, you will," Randt says assuredly. "And perhaps some of my people will join you." I start, caught off guard, but Randt keeps going, growing excited, getting to his point. "But I must know, *what brought you here?* Did you come by accident? Did you follow your father?" He pauses, his eyes locked onto mine, the strange feeling in my head going on again. "Or did something point the way?"

He's talking about the map, I'm sure. I glance at Rob but Randt just follows my eyes. Almost immediately the odd sensation in my head stops as the Keeper shifts focus. Rob's hand drifts into his pocket, probably touching his phone. I feel an odd sense of selfishness take hold. I was the one who found this place. It's my answer to give. "The map told me," I say.

"You say the *map* told you? What map? Describe it." Randt says, taking an eager step forward. He looms over me, and I can feel the railing press into my back.

"You didn't put it there?" I reply, puzzled. "Didn't you make it so that we'd come? If you can see what's going on in my world, how can you not know about the map?"

"I know of the map, yes, but no matter how hard I have tried, I cannot see what is *on* it. Where did you find it?" Randt says, speaking through clenched teeth, as if to contain his eagerness.

"It was a painting on the wall, near the well that brought us to you. My father found it, cut it out of the wall and studied it for years."

Randt eases back slowly. "I can see you speak the truth. When was this?"

"Thirty-four years ago," I reply. Crazy that I just learned that yesterday. That it was exactly double my age that dad found the well.

"Two cycles," Straoc says, counting out loud.

"Yes," Randt agrees, as if they've just figured something out. "That would make some sense. It is when I first began to feel the map, when I first knew of its presence." He turns back to me. "And you have memorized this map?"

I shake my head. Not completely true of course, but apparently true enough to pass his mental lie-detector. The images I remember are seared into my mind, but I don't know what's on the rest of the map. I wish I had had more time with it. "No, but dad has. If you let us speak to him, he can tell you what's on it."

Randt's thoughtful. "If only it were that easy. A tension swells the city. Keeper Feileen's brutal death calls for a successor. There will be conflict for the first time in memory, if I do not act quickly. Clans divided. More death. We are not used to that word. It represents a horrible waste of water."

"I thought you ran this place?" I ask, confused. "Straoc said we'd get to go to the Lock. So why can't you speak to my dad?"

"Capian is at arms, young Mia," he says, motioning to the buildings below. "Your father is held out of my reach by Keeper Arcos, who is as strong as I am. He knows of the map as certainly as I do, perhaps even sees it better than me, and he will gather everything from your father before he dares allow me near."

"I thought you were part of the decision-making. I mean, don't you have to consult one another over decisions or something?" Rob asks, his nose wrinkled in confusion. It's still distracting to see him without his glasses.

"I am one of the Three, yes," Randt replies, with a wry smile. "One of the Two, now. But I have no power over him. What we see, what we interpret, is of our own abilities." Randt grabs the railing and looks over Capian. We're quiet for an awkward moment.

"Keeper Randt," Straoc finally says, "if this Topsider knows the map, and Arcos gathers from him, then all of this . . ."

Randt raises a hand, silencing Straoc. The big Keeper cringes at the chastisement.

"You are right, of course." He turns back to us, a smile in place. "Now, you three, you will stay here with us? Our guests until we resolve the order of things?"

"What?" I say, incredulous. It's strange, him asking. Like we aren't already at his mercy. "We can't just stay here. We have to get my dad."

"I agree," Randt replies. "We *do* have to retrieve your father. And you, with no knowledge of this city, of the people here, you will only get in the way. Straoc, here, will go for your father. And you will stay."

"No," I reply firmly. "We're coming."

"It is not your choice," the tall Keeper's eyes flash, and for the first time I see a glimpse of real anger in his face.

"We don't want to be your prisoners," Jo says fiercely, her teeth clenched.

Randt calms himself, raises an eyebrow. "I assure you, young Jo, that I could make you *feel* like a prisoner. Instead you will merely not be allowed to leave. Every other luxury I can offer is yours."

"Remember the Exchange?" Straoc adds. "We Keepers, some of us want to know you, to learn what it's like Topside. But most are very hurt. To have had one of the Three die . . . It would be dangerous for you. You must stay here."

"It's the same thing," Jo presses, now speaking to Randt's back—the Keeper has walked to the balcony door, our meeting apparently over. He turns his neck, his profile like a statue chiseled of marble.

"Perhaps. As long as Mia's father tells us everything he knows about the map, when we find him, you will not feel like a prisoner at all."

"But I still don't get why you don't you know what's on the map," I say again. This seems key.

Randt looks at me as if he's deciding whether the answer's worth sharing. "There was a time when there were ten Keepers who had drunk of the source, not three. We could see most everything. We could do most everything. The source flowed through us and we built this city and watched the Topside, keeping the water safe. But as the time passed, we grew restless. There were no trials. There was nothing to keep the water safe from. There was no *purpose*. Why were we set on this task? It became too much. So, many, many cycles ago, seven of my sisters and brothers left to find their way Topside, and we three remained to keep. The seven were supposed to return after the first cycle, but they did not. Not ever. Over time, their clans absorbed into ours. We have not heard from them or felt them or caught a glimpse of them since, and if not for the source, which tells me so, I would not believe them still alive. I cannot see what my brothers and sisters have put before me, the seven who have left, or know their purpose. But two cycles ago I began to sense something. I began to feel the map through your father and his friends the moment they found it. That is how the water works, through you, through us, through everything that drinks it." He grows quiet, lost in years of thought. "I can only sense the map, but last cycle Feileen and Arcos united against me in judgment before all of Capian, forbidding me to leave. If the map is truly of the lost Keepers, it must show us why they have been gone for so long, and where they are now. If there is a greater threat to my city and the source, I must know. If there is a greater purpose, I must discover it. That was the entire function of their journey. And if my sisters and brothers found out what it is we keep from, why we were put here, then it is worth as much as the source itself."

"I don't think the map says that stuff," I say, dubious. The words just come out. The Keepers who made the map had drunk the source, and left here eons ago. Did they make it for us, then? Or for Randt and his people?

Randt snorts. "How can you expect to know and understand anything of this place, little one?"

"Why don't you just go Topside and see?" Jo asks.

"Yes, we should," Straoc says, earning swift look from Randt. Straoc seems to love the idea of the Topside, like a kid dreaming of Hollywood.

"We cannot just leave the source. If I leave, then Arcos alone keeps the city." He stares hard at Straoc. "We must get the other Topsider. We must know what the map says before Arcos does."

"And if he doesn't tell you what's on the map?" Rob asks.

Randt shakes his head, as if that could never even be a possibility. When he does speak, it's with the sigh of a busy man at the end of his day. "That is why you will be my guests, to ensure he does."

"Sounds like a threat," Jo says.

"He will speak or he will not." He looks at me now, smiling kindly. "But if not . . . well, we will just illustrate on young Mia, here, show him just how many times we can break her arms and legs and heal her with the water while keeping her conscious." He studies me, like he's looking for an answer. "Quite a few times, I'm sure."

He pauses. "Welcome to my home." And then he's gone, the door swinging shut and leaving us with the dark city pressing in.

8

STRAOC HOLDS THE DOOR FOR US LIKE A GENTLEMAN,
letting us inside as if nothing's happened, as if we weren't just
blatantly threatened. The Keepers standing guard in the hall don't
look our way, which is similarly unnerving.

"Randt and Sutton should become best friends," Rob says.

"Not the time, Rob," Jo replies.

"When, then? It's not like we're going anywhere. We thought we
were getting help but instead we're held for potential torture."

"Friend Rob," Straoc says, somehow looking hurt. "That will
most probably not happen. I certainly would not want that. You
have to show me the Topside."

"Oh fun. I'll take you to Baskin-Robbins."

"Good, I would like that." Straoc replies, oblivious. He rolls his
massive shoulders. "Now I must hurry to find your father. We shall
speak of your home again soon."

Straoc says something in their foreign language to the Keepers
guarding the nearest door. The words are guttural, more like He-
brew than, say, Italian, but pleasant to the ear. Afterward, he doesn't
even look our way, he just hurries to the foyer and disappears.

The Keepers both have long hair tied up in buns, both wearing
deep blue tights and blue and yellow striped sleeveless shirts. As

soon as Straoc leaves they order us down the hallway. The woman leads, the man follows us. They hold thin, short swords, unsheathed, and walk with practiced ease, swinging the bright blades close to their bodies.

"Do you have any guns?" Rob asks, as we walk through a narrow passageway.

"It is forbidden," the woman says, her voice deep and scratchy, like a lifelong smoker.

"Sounds like lots of stuff's forbidden," Rob says, half to her, half to us. "Electricity, guns. What else?"

"Please stop your talking," the woman says.

"What's your name?" Jo asks, ignoring her order. Her face shows a mixture of genuine curiosity and intentional disobedience.

The guard doesn't answer. And we walk in silence for another hundred yards, down two flights of stairs, and finally to a set of double doors painted white. The man, the first Keeper I've seen with facial hair—a tuft below his chin—opens the door and ushers us in. But it's the woman who speaks. "This is your room. You are not to leave. We will be here if you need anything, and will bring you food presently. There is a font, of course."

"Right," I reply, not sure what she means.

"My name is Jo," Jo says, reaching out a hand. The Keepers stare at it.

"I am called Sratha," the woman finally says; you can feel the reluctance in her voice.

The man juts his chin out, refusing to speak, maybe under orders, or maybe he's angry like the ones in the Exchange. With the flat of his sword he taps Jo on the back, pushing her inside. The doors close behind us.

The room's simple but elegant. The kind of thing you'd expect to see in a schmancy modern apartment in New York City. There are three beds, each level with the floor, set into the ground. Pillows and crisp white sheets. A thin gray stone table and wooden chairs. A leather-lined bench. It's like a minimalist paradise.

The 'font,' I suppose, is the little water fountain that's near the door. Like a birdbath. I dip my finger in and take a taste. My mouth goes warm. I'm growing too pleased with that feeling.

Rob's like a kid exploring a hotel. He goes behind an opaque piece of glass in the corner of the room and shouts, "They only have a hole in the ground."

"At least they have something," Jo replies.

The noticeable thing missing is a TV. No guns, no TV. I wonder what other technologies they haven't developed, and whether it's by choice. They've clearly surpassed us on a few things as well, considering that smooth elevator ride, the buildings, the gigantic gates. Divergent civilizations, different growth.

Jo plops into a chair. She looks ridiculous in her blue scrubs and red winter coat. I glance around and see that on the beds there are three changes of clothes, white cloth, folded neatly into little perfect squares. I think of Dad, and how he's in the Lock, and I wonder whether he has his own inset bed. If all jails here are this comfortable. I wonder if Arcos's men told him that we were here. I'd rather they didn't, if only so Dad won't worry.

"I could use a shower," Jo says, pulling an elastic out of her blond hair. She holds it up and examines it critically, as if it were the problem instead of her unkempt and sweaty hair. "Though it seems like such a waste of the water."

"Here, maybe this will make you feel better," I say, and throw a square of cloth at her. She unfolds it, looks at the shirt with amusement, then shrugs. I'm reminded of Saturday nights before she went out, her standing in front of the full-length mirror, trying on dress after dress. Sometimes I wondered whether she took so long only to have more time to convince me to go out with her.

"Fine," she says, and begins to take off her jacket. "Rob, stay over there, I'm changing."

"Oh, I want to change too!"

I toss him a set over the glass screen of the bathroom. I can see the vague shape of him ripping off his clothes.

"You realize it's your birthday, right?" Jo says suddenly, a guilty look flashing across her face.

"Kinda hard to keep track of the time down here," I say, turning away from her. I don't really want to talk about it. There's nothing to celebrate. My birthday is just a reminder of the way things will never be again. No birthday cupcake in our dorm room, no cheesy photoshopped picture of me on Lionel Messi's body that Rob taped to the door. No time before a virus. They must have heard the disinterest in my voice, because no one says anything more on the subject, and I'm happier that way.

I do a pocket check of my coat and find two things I've already forgotten, both which I stuffed into my jacket before we left. One, a small paring knife I took from Furbish Manor, the last holding cell we were stuck in. And the other, some berries Odessa told me not to eat. Blue ones, from the exotic greenhouses back at the Cave, where Dad and his scientist buddies were using the water to experiment on crops. Most are crushed but there are a few survivors. Strong breeding, I guess. I can't believe I forgot these things, and even more so, I can't believe they didn't check me for them. I suppose they aren't used to stop-and-frisk down here. I slip on the new clothing, breathing a sigh of relief as the soft material shifts over my body, surprisingly warm. Suddenly the bed looks inviting.

I give myself an internal shake of the head. *No, not now. What if Dad gets here?* I take another handful of water and let the tingling sensation push away my exhaustion.

Ever since we arrived here, we've been forced to follow someone else's lead. Judging from Straoc's reaction, I'd imagine that the arrival of a Topsider might normally have provoked a positive reception, but with the assassination of that Keeper they spoke of, one of the so-called Three, it's like we're terrorists.

"We have to get out of here," I say, mustering my energy.

"How, Mia?" Jo replies. "This isn't like the backwoods of Westbrook, where we at least know where to go. How are we supposed to get out of this tower?"

"Um," Rob says, peeking from the bathroom. "You do realize that Randt said he'd torture us if Mr. Kish doesn't talk."

"Rob's right," Jo says. "But he'll definitely torture your dad if we leave. We don't know anything about this place, and if Straoc's going to break your dad out of prison and bring him here, I say we wait until we're all together."

"But how do we know that as soon as they get what they want from him, we're not all tossed out that window?" I say.

Rob comes back into the room and throws his old scrubs on the floor. The white suit fits snugly, as if tailored for him. He looks remarkably cool—like a ninja speed skater. "Mr. Kish *will* talk. Why wouldn't he? He came here for a reason and it seems more and more likely that he wants the source and all of its powers and maybe the map is helping him get there, but you don't really think he'll stand up to them threatening you?"

"Right," Jo says. "We're safer here."

I shake my head. "We aren't safe anywhere that we can't leave on our own."

Rob waves his phone and then tosses it to me. "Why don't you see what the map tells us to do?"

"Does it work that way?" Jo asks, crossing her arms on her chest.

"It has so far, right?" he replies.

I scroll through the images, and immediately get why Dad's been obsessed all these years. Each one could have so many meanings. After the city, where I assume we are now, there's still another dozen or so paintings. In the first image there are three blue circles in a tight clump. And a red stripe—not even a real shape to it. Then a Keeper with a spear in his eye and a waterfall and a cup with a shining rim.

"Well?" Jo asks. I glance up, dazed. How long have I been staring at the phone? I shrug and give it to her. "It's not exactly easy," I say.

She looks at it, biting her lip, her brow furrowed intensely. I realize I've been at odds with her on most things since we've gotten here. But I can't just decide to stay here, trapped in this room, to make her feel better.

I put my hand on the glass wall, looking for the door to the balcony, when outside on the railing, I see a hand.

"Oh, my God," I shout, and almost fall over.

"Damn it, Mia!" Jo says, dropping the phone and clutching her chest. "Don't do that."

"But look!" I shout again, pointing.

There's another hand now. Pale. Fingernails painted red. Someone's dangling off the ledge of our balcony. Then a head pops up, the head of a young Keeper, her eyes smaller than any Keeper's I've seen so far, only plum-size, like those of a perpetually surprised Topsider. Her hair's short and spiked and blue as can be and she sees us and smiles. I've seen that hair before: it's the girl who was forced to look away from us down in the gardens. For some reason, hers is the first smile I've trusted so far.

"What the hell's this?" Jo asks.

"Who is she?" from Rob.

The head disappears, but not the hands, and then suddenly a whole body jumps over the railing and onto the balcony. She straightens, a lithe grace to her movements, something I recognize from years of watching divers like Jo. She's wearing similar clothes to ours, only hers are the same colors and design as Randt's: chain-mail silver and deep blue with gold thread. She motions for us to come outside, but after I make a few tries at pushing on the glass, she rolls her big eyes and opens the door for us.

"You are the Topsiders?" she asks needlessly. She's breathing fast and speaking low, like she's ready for trouble.

"I guess we are," I say.

"You're Randt's daughter, aren't you?" Rob asks. He's gotta be on the mark, because she stiffens in surprise. Her skin is so milky white I can see some veins underneath. Her eyelashes are long. Her eyes are a gorgeous green, the irises thin discs around her pupils. And her lips are full and curved, thick and red. She's taller than me. But my swimmer shoulders are broader than hers, a fact that makes me oddly proud.

"How did you know?" she asks.

Rob shrugs. "Your clothing is as nice."

She laughs, a hearty sound, and somehow more genuine than Straoc's. "Normally that would not be the case," she says, fingering her glittering top. "But my mother has passed not a cycle and so I wear her clothing. I am the clan heir. It is tradition."

"So the guards outside, you're their princess?" Jo asks.

"Every clan owes allegiance to one of the Three, and must wear their colors when on duty. Our blood has mixed with these Keepers for generations. When not on duty, they wear more colors, but even then there must be blue and yellow." She smiles and points at her head. "My favorite are the cousins who dye their hair."

I wonder how many clans there are. "Do you want to come in? What're you doing here? Why'd you . . . *how'd* you come up this way?"

"No, we should stay out here, so your guards do not hear us," she replies. "And how can I not be here? You are Topsiders. The whole city is speaking of you. And I get you all to myself under my roof. You have no idea how much I want to go Topside. And now here you are coming to me. I could not resist. My own rooms are two floors below, and my father does not want me out, especially now, so I jumped up."

I run to the edge and look down, instantly vertigoed. "Are you crazy?" I say to her.

"No," she responds gravely, and I wonder if she's missed something in translation.

"What's your name?" asks Rob. A much smarter question.

She looks at Rob. "I am Lisenthe."

"Lisenthe," I try, butchering the pronunciation.

"Kind of like our 'Lisa,' " Rob says, a shy smile on his face, which she returns.

"Please, to you, call me Lisa."

"I'm Rob, that's Mia, and the blonde's Jo."

"Lisa," I say, ready to get on track. "What's going on down here? Why does everyone think we killed Feileen? How'd she die anyways?"

"Those are many questions, Mia," she replies, sounding out my name slowly, making sure she gets it right. "I do not know why Feileen is attached to you. I know only that she was found with no life, and no injury. It is a mystery, and so are you. So you are the same, in that way. But I do not know much else. I am not allowed to leave this tower."

"You're a prisoner too?" I ask.

"No, no," she says, some skepticism in her voice. "It is dangerous in Capian. Feileen has long been my father's opposite on the Three,

81

with Arcos choosing at whim who to support. Now that Feileen is gone, I am a target." She pauses. "We do not die often. It is a sad thing. I always liked Feileen when she visited our tower."

There's a voice down below, on another balcony, a loud laugh that makes me want to duck, as if we're in trouble

"My father once told me that my mother was ready to pass, and that the water allowed her to do so," Lisa says quietly, looking over the railing to the inner garden below. "But he says that Feileen's life ended differently. That she had no choice in the matter. That she was killed."

My mother wasn't ready to pass, and I wonder what I'd have given for some of this water to save her life. How could Lisa be so calm about her mom but so sad about Feileen? Down here, I guess, death is just a different thing. Either the water heals you of all illness and injury until you are ready for it to take your life or you go like Feileen, mysteriously and out of synch, an event big enough to throw the city in upheaval.

"Lisa," Jo says, filling the gap in the conversation, "how does it all work? The water, the source, your dad being able to see that we arrived? If he can see so much, why does he have to keep us prisoner? Couldn't he just find us anyway?"

Lisa pauses. "He just wants to help. He *told* me about what the water could do Topside, about how much you need it."

"And you believe that's the reason he suddenly wants to go Topside?" she presses, her voice angry enough that Lisa seems to shrink in on herself.

"Give her a break, Jo," Rob says.

Lisa sighs, and for a moment she seems just like any other girl, annoyed by a text from a boy, or a question from her teacher. In fact, I kinda find myself liking her, despite who her dad is.

"I told you, my father does not tell me anything real. But I know for truth that he is watching the Topside now more than ever."

"I get that the source is helping him do that, but not *how*," I say. "What, is there a mirror he looks into that talks to him?"

Lisa sighs again, but then puts on a wry smile. "For all the wide world you live in, you know so very little. I guess I shall have to show you."

9

FIRST LISA TRIES TO GET US TO CLIMB THE RAILING AND jump to another balcony, but only Jo seems up for the challenge. Poor Rob can barely watch her demonstrate, much less try himself.

"Okay then," she says, thinking fast. "You say there are two guards?" I nod. "Give me a small moment." And then she's gone, off the railing and down a floor like a parkour champ.

"Could you have done that?" I ask Jo.

"I'm a diver, not a gymnast," she replies, bending over the ledge, letting her blond hair dangle in front of her face.

"What now?" Rob asks. He rubs his stomach, like he's in love with the soft fabric of the shirt.

I shrug. "We go inside and wait?" I slip through the door and grab the knife and remaining whole berries. There are two small pouches, lined with a plasticky material, sewn into the shirts we wear. Convenient for the berries, less so for the knife. They feel waterproof—maybe to store water?

I fumble with the knife, unsure what to do, and finally just cut a hole in the lining of my other pocket and fit it through, angling it so the blade doesn't butt up against my skin.

Suddenly, there's a voice outside the door, loud and

commanding. Then an argument. The door pops open and for a moment it feels like we've been caught doing something wrong—but it's only Lisa who peeks her head in.

"I sent them home. Come now," she says, and vanishes.

Jo lets out a shaky laugh.

"That easy?" I say.

"Well, she *is* the boss's daughter," Rob replies.

We follow her at a jog through the halls, no sign of the other Keepers. It's like she disappeared them. We run up a flight, then another, back to the penthouse floor. At first, I wonder if we're going to the elevator, if this is a jailbreak.

But then we arrive at a marble alcove with a spiral staircase, a single corkscrew of iron steps that rises into the ceiling. The room is square and constructed entirely of glass; the stairs pop up directly from the middle of the floor. Lining every wall are shelves about four feet high, stacked so perfectly with scrolls that at first they look two dimensional, like wallpaper pocked with holes. But then Lisa pulls one, seemingly at random, from its place and the room settles into the third dimension.

It's a greenhouse of scrolls. The room's cooler than the rest of the building, maybe temperature controlled like the rare-book room at Westbrook's library. It smells the same, a comforting, musty tang to the air. Lisa unrolls the scroll on a large wooden table, spreading it out expertly and placing bright gems shaped like flat eggs onto the corners as paperweights. The gems must be a hundred carats.

I tear my eyes away because I notice something else: the art on the scroll is familiar. My breath catches.

"It's like the map," I say, unable to help myself.

Lisa looks up at me sharply, making it clear that Randt has told her about it. "You have seen the map?"

"Yes, we've seen it," I say hurriedly, reminding myself that the Keepers don't realize we have a copy of the map on Rob's phone, "I just don't remember most of it. That's why your dad's looking for mine. Wait, how much do you know about it?"

She's mollified and motions to the scroll. "My father speaks of the map often. Many, many cycles ago, instead of the Three that rule Capian, there were Ten. Ten Keepers who had partaken of the source. My father was one. My father says he did not want to leave; he thought some of them should stay below and keep. So did Arcos and Feileen, and the others did not disagree, but they themselves wished to explore. We do not know what happened to them, only that once they were Topside they were supposed to each go their own way to explore, and then return in one cycle. But they did not."

"Why doesn't someone else drink the source?" I ask.

"Because there cannot be more than the Ten. The source will not allow it. And because no other Keeper can take the source— they tried—the other Seven must be alive," Lisa says. "My father says he believes the Seven found their answers but refuse to share with us, that they live happily in their lives, knowing the purpose of the source and of us and of everything. He was angry at them for this. Furious." She frowns. "But when he began to sense the map, his mind changed; he believes the Seven are trying to communicate with us. He says they left us the map as a guide to them." She's staring into the scroll but her eyes are glazed. "This scroll," she thumbs the parchment, "this is how my father uses the source, how he watches the Topside and how he first felt the map." The scroll's a rendering of a mountain carpeted with pine trees. Sun, clouds. A rough drawing of a summer's day in the Rockies. Topside.

"I thought you didn't go Topside," Rob says. "How do you have a painting of Colorado in the summer? This is like that image of the aqueduct you have near the elevator."

"I do not understand everything you say," Lisa responds, her brow furrowed. " 'Colorado,' 'summer,' I do not know every word. But the paintings on these scrolls, like your English, are brought to us through the water."

"The water taught you English?" I exclaim, incredulous.

"Yes and no," Lisa replies. "The source connects to the Topside, and the Three are connected to the source. Randt and the others have been listening for a very long time, recording, tracking, looking for the Seven, watching you. When the gates are open, they hear much. When they are closed, only impressions." She pauses, motions to the painting on the scroll in front of us, as if to say *this* is merely an impression painting. "But the Three are very talented at understanding the impressions. It is their duty."

"Why?" I ask. "Why do they care?"

"We are the Keepers," she says, as if that explains everything. And maybe, to her, it does.

"Wait a minute, your dad painted all of these? There must be thousands. He just sits here and paints watercolors?" Rob asks.

"For a time every day, yes," Lisa replies. "It is his greatest task." She's defensive, but proud of her father. I understand. My dad has strange hobbies too. Lisa starts rolling up this scroll, and we all stand there awkwardly for a moment. Then she smiles. "And ten cycles ago he made everyone learn as many Topside languages as they could."

"Your father's progressive, huh?" I say, not really asking. I imagine Keepers sitting at tiny desks with their massive bodies, learning the present perfect tense.

Lisa doesn't seem to understand the word and shrugs, an act that seems odd on her tall frame. "You cannot spend your days faithfully reproducing another world's reality and not become obsessed with it to the point of mimicry. *I* am obsessed. My father believes that one day we Keepers will see you Topsiders, know you, be among you, and we must ready."

"Why didn't Randt go Topside before?" Jo asks. "I mean, I get that now's not the best time, but what about before Feileen died?"

Lisa stares at her as if she's stupid. "I do not understand what you do not understand. My father is a leader of the Keepers, his entire duty is to remain here and rule Capian in a balance of Three. If he went Topside, how could this continue?" She gestures at the maps around her. "The Seven left and he watched, and waited, doing as he should for our people. It was only of late, with the map, that his mind was changed. Now, to him, it is just as much his duty to find the Seven as it is to keep the source."

I think of Randt, the looming, threatening man who's holding us hostage, and wonder if Lisa knows that side of him. Or if it even matters to her. If Sutton had kids, would they see him as a monster?

I walk alongside one of the shelves, running my finger along the scrolls. "Which one tells us about the water?"

"All of them," Lisa replies.

Rob laughs and Lisa's eyes drop to the floor, embarrassed. Maybe she doesn't get that Rob likes her answer, and isn't making fun of her.

"Come on, Lisa," Jo says, turning serious. "You brought us here for a reason. Why?"

"Because I have seen the sickness you face in these scrolls." Lisa motions to a pedestal on the far side of the room. There, a scroll is already unfurled. "My father has felt the sickness, he has made impressions of it."

We gather round the scroll, eyes wide. The scroll is painted green, and in the center is a splotch of black with tendrils snaking everywhere. Like a mutated spider. She rolls the scroll forward, and there are a hundred bodies piled on top of each other, hair long, eyes closed, blood dripping from their mouths. Just like the infirmary back at school. How can this be possible?

"The virus," Jo says, grim.

Lisa looks at her for a moment, then nods. "I think it is a sickness, yes."

"Can you zoom in somehow?" Rob asks. "Can you see what's going on with our friends right now?"

She shakes her head. "Maybe my father could. But I have not drunk the source. I cannot say precisely what he knows."

"But what's the point of showing us this, then?" Jo asks, getting flustered. Her pale lips tremble in anger. "We're stuck here. We can't do anything about it."

"You wanted to know how my father used the source," she says, confused. "This is how. You can find yourself here, if you look hard en—" Lisa freezes, remembering something.

"Lisa?" Rob asks, but she ignores him and runs to the wall, where she pulls a scroll, seemingly with purpose, but heck if I see a cataloging system. She unfurls it fast, flinging it open with a *crack*. There's no dust that I can see, but it *smells* old. The scroll is stitched together with sheets full of color.

The image is of a Keeper on his knees, bent over. It would look like he was praying if not for the blood gushing from his head.

"What does this have to do with anything?" I ask.

"I found this scroll many dreams ago," she replies, speaking fast. "I thought nothing strange of this except that it was old and my father might not have painted it." She thumbs the edge of the parchment. "Maybe made before the Seven left, when there were still ten, when those who drank the source could see far more. But then," she continues, moving forward a number of panels in the scroll with an eager hand, "I found an image of myself."

Alone on the scroll is a Keeper, small and female with spiky blue hair. The rendering is generalized, it could probably fit a number of Keepers, except for that hair. That definitely narrows it down.

"So," Rob says, speaking slowly, frowning his way through the logic, "if this old scroll has an image of you, then it can tell the future?"

She bounces on her feet, frustrated. "You do not understand! It speaks in riddles. I have studied all the scrolls and could find nothing more about me." She rolls the scroll back to the image of a bloody Keeper. "But I just remembered this, and that Straoc went to the Lock to gather your father . . ." She indicates the page and a new image, runs a finger on the parchment, tracing the edge of a doorway behind the fallen Keeper. "There are bars here, closed doors, dark. That is the Lock. And this Keeper is Straoc."

"We have to get there," I say, a cold creeping into my stomach. "If Straoc's hurt, then something bad has happened. Then Dad isn't coming back here."

"I have to tell my father."

I shake my head. "There's no time."

Lisa hesitates.

Jo pushes her. "If you want to help Straoc, we need to get out of here *now*."

Lisa frowns, but grabs one more scroll, and as soon as she opens it I see that it's a cross section of Capian, complete with the tunnels and gastrain tracks. There's a key in the corner, and corresponding symbols over various buildings. Blueprints to the city.

I catch my friends' eyes, surprised and pleased. I'm feeling an energy thrum through me, and I'm suddenly impatient. We're not stuck here anymore and now I'm eager to leave.

There's a shout downstairs, still far away, but we all jump.

"The guards discovered my deceit," Lisa says. "They will check your room and then everywhere." She tugs a small bag free from where it was attached to her belt. She dips her fingers in and licks the water from them.

"You take water everywhere?" I ask.

"We are never far from the water," Lisa says. "That is why you are so different from us. You are separated from the water. Your life is quick and scary and is like climbing too high. If you fall, you cannot be healed."

"Let's just hope we don't have to climb any balconies to get out of here, then," Rob replies.

"Lisa," I say. A part of me is feeling guilty all of a sudden. "This isn't some prank, you know, sneaking us out?"

"Mia, friend. I will be fine. Straoc and your father need us, and I say my father would want me to help you." She takes my hand, her skin warm and clammy. "Now follow me and trust. I have not been from this tower before but I am the daughter of Randt and I will see you safe."

Lisa brushes past me and down the stairs, her shock of blue disappearing from view last, leading the way. Jo and Rob run after her, and so do I, but it's hard not to take one more look at the image of Straoc, his body broken and exactly where we're running to.

10

JIMMY

JIMMY STARES AT THE DOOR MARKED WITH THE NUMBER 4. Inside, he knows, are all sorts of nasty things. Viruses, poisons, death in a jar. Each gathered so the Westbrook alums could experiment with the water. It's this place where Sutton must have thought up the virus that's ravaging Westbrook.

Odessa's holding the pistol in her hand like she was born to. Though he doubts she knows how to use it. He doesn't know anything about guns either, not really. He was never into the whole hunting thing. And even though he can tell the difference between a 12-gauge and a deer rifle, it's not like people have been showing him their handguns. They're called concealed weapons for a reason.

Maybe the best move would be to suit back up and grab some super-serious virus and infect Sutton and his men. Of course, Sutton and his team have the water now. And clearly it's capable of stopping a virus. Jimmy finds himself looking at his massive hands. Get the water, save the day. That's the plan.

So the options are simple. Find a way out and get help, or find Sutton and shut him down. Jimmy remembers the sheriff cruisers outside, but he's not sure whether they were confronting the soldiers or helping them. Maybe the police were fooled into think-ing Sutton's men were legit, and that they're here for an outbreak. Shouldn't be too hard, what with the way everyone in Fenton gossips about the Cave.

Jimmy's not the type to pass up on heroics, but he's also not flying solo. He has Odessa to think about. Just watching her hold that gun, the steady hand but shaky breaths, he knows the right move is getting help from the outside, however he can.

He takes Odessa's chin in his hand and gently focuses her. Her eyes are dazed, but zoom in on him. She's here now. Jimmy can't really remember a time back at Westbrook when she gave him this much attention. It's hard not to revel in it.

"Follow me?" he asks. He doesn't order.

She nods.

He inspects the machine gun he took from the soldier, and looks for the lever that people are always pulling back in movies. He finds it and pulls and it gives a satisfying *kachunk* when cocked.

"You know how to use that?" Odessa asks. No joking, no smiles.

"How hard can it be?" Jimmy grins.

She shakes her head, but he doesn't mind. He jiggles the heavy gun in his hand. No problem.

They exit the lab moving slowly, Odessa keeping a lookout at their rear. Jimmy doesn't know where they're going, but he knows that if he keeps looking, he'll find it. That's good enough. Every-thing has to be good enough now.

They hit a T junction and take a right, and about ten feet later, Odessa fires behind them, the shot so sudden and loud he nearly drops the machine gun. She's screaming and runs by him to hide behind his back.

Jimmy curses, and stares at the soldier splayed awkwardly on the floor. Jimmy's about to go see if he's okay when the soldier pulls out his own pistol with shaking hands and shoots him. Or he tries to. Instead, the bullet smacks the wall next to Jimmy's head. When he pulls the trigger it's as much reflex as self-defense. The machine gun's so much stronger than he expected, like ten of his offensive linemen punching him all at once in the arm. The bullets spark on the ground and against the wall but not into the soldier—not that he sees. Jimmy pants, about to shoot again. He knows he should finish the soldier off, but then he'd be a killer. He doesn't want to be.

They run for a while with no destination in mind. When Odessa stops, she's breathing hard, her red hair all over the place.

"You okay?" Jimmy asks her, watching her wide blue eyes tear up. Her cheeks are flushed and her lip are pressed so hard together you can barely see them. "It's okay, Dess. You saved us back there. You did the right thing." But she's not paying attention. She's staring at an open door. It's the Map Room. And Chuck, the other Westbrook alum running this place, is lying knocked out or dead on the floor.

"Do you see that?" Odessa asks.

"Yeah, he needs to get to a hospital."

"No, Jimmy, look at the map!"

He does, but can't see anything special. It's just as strange as it was before, filled with pale skinny dudes and waterfalls.

"I don't get it."

"There's tons different! You don't see it?" She looks at him skeptically. "That one there, the water's flowing, for one, when it used to be a black hole. That makes sense, in a crazy magical way, cause there *is* water now. But look at that city, it's got a ring of fire around it now. I swear that wasn't there before. And the waterfall is smaller. And the last image, that image within the image—the map within the map—it's black. The map's changed!"

"How's that possible?" he asks.

"No idea," Odessa says. She's ready to step into the room to investigate the map further, but Jimmy knows they don't have time for this. He takes her arm.

"Let's worry about ourselves for a moment," he says, looking around. "We're back up in the center of the Cave. Where's the greenhouses and the back entrance?"

Just then they hear voices, boot steps.

"Behind the map. Hurry!" he whispers, and pushes her into the room. They step over Chuck and dive behind the enormous map. It's in the center of the room and hung in place, so the best they can do is crouch behind it and hope no one decides to walk into the room. Jimmy gets his gun ready, and takes Odessa's pistol from her shaky hands and puts it into his waistband. She doesn't even seem to notice.

The voices get louder. Veronica. And Sutton.

". . . sure what you were trying to accomplish. You have to stop this now."

"Don't you think I know that?" Sutton replies. They're in the hallway, almost to the door. The Doppler effect in full force.

"Then *do* something," she replies. "Grab a ten-gallon jug of the water and send your men out and help everyone. And give some to Chuck."

"Screw Chuck. The condescending bastard," he says, stopping at the door, probably to look at his former colleague. "He can rot in there." Jimmy can hear a few other footsteps pulling up. Must be a couple guards with them.

"There's not much I can do now—I meant . . ." He pauses to gather himself. "I meant for this to be easy, you know? Greg's too stubborn."

"Blake, that's bullshit. You've *killed* people. Hundreds of them, maybe. This could get worse, this could get catastrophic!"

"How was I supposed to know our hazmat suits wouldn't stop the virus? We were supposed to contain it at Westbrook."

Jimmy can almost see Veronica throwing up her hands in disgust. "That doesn't matter now, Blake. You can *do* something."

"There's no more time, Veronica," he says. "It's too late." For a moment it's so quiet it's hard to believe they're still standing there. "Listen, Greg went into the well for the source . . . It's *real*, just like he said. And I need it."

There's a loud noise. Sutton grunts. Then Veronica cries out in pain. She slapped him and what, a guard clocked her? Jimmy tightens his hands around the gun. Odessa shakes her head no and grabs his arm.

"Hey!" Sutton shouts at one of the guards. "Don't touch her."

"Leave me alone," Veronica yells, and Jimmy would like to think it's because she's refusing Sutton's help. "You can't just run off, Blake. Your quarantine didn't work. Whatever it is you are trying to prove has gotten out of hand. So you have to fix things. Now, as much as it pains me to say it, *you* are the only one who can save us." Her voice softens. "I know you. I *know* you, Blake. Please."

It's quiet. Jimmy's heard that tone of voice before. It's the same one his mom uses on his dad after a fight. Not surprising, considering that these two used to be married.

"Fine," Sutton says, relief palpable in his voice, as if he were wrestling with himself and his better side won. "Gutierrez," he barks in a commander's tone, "get down to the well and take as much water as you can carry and go straight to Furbish Manor. Hand out water to the boys and then get to Westbrook." He pauses, his voice sounding weary. "Last report was that a group of kids barricaded themselves up in a dorm and haven't been infected yet. Distribute the water, just a few drops per person. I want you radioing everyone left to come in on rotation and get their share, then report to me here at the Cave. Everyone gets, no exceptions, understood?"

"Yessir!" Gutierrez shouts, and then he's gone, his boots squeaking on the floor. Jimmy and Odessa share a smile, the news about their surviving classmates a ray of hope.

"Happy?" Sutton asks.

"No," Veronica replies. "But it's a start."

"I can't deal with it myself. I need the source," Sutton says.

"I thought you sent your little Judas for it," she sneers. Jimmy's blood boils at the reference to Brayden. He replays the image of Sutton ordering him to jump in the well.

"I don't want to take any chances."

"Then what're you going to do?"

A pause. "We're gonna go get it."

"What now?" Odessa asks after their footsteps recede.

"I don't know," Jimmy says, racing through options. He was never very good at this part—the brainstorming.

"Sutton's sending out water, so we're okay, right?"

Jimmy shakes his head. "What if it's spread to Fenton? What if our parents have it?"

"But they're going to follow Mia and the others. They're going to go after them."

Jimmy wonders, not for the first time, where they went. Must be an underground cave or something that they swam to.

"We can't do anything about that," he says. "We need to get some water ourselves to help others, and then get out. Find our parents, tell people. Call CNN."

Odessa runs her hand through her brush-fire hair. "How do we do that? I don't know where the well is."

Jimmy only knows two people here who do.

It doesn't take long to catch up to the sound of the boot steps and the voices. They sound muffled, but Jimmy resists the urge to get close enough to hear. That would be stupid.

After a time, the voices fade. *Stay back*, he motions to Odessa, then sneaks a peek around the corner. It's the elevator they used yesterday to get to the well, down at the end of a bright corridor. The door's been wrenched open, exposing an empty shaft, and Jimmy sees the top of a ladder propped against the entrance.

"We're there," Jimmy whispers. "The elevator's busted."

"What now, then?"

"Give me a sec." He frowns, then tiptoes to the shaft and glances down the open hatch in the top of the elevator. The inside is scarred black, from some sort of fire, and a ladder reaches through the opening all the way to the floor.

"If we go down that, we're cornered," Odessa says, leaning out over the edge, holding his arm to get a better look.

"But that's where the water is," Jimmy says.

"I know, I know. Okay, I got an idea—"

But she never gets a chance to say anything. There's a *clang* below them, someone climbing the ladder. Odessa turns to run, but Jimmy grabs her arm and pulls her back.

"What?" she mouths, her blue eyes flashing.

He makes shushing motions and lays himself carefully down on his belly, aiming the gun right at the head of the ladder. He waves behind him for her to move back, and she finally does, far enough away that he can't see her. He can't see anything really, nothing beyond the end of his gun. The ladder rings louder, step by step, and then he sees one hand, and another. Adult, male, trimmed nails and dirty fingers. Jimmy tightens his grip on the gun.

A black knit cap tops the ridge, then a pair of eyes.

"Shout and I'll kill ya," Jimmy whispers.

The eyes stare for a beat, then the hat nods.

"Come on, keep coming. Slow, hands where I can see them."

The soldier climbs. Dark eyes, round jaw, tight black gear. He has a large backpack that's open, its maw stuffed with bottles full of water.

"Gutierrez?" Jimmy guesses, recalling the name of the man Sutton ordered to grab water.

An eyebrow raises. Jimmy remembers, suddenly, that he looks ten years older than this guy. That's why he's getting real respect. The gun helps, of course, but who's holding it matters just as much.

"I want you to follow me, quietly. Got that?"

Gutierrez nods. The problem, Jimmy realizes, is that the narrow hallway isn't exactly conducive to this move. If Gutierrez passes him here, there'd only be a foot or so between him and the gun. Too close for comfort.

"Odessa, you there?" Jimmy calls as loudly as he dares.

"Yeah, Jimmy."

"Check the hallway, make sure no one's behind us. Find me a room. Quickly."

She doesn't even reply, just squeaks away.

Jimmy and Gutierrez keep a wary eye on each other. In movies, this is where the professional soldier calmly steps forward and takes the gun from the amateur's hand, then explains that the safety is on. Jimmy knows the safety's off, but he's still sweating. He doesn't want to shoot anyone. He wonders, idly, if he could push Gutierrez into the elevator shaft and somehow keep the bag of water bottles if he had to.

"I got one," Odessa says behind him, her voice low and urgent.

"Okay, this is what I want," Jimmy says, trying to channel his outer adult. "I'm going to walk backward and you're going to follow, your hands raised, and that's all you're gonna do, got it?"

Gutierrez nods, but he also runs his eyes over Jimmy, sizing him up. Jimmy doesn't like that, he can almost feel the calculations going on in the soldier's head.

Jimmy walks backward, desperately hoping Odessa is watching and will tell him if he's about to hit a wall. He hits the intersection and feels Odessa's hand on his back, like he's docking gently into a space station.

They reach an open door, not twenty yards later, and Jimmy orders Gutierrez in. He feels a small moment of triumph. It's like he just won a level of a game: "Get the bad guy down the hall while walking backward." It's a storage closet, loaded with mops, brooms, cleaning supplies, metal shelves and stacked chairs. "Give me the backpack."

Gutierrez takes it off slowly, and risks speaking for the first time. "What do you want with these? I need them. People will die."

Jimmy pauses. "I know, and I want you to follow your orders as soon as you can. But I need the water too, and I'm not about to go down that elevator shaft. I'm taking the water to Fenton, to make sure everyone's okay there."

"But there's no one sick in Fenton," Gutierrez insists, shaking his head, his voice unsure.

"You don't want to be here, do you?" Odessa asks, surprising them both. She's staring hard at Gutierrez, as intimidating as a woman in scrubs and slippers can be.

He doesn't reply, but watches her carefully. The room feels suddenly smaller. Jimmy feels the weight of the gun in his hand.

"You were hired by Sutton for what? To guard the school?"

"We didn't know what he was gonna do," Gutierrez admits.

"Doesn't that matter?"

"Not to some."

"But it does to you?" she asks.

He shrugs, like a little boy admitting his guilt. He puts his hand on a shelf to steady himself, but all Jimmy sees is the Raid bug spray nearby. This room is full of MacGyver-style weapons.

"Okay here's what's gonna happen," Odessa continues, not missing a beat. "I'm gonna take this water, and Jimmy here's going to guard you. In five minutes, Jimmy'll let you go, and you'll just follow your original orders to bring water to Westbrook all over again. Clear?"

"What are you doing?" Jimmy asks. "Don't split us up."

"Saving as many people as we can," she replies. Her face is hard. "Oh, come on, Jimmy. How else are we gonna get out of here? If we let him go now he'll run to Sutton and we'll get caught." She wheels on Gutierrez: "And do you *really* think Fenton is okay, when the virus spreads through hazmat suits? Get your head on straight."

Chastised, Gutierrez looks away from her.

"You sure there's no one sick in Fenton?" Jimmy asks.

Gutierrez's quiet. "Not from the last report."

"But you don't know."

He shakes his head.

Odessa jumps in. "You want to save your soldier friends at Furbish Manor, right? You actually want to help the kids at Westbrook?" Gutierrez stares her down. He doesn't like being spoken to that way. She's not phased though. It's clear the soldier's uncomfortable with Sutton and what he's doing.

"Then pretend we never existed."

She hefts the backpack and steps close to Jimmy. "You'll come after me, right?"

"I want to go *with* you," he whines. This, to him, is far from the plan.

"Jimmy, there's no way we'd get the water, aside from this, right here right now. We *have* to take it. And then you *have* to let him go. Even if he sounds the alarm. If he doesn't get water out there too, everyone's screwed. We need each other."

"Girly," Gutierrez pipes up. "I'm not gonna tell."

Odessa considers, but shakes her head. "I can't afford to believe you. Jimmy, just watch him for ten minutes. Give me enough time to get ahead, okay?"

"You sure?" he says, feeling absolutely helpless. Just a week ago she'd have wanted to Instagram this.

She smiles, slapping the water-filled backpack. "What can hurt me?" Then she turns to Gutierrez. "Hey, flyboy. Which way's out?"

He nods his head to the right, as if that's really helpful. And then she's gone. Just gone.

Jimmy pulls a plastic chair from a stack and sits there, watching Gutierrez and trying his darnedest to hear Odessa's footsteps recede down the hallway.

11

LISA'S GONE. TO DIVERT THE GUARDS, SHE SAID. BUT it's odd having the run of the place. We tiptoe through what is essentially Randt's throne room. It's like sneaking around the principal's office. But true to her word, no one's around as we ghost to the foyer. In fact, there's no noise at all aside from our steps. It's unnerving.

The trickiest part is activating the elevator, even with Lisa's instructions. The keys are in another language, like the cursive version of the hieroglyphics on the map. Lisa told Rob what to look for—a tall tree and a man with a fire at his feet, both separate buttons—but now that we're here, the air drafting up from below, urgency beating in our hearts, finding these images is like playing memory with cards. There are hundreds of them, as if the elevator was built to fly into space.

"There it is," Jo says, pointing at a tree. But Rob stops her hand and says, "No way, look. That's a *small* tree. That's not even the same type of tree that Lisa described."

"Wow, thanks, Odessa," I say with mock admiration, comparing him to our genius botanist who's back in the Cave.

Rob smiles, but doesn't answer as his finger quickly traces the line of glyphs. He's good at this stuff, I know, almost bred for it, what with the hours of online gaming, the coding he does. I hear voices; one of them might be Lisa's. "Hurry, Rob," I say. What if he gets it wrong? Will an alarm sound? Will we go to a random floor? Will we just sit here smiling while a troop of Keepers storms in with their fighting ribbons?

"Got 'em," he whispers, triumphant. He presses a tree image, one that, for me, is hard to distinguish from what Jo pointed at, and then a man on fire and suddenly we're moving, the elevator descending as smoothly as it rose and then just as suddenly stopping. We only went down maybe thirty feet, and are at the edge of a dark and empty foyer, encased in shadows, just like Lisa said.

"Hurry," I say, and jump from the elevator. Jo joins me but Rob's still on the elevator, futzing with the glyphs.

"Rob, come on! No time!"

"We have to send the elevator back," he says, whispering harshly. My fear spikes. He's right. What a basic thing to forget. The guards will come out to get the elevator and see that it was parked one floor below and there goes our surprise.

Rob pushes a couple buttons and sprints toward the edge but before he takes three steps, the elevator begins moving, rising up quickly. Rob trips and lands on his stomach, halfway off the elevator, his arms dangling over the side.

"No!" Jo shrieks in horror, rushing ahead to grab him. I'm right beside her. If the elevator keeps going, Rob will be cut in half by the ceiling as the elevator zooms upward. I jump, take his left hand and immediately lose my grip, falling hard on my ass. Jo's got his right hand, though, and she flings herself backward. Rob slides off and into her lap and they lie breathing hard, but alive. My whole body shakes with relief.

"That was supposed to be the easy part," I say, and Rob and Jo laugh. Rob pats his body over and over to make sure he's in one piece.

We hear voices above again—Lisa instigating part two of the escape. That's why we're here. Apparently, Randt left the floor we're on empty to give to Lisa when she's ready to take a husband. Part one: Lisa somehow persuades the penthouse guards that she didn't lie to them. But we can't just go down to the garden, because the Keepers there would see us. Part two: Lisa goes ahead of us to clear the way.

The elevator descends, very quickly, and from the shadows we can see the two guards on the platform with Lisa, heading down, her hair leaving a trail of neon blue behind her.

The emptiness of the dark room is unnerving, and we sit with our backs to it, looking out on the atrium, waiting for five minutes to pass. My body's tense, wired to go. It feels like that moment back at Furbish Manor, when we were lined up against the wall before running through the firefight and into the woods. Brayden was there, but that was the beginning of his betrayal. Just a hundred feet away his parents were bound, gagged, locked up in the basement and he was let go.

Finally, Rob gets up and calls the elevator, which begins its upward climb once again. "Now we just take this down and hide in the trees directly in front of the elevator. Or that's what Lisa said. Sounds easy enough."

"How's she supposed to clear the courtyard?" Jo asks, getting on the elevator.

"I don't know, Jo," Rob says. "She's a princess. She gets what she wants."

Jo doesn't say anything. She looks over the edge as we move. It's fast, like last time, and my hair whips into my face. It smells oily, feels oily. I almost moan aloud trying to calculate when I might get my next shower. *If* I get one.

The elevator stops, and for a moment I'm certain there'll be fifty Keepers strolling about, but Lisa is as good as her word, and there's no one in sight. The gardens are big and spread out and there is, indeed, a clump of thin but leafy trees not thirty feet from the elevator.

We sprint to the relative safety of the branches, tucking down to make ourselves small. I'd rather not be wearing white, which stands out against the trees. The bark is black, corkscrew and thick, and the leaves are lined with the same familiar shine as the glow-flowers. Quiet, our breath settling, I can hear birdcalls. Water flow. And then, suddenly, the steady pacing of someone walking. I can't see or tell who. I feel as helpless as I've ever been.

The footsteps get closer. I squeeze my eyes shut, for once just trying to disappear.

"Rob?" comes a tentative voice.

"Lisa!" Rob whispers. I open my eyes to see a shock of blue; she's ducked at the waist and peering into our hiding place. It's normally hard to read the Keepers' expressions, but there's no missing the alarm written across her face. She's not having as much fun as she was back in the penthouse planning this all.

"We have to hurry at the moment," she says, peering back over her shoulder. There's a shout from the way she came and through the trees I get a glimpse of a dozen or so Keepers running in all directions, a hornet's nest of yellows and blues, all looking for us.

"This way," Lisa says. She runs fast through the garden, fast enough that we all have to strain to keep up. There's another shout and maybe someone's seen us but we don't stop, and soon we're into the city's underground tunnels. We move through the tunnels in bursts of speed, and then random standstills in doorways as we wait for armed Keepers dressed in Feileen's black and white to sprint by. Now that we're out of Randt's tower, Lisa's in new territory, but she never seems to hesitate, and moves unerringly toward wherever we're going. I guess she has Capian's blueprint seared in her mind.

"Lisa," I say, "you're taking us to my dad, right?"

"Yes, Mia. We go to the Lock. Keepers who are unfaithful to the water are put there."

"How do you know where that is, if you haven't been out?"

"There's a big difference, friend, between being allowed out and going out." She grins, but turns pensive. "Of course, we might have to subjugate the guards."

"Subjugate?" Jo responds, sharing a glance with Rob and me.

"Did I use the word wrongly?" Lisa asks, her voice clearly pained. "We will have to overcome them."

"Knock them out?" Jo says, incredulous, and I agree. I think about Straoc, about how big he is, and about how impossible knocking out one of these semi-immortals would be.

"Yes, Jo. We cannot take their lives before their natural time, so we must bring them as far from awareness as possible, so that the water might still bring them back." She says it gravely, at once innocent and earnest, like she understands what she's saying but only in theory.

Rob holds up his hands to look at them, unsure they can do what she's asking. "I don't know, Lisa. Can you distract the guards? Get them out of there or something?"

Lisa closes her eyes, which is a striking thing. Her face becomes more Topsider than ever, her blue hair cool and perfect, and I see that she's quite a pretty girl. My stomach feels queasy at what we've got to do, as if I didn't have enough to worry about.

When she opens her eyes again she looks resigned, as if we just made her job harder. "It must be done. I will approach the guards, you will not let them touch the water," she says, jiggling the pouch at her belt. She takes off again and we follow because there's no better option. We're all amateurs here.

We reach the prison suddenly, stopping abruptly enough that I'm surprised. Lisa seems to be too, though, because the heavy metal door that she stops at is wide open. The Lock's entrance is situated at a bend in the tunnel, with two bright torches on either side. The walls glitter in the torchlight, and we can't see a thing past the flickering light. The door is black and gaping.

"This should not be usual," she murmurs. "You should stay here." Without waiting for us to answer, she disappears inside.

But it's bright out here. And we can hear the sound of voices, of footsteps, of heavily trafficked routes nearby. "I don't know about you," I say, "but I'd rather get off the road than be standing with our thumbs out when a group of guards come back."

"Agreed," Rob says, and we follow him inside to near blackness. There's a hallway I can make out that goes on for a while, but I can't see much else. There are no gas lamps in here. No glowflowers. The room feels hot, sweat lodge style. I wait a beat, letting my eyes adjust, but still can't really see anything. I hold Jo's and Rob's hands and we shuffle ahead. I feel like I'm in a haunted house.

I'm about to call Lisa's name when she bursts into view, inches from our faces. We scream, all three of us, loud and scared, and I almost pull Rob's arm from its socket.

"Now is not the best time for those noises," Lisa says, her face worried.

"You scared the shit out of me," Jo replies.

"I am sorry, Jo."

"Where's my dad?" I ask.

Her eyes dart around behind us, her movements jerky and filled with unease. "I think he is farther. But I found the guards, and they are not alive," she says, her voice rising in panic. She puts her hands to her forehead and moans. "More dead and more death. More dead and more death."

"Was it Straoc?" Jo asks.

Lisa takes a few shuddering breaths to gather herself. "Maybe," she says. "But I have known Straoc for the entirety of my life. He is . . ." She pauses. "He never hurt me."

"Where are they? Where are the guards?" I ask.

Lisa doesn't reply, just motions ahead, and we move farther into the dark. The hallway is lined with doors, and the first one is ajar, kept open by a shadowed, muscled foot.

"There is another floor," Lisa says. "I saw stairs at the end of this hallway. We should keep looking."

"Lisa," I ask. "Do you have a light?"

Her shape, now just a shadow before us, pauses. "I have my eyes. Stay close."

Jo squeezes my hand and we creep slowly down the hallway, following the bare shaft of light that is Lisa as she guides us farther into the prison. We walk unsteadily down steps, and for the first time I'm beginning to pick up a smell, something unclean and sweaty, like the air itself is dirtier down here.

But there *is* a light. It comes from an open door maybe halfway down this hallway. Not especially bright, and it flickers, but I can see and that gives me strength. Rob and Jo let go of me. The light makes us brave enough to walk on our own.

I put my hand in my plastic pocket and pull the knife. Jo gives me a look, and I shrug. I'm not going in there unarmed.

Lisa starts moving slower, barely making a sound. She is peeking around the edge of the door when we hear a voice I know very well. It's loud and ragged and desperate.

"Please, please stop. Don't do this!"

"Dad," I whisper, and unable to help myself, I leap into the room, my knife clenched tight, ready for everything and nothing at all.

But it's not what I'm expecting.

Dad's there, yes, but he's in a corner of the room, crouched, his face swollen and mottled in colors, blood dripping from his mouth and nose. His knees are curled up to his chest and his hand is in the air, begging. But he's not begging for himself.

In the center of the room, lying faceup on a wooden table, is Brayden. He's pale, a rivulet of blood dripping down his cheek from the corner of his mouth like half the Joker's smile. My stomach lurches and I almost drop the knife. Behind him, facing us, Straoc stands in the flickering light of a gas lamp. The scroll was wrong, he's not hurt at all. Next to him, there's a small birdbath of water. He has his own knife, a big beast of a thing, slick with blood.

My eyes adjust to the light, and I can see the cuts now. Dozens of them scored across Brayden's forearms. Two thick ones on his cheeks, as if he were a bloody football player. His eyes are closed, his body slack. He could be dead for all I know.

Straoc's stunned at our arrival. He looks sharply at Lisa and barks at her in their own language. For her part, Lisa manages to stay fairly strong in the face of his yelling. She points at Dad and says something. Straoc clicks his tongue and shakes his head.

"Mia," Dad croaks. He makes to rise but Straoc casually steps over, plants his foot in the middle of his chest and pushes him back down.

"Let him go," I yell, my voice cracking. I raise my knife, but my hand's shaking.

"You Topsiders work fast to have so quickly corrupted a Keeper, the daughter of Randt no less," Straoc says to us, his tone more annoyed than anything.

"I brought them here of my own mind," Lisa spits. "But I did not know we would find *this*. I will tell my father and you will be cast from the clan."

He laughs. "You do not understand a thing, little girl. Your father sent me here to find out what the map said. It is your father who ordered this." He flicks some blood from his knife as if to emphasize the point.

"I do not believe you," Lisa shouts.

"Then you do not know your father, Lisenthe. This is what the Topsiders are like. These ones"—he points his blade in my direction—"show up and threaten our world. We are Keepers, we are to keep by any means."

"But what are you doing?" I ask, unable to mask the wobble in my voice. "Why are you torturing them?" I look at my father. "Dad, why don't you just tell him what's on the map? Why does it matter?"

"Because, hon," Dad says, his voice weak, tired, "as long as they want what's on the map, they need us. And until they let us go, I won't give it to them."

Straoc whirls on Dad, and without the slightest hesitation he slams the knife into Dad's shoulder. Dad grunts, his mouth open, somehow unable to scream. So I do it for him. Lisa lunges at Straoc but he backhands her across the room. I step toward him and he pulls the knife from my father's shoulder with a sickening sound and holds it in front of me, waving me forward, smiling.

"Stop," Rob shouts, digging into his pocket for his OtterBox.

Smart Rob, gentle genius Rob. Hand over the map so my father can live.

"What, young Rob? What do you have in your pocket?"

Rob pulls out his OtterBox. I doubt it will make much sense to Straoc, but Rob turns it on and shows it to him. Straoc's puzzled, watching the apple on the screen as it boots up. Lisa slides herself up the wall into a standing position, nursing her elbow. She dips her hand into her pouch and licks her fingers, using the water to heal herself. Just like Straoc is doing with the birdbath here: he's cutting Dad and Brayden up and then healing them, able to torture them forever.

My dad coughs, and as if Straoc were reading my mind, the Keeper cups a handful of the water and tosses it at him. It lands all over, but some does hit his face and his arm, and I can see Dad lick his lips; immediately he begins to breathe easier. And I do too.

The iPhone turns on, and Rob flicks the screen to the map, then hands it over to Straoc.

Jo's been quiet up to this point, but I can see her, sidling down the wall to my dad. Lisa's looking at her, making eye contact, and she begins to move as well, slowly, toward the far side of the room.

"What is this? How does it have the map? It is so small." Straoc seems to forget himself, his Topside fascination overwhelming him. He's almost eager, bouncing on his giant calves.

"It's a Topside thing," Rob says, taking a slow step forward, his hand out, pointing at the screen. "Here, let me show you." He takes the phone back from Straoc, who's lowered his knife, his eyes rapt and on this new gadget, and just as pleased with the luck of finding the map, whole, in a perfectly replicated image.

Rob holds up the phone in front of Straoc, the images facing me, so I can see when Rob taps the toolbar at the bottom. I get what he's doing. I'm actually ready when he pushes the button for the flashlight.

It might not work so well on someone in Fenton, but to a Keeper in a dark room who has eyes as big as apples, the light comes as a complete surprise, blinding Straoc. I'm not sure if Lisa and Jo were expecting it, but they're as ready as I am, and we all charge together, smashing into Straoc and sending him sprawling to the floor.

I fall with him and land hard on the hilt of my knife. Straoc gulps and pushes me off him, but that's not too hard to do; I can barely move, my body frozen by the nauseating feeling of his warm blood pumping onto my hands.

Straoc stumbles to his feet. My knife is still in his belly, the hilt so small against his enormous frame that it looks like a toy. He pulls it out, grunts and drops it to the floor with a *clang*. I step back, my nerves seizing, the room suddenly too small.

But Lisa doesn't wait. She charges, ducks a huge swing from Straoc and kicks him in the knee, sending him panting to the ground. "Rob, knock over the water," she cries.

"What?" he shouts.

The water. Straoc can't be allowed to get to it. She's standing in front of the birdbath, blocking it, and Straoc's up again and moving her way, slashing deep into her arm with his own knife. She gasps in pain. Rob hurries to the water and kicks the stand over, sending it splashing onto the floor and into a drain underneath Brayden's table.

"Help her," I shout. And that seems to spark everyone in the room. Dad drags himself forward and wraps his arms around Straoc's leg. I grab Straoc's arm, Jo pushes hard on his wounded stomach and Straoc's on the ground again. Lisa stomps on his wrist, breaking his grip on the knife, sending it clattering to the stone. Jo pulls Straoc's pouch from his belt, spilling the rest of his water on the floor. He's on his back, tendons in his neck straining tight, bellowing in rage.

I grab my little knife from the floor and hold it to his throat.

"If you move, Straoc, I *will* kill you." I don't know if I believe myself, but I sound threatening enough. I stare in fascination at the wet blade resting lightly against the skin of his neck, a thin line of blood already forming.

Straoc stops, his eyes wide, breathing hard, a wounded beast.

Lisa's grimacing, her arm split along a seam—it's amazing she's not passed out from shock. She looks around at us. "You need to go get someone. We need more Keepers here. We need to restrain him."

"Mia," Dad says, staring at my left hand, at some blue stains on my finger. "What's that?"

"What? Nothing. Berries," I say, keeping my focus on Straoc, on the blade pressed to his neck. "I took them from the greenhouse. Who cares?"

I can't move because I'm the one keeping Straoc in check, so there's nothing I can do when Dad slips his hand into my pocket and pulls a few berries out. A rising dread courses through me as he rolls them in his hand, three blue circles—just like on the map—and then slams his palm over Straoc's mouth.

"Dad!" I shout, but it's too late. He pulls his hand away and Straoc's mouth and teeth and lips are bright blue. He tries to spit, his big tongue working past his lips. He's like a guppy gasping in the air.

"Oh man," Rob says.

"What?" Lisa asks. "What is 'oh man'? What is going on?"

Straoc seems to get what's going on because suddenly he comes to life, pushing me off him—getting his cheek cut halfway open in the process—and scrambling to his feet. Before we can even move, he's out the door, faster than I would have thought possible. But I hear him slam into the wall in the hallway. I run after him but he's already on his knees, breathing slow. Blood or saliva drips from his mouth onto the stone.

Lisa pulls out her own pouch and takes a shaky step forward, but Rob holds her good arm.

"Not you," he says, taking the pouch.

Rob moves alongside Straoc and bends at the knees, pouch shaking in his outstretched hand, but before he gets a chance to give water to the Keeper, Straoc slumps forward, head onto the stone. Lisa closes her eyes, unable to watch any more, and I put my hand on her shoulder.

"Are you okay, Mr. Kish?" Jo asks after a while, trying to fill the silence. He smiles at both of us reassuringly. It's so strange to see him here, the relief in me so palpable that I feel spent, as if there's nothing more to do. Let's go home, let's ignore all this and get home and make pancakes and watch *Dead Poets Society*. But then Dad's face shows alarm, remembering something.

"Brayden," I say, reading his mind.

Jo, Dad and I rush back inside, and all I can think is, *Maybe there's water somewhere, maybe on the floor, can I find some on the floor?* But when I see him I can't focus on saving him. Brayden betrayed me, I know this, but right now, seeing the skin along his chest curled open like a peeled orange, his face streaked with blood—right now it takes everything not to put my hand on his forehead and sob into his chest.

Dad feels for a pulse. He looks tired, grim. "He's alive, barely."

Lisa stands in the doorway, blood all over her shirt. She's looking ragged. We all are. "We have to get him to water. I'll carry him."

And she does, tossing him over her shoulder with no preamble. It's like she can't allow two people to die today. We follow, my father leaning on me and Rob. I smell his sweat, his blood. He's heavy, but he's trying. He needs more water himself.

We pass Straoc. I step on his hand accidentally. I feel his finger break beneath my heel. I don't think I'll ever forget the sound.

Up the stairs, in the light, Lisa bears a look of stark resolve. "There is no easy water here. The nearest font will be with Arcos and his clan. No one speaks but me, understand?"

We all nod, confused, and then she raises her head and screams like a banshee in the wind.

"Lisa, what're you doing?" Rob says, his voice straining. "You'll bring Arcos's men."

She looks at him, her face impassive. "That is exactly the plan."

12

IT DOESN'T TAKE LONG.

They come as a troop, more soldierly than I have yet seen, nine Keepers running three abreast. Both male and female, they're dressed in thin, tight silver shirts and pants that appear to be hybrid armor and clothing. They shimmer as they run. Each has the same long black hair twisted into a bun on top of his or her head. They are big and scary and stop fifteen feet from us, watching warily.

One of them, the collar of her shirt lined in a shimmering red, calls out to Lisa in their native tongue. We've gathered together in a clump, a pretty pathetic group. Dad can't stop rubbing my back, as if he's not sure he can believe I'm here.

Lisa responds in English, presumably for our sake: "Please, friend Keeper. We need safe passage to a font."

The Keeper is tall, fierce looking, and I notice that she has a paint streak of that same red down the ridge of her nose. She glances at the open door to the Lock and squints suspiciously. With her large eyes, it makes for a very intense expression.

"Where are those who guard the Lock?" She looks us over. "Why are you carrying a Topsider?"

"I understand, and I am sure the seeing of us now and at this moment brings questions to your heart," replies Lisa. Keeper diplomacy seems very proper, a slow way of doing business. "I am Lisenthe, daughter of Randt, one of the Keepers of the Source. You know of me, surely. We surrender ourselves to you and Arcos, Keeper of the Source, so that we might have your protection and speak to Keeper Arcos." She motions to Brayden with her head. He's bleeding down her shirt. "But most of all we need a font, all of us."

The officer considers this. "I am Palu, commander. And who does not know of the daughter of Randt, kept in his tower? You look of your father, and Keeper Arcos has little to trust in him at the moment. You will come, and you will be bound."

At a gesture from Palu, the soldiers fan around us, giant pale shadows, and without a word we're trussed up and organized. A Keeper takes Brayden from Lisa and puts him on his shoulder; another carries Dad, who winces with each step his carrier takes, but I get it: he'd only slow us down if he walked on his own.

Once we're lined up we move quickly. I'm tired, both physically and emotionally, and soon the hallways blur and I'm lost in the rhythm of running, just trying to keep up. Like the end of a day doing laps at the pool, exhaustion fading in. I stare at Rob's feet, watching him stumble over and over again.

I don't realize we've entered a new tower until the stone under my feet turns abruptly to wood. Long wide boards, dark with a distinctive wood grain, laid in crisscross pattern. The boards must be thick because they don't give at all. I catch my father looking at me as he dangles almost upside down from a Keeper's back. He shakes his head. I'm not sure why.

We're in an enormous spherical courtyard at the center of a huge building, like the inside of Epcot. Everything's wood. There are wooden beams lining the walls, balconies supported by columns as thick as redwoods. On the floor there are trees, like at Randt's tower, except here they jut from huge planters dug into the floor instead of grassy gardens. The place is empty, the vastness reminding me of the inside of a cathedral.

Palu takes us directly to another gazebo/elevator, this one with a wooden door, but we head down, not up. Levels flash as we go, exits into foyers like at Randt's tower. Five, six, seven of them until we stop.

Palu motions for us to rise. "You must not speak unless spoken to," she says, her voice deadly earnest. "I cannot repeat myself enough. To speak will be to end your lives. Have patience. Is this clear?"

We nod our heads like schoolchildren. I'm tired of the surprises this place brings. I can hear the sound of Straoc's finger under my foot. I can see the faint bubble of breath on Brayden's lips. I just want to get this over with.

Palu opens the door and steps out, guiding us into an amphitheater filled with Keepers in all manner of clothing and style. It's like the Exchange, only quiet. Five hundred pairs of bright eyeballs stare at us from their seats as we're ushered in, but no one makes a noise. I wonder why they're all here; surely not because of us? That would be impossible. Palu walks down the center aisle and motions for us to sit in the first row, which is empty. She lays Brayden down on the thick wooden beams in front of me, then steps off to the side, as if she doesn't want to obstruct the view of the Keepers behind me.

In front of us, onstage, is the fattest Keeper I've yet seen. He's huge, easily five hundred pounds, but at seven feet tall his bulk seems manageable—at least mobile. He's got several chins, and a long black braid that goes over his left shoulder and drapes down his ruby red robe. His eyes are fierce green and he's staring blankly at the crowd, as if in a daze. Beside him is a font, and behind him is a large white canvas, mounted between two gray and stiff pieces of petrified wood, gas lamps and glowflowers positioned all around to provide light.

I lean over to ask Dad what he thinks is going on, but he waves me away, and I remember the rule not to speak. Dad winks reassuringly, the crows' feet around his eyes wrinkling, and it's just like him to try to make light of a serious moment. An irrational anger flares; why can't he see that I got us this far, that I'm not some helpless kid who needs his comfort?

What are we doing here? Jo mouths to me. Her knees bounce and I wish I had that kind of energy.

The Keeper onstage dips his fingers in water from the font and sucks them greedily, then picks up a large brush from the ground. It's the size of a broom, though the head is smaller and more refined. He dips it in some paint—it looks like there are dollops of color at his feet, as if he's using the floor as a paint palette.

This must be Arcos himself, one of the Three, and like Randt with his library of scrolls he must paint images, except that Arcos seems to prefer a bigger canvas and a larger audience. Watching his robes shift and his massive bulk move gracefully back and forth is entirely surreal. I feel like I'm at some bizarre performance for the Postmodern Club back at Westbrook. But it's what Arcos draws that actually matters.

He divides the canvas in half, right down the middle, and on the left side he draws Capian, just as I remember it from the gates. It's stunningly accurate, identical to the memory I have of the view from the steps leading in. He finishes the towers quickly, and then he turns to the empty canvas on the right. He's pushing his brush hard, scraping the paint on. At first I think he's just drawing something from Capian I haven't seen before but then, suddenly, I know. My stomach curls. I've seen that view, I *stood* there, on the hill above Westbrook by the broken statue of Socrates. I could see the school and Fenton beyond. There was snow and soldiers and spotlights and we escaped Sutton's quarantine by knocking the statue down and racing across the frozen lake. And in less than five minutes Arcos has dipped into my memory and sketched exactly what I saw. He paints a line of blue between the cities, and underneath them, like an aquifer.

Arcos steps back and examines his work. He picks up a fresh paintbrush and dips it in a bowl of red and then yellow paint and smears it violently across the Keeper city, lighting it on fire. I can feel the breaths behind me suck in. The hair on my arms stands on end. Even Palu looks queasy.

Then he dips the same brush in black and red and splatters Westbrook, and only Westbrook. But he draws little tendrils up to Fenton, and I'm sure Rob and Jo and my dad recognize that the tendrils aren't random, but follow the exact line of Highway 504, snaking through the mountains.

Arcos drops the brush, turns around and stares right at me.

"The source speaks of a falling city, of Capian in flames, but I do not know why." He squints at me, then at the rest of us, settling finally on Brayden on the floor. "Palu, I do not want sickness and hurt here. Take him to my personal font."

Palu nods, then hurries to lift Brayden from the floor onto her shoulders. His hair falls down his face and a drip of blood streams from his nose. Before I can do anything she runs up the steps and is gone. I stare at the blood he left on the floor, shuddering.

"I know why Capian falls," Lisa says, standing slowly.

"Oh yes, Lisenthe, daughter of Randt, youngest of us all. Your father has finally shown you his scrolls, where he stores the visions the source gives him? The ones he locks away and guards like a treasure. I paint what I take from the source for all to see. I do not fear you reporting back to him. It is a shame that we no longer share our visions, that we are shown such different realities. When the Seven were here, when Feileen was alive and your father cooperative, we came together and could grasp the full meaning of the source every time. And now we are left with this," he says, indicating the canvas. "An imperfection."

"The city falls because of the Seven you speak of, and the map they made," Lisa says, her eyes fierce and defensive. Alarm bells go off in my head. Arcos shares his visions with his Keepers, which means they know of the map too. It is no secret at all.

"Lisa, no!"

But she goes on as if she hasn't heard me. "The Topsiders here, this one"—she points at Dad—"he has seen and memorized the map." The room erupts into shouts, not just shocked whispers but full-throated shouts.

Arcos stares at Lisa, and then at my father, his great brow clearing. He steps closer. "The Seven, my sisters and brothers, left when we were young. Did Randt tell you why they left? Does anyone here understand why they left?"

No one says a thing.

"They left to ensure the source. To keep us safe. And any map they left was created for the same purpose."

"My father thinks differently," Lisa replies, speaking loudly, defensively, as if on trial. "He believes the map is a guide to the Seven, that when we were ready enough to go Topside, it would be there to show us the way."

"We all know of your father's politics, Lisenthe. Feileen has long opposed his wish to go Topside, to abandon us like the Seven. The map we sense is an excuse for Keeper Randt, nothing more. We Three made a vow to await the Seven and until then we will not allow anyone to leave, even if that involves force." There are rumbles of approval around the room, but Lisa just takes it all in stride. She believes her dad, she has faith in him.

"You don't understand the map," Dad whispers, so quiet I can barely hear him. But apparently loud enough.

"Speak, Topsider, speak for your kind. There is little else you can do," Arcos says. He holds out a huge hand to silence the crowd.

Dad stands gingerly, his face a flower patch of bruises, his lips swollen. He cradles his arm awkwardly. But he still manages to look strong, smart, someone to listen to. I feel my heart swell in pride. It occurs to me that it's not Lisa who's on trial, but us.

"Two of your cycles ago I found the map. And I can say this clearly: it will not lead you to the Seven," he says, easily picking up the lingo. "I believe it was created to guide me," he pauses, looks at me, "to guide us Topsiders to the source."

The crowd goes crazy, lurching to their feet with roars of indignation. The closest Keepers begin to spit all over us, disgusting warm globs that smack. We jump out of our seats and climb the stage, but guards are there immediately and hold us in place. Dad, though, won't be cowed.

"How do you think we got here? Why is this the first time a Topsider has found you? It's because we were shown the way. The Seven *want* us here." He struggles against the Keeper who holds him tight. "Keeper Arcos of the Three, you see the sickness that's spreading among our people. The Topside needs the source to survive. Not just the water, but the source. Do you know why?" He's still looking at me, as if this is all for my benefit. His years of secrets and theories laid bare. "Because we're too late. Because the water has been tainted and turned evil and spreads too fast. Because we need a source of our own Topside to heal from the death that is coming. We need its visions and water and life Topside, not every seventeen years."

"The source does not work that way," Arcos says after a moment. "Its powers differ for each of us, its gifts work best when we are all together. It cannot be moved. It is for us alone."

"I've seen the map," Dad replies with conviction. Everyone's listening, they can't help it. "You are here, keeping the source safe, protecting it. Right? But for what reason? I believe you keep it for *this very moment.* Keeper Arcos, the Seven sent me to ask for your help."

I'm watching him in awe. Part of what he's saying is totally spot on. There's no way at all we'd have known to go through the well without the map. There's no way I'd have jumped in without having seen the images on the map change to give me the hint I needed to find this place. Dad's had the map for years; who knows how much more he could have deciphered. Maybe he's right—maybe we're here to bring the source home.

Arcos looks back at his painting, at his burning city and the dark Topside. "And does the map tell you what the source is? Do you know what it truly does?"

"I don't," Dad admits, rueful. "Not completely—"

"I do," I interrupt. "I know you and Randt use it to find people, to *feel* people, to understand what they are thinking. But you have to *look,* it won't just tell you what's going on in everyone's minds. I know that if the virus spreads, we could use the source to find those who are sick and heal them."

I flinch, expecting the crowd to erupt again. But they don't. They don't make a sound, and in some ways, that's scarier. Arcos blinks once, slowly, taking it all in. His eyes bore into my father, then me, and I feel it—the same thing I felt when Randt stared me down. Like he's looking inside me right now, digging into my mind in some way. I squirm against the feeling, but it doesn't stop.

"You sound like Keeper Randt," he finally says, relinquishing the grip on my mind, apparently satisfied with whatever he was looking for. "You are so focused on the Topside that you forget that we have been here long before you. It is not our duty to venture forth. We tried that once and lost our sisters and brothers and I will stop any Keeper who tries to do so.

"Take them to my chambers," he says to one of the guards, then turns to the crowd of Keepers. "My sisters and brothers, we do not have much time." He points again at the burning city he painted. "Do you see? The source tells me that we must serve our purpose, that we must keep the source safe. Quickly now, go. Call our clans to arms. I feel something coming and there is not much time, not anymore."

13

JIMMY

SIX MINUTES, APPARENTLY, IS ABOUT AS LONG AS JIMMY can stay still.

Gutierrez sits, tapping his combat boot on the concrete, his eyes never leaving Jimmy's gun. "When you let me go," he says, "what you gonna do? Go after her?"

"Obviously," Jimmy replies.

"Won't work," he says.

Jimmy's trying not to listen. He looks around the room. It smells of ammonia and showers.

"You want to know why not?" Gutierrez asks. " 'Cause even if I lie to Sutton, he's going to send someone after you. And if you follow her, they'll find you both." He shakes his head. "Look man, I'm just trying to help. You want to give her a real head start? Makes some noise on the way out, and go the *other* direction."

Jimmy's body is so full of adrenaline it's leaking from his pores. He checks his watch, seven minutes. Good enough.

"Stand up," he orders. Gutierrez gives a resigned smile, but does as he's told, pushing his chair out of the way with a loud *squeak*.

Jimmy raises the gun, butt first. Gutierrez holds up his hand in protest. "Don't knock me out! I can't help you then. I could be down for—"

Jimmy clocks the guy hard in the gut, knocking the wind from his lungs and sending him slumping to the floor. He happens to agree with the soldier; knocking him out would be stupid. Jimmy needs Gutierrez to be able to hurry back for more water, but he can't just walk out the door arm in arm with the man.

He watches him cough and curl on the concrete and then he moves, out into the hallway in a flash and sprinting down the halls.

He can't go the back door route, the way Sutton came in, the way Odessa's gone. He's looking to walk out the front.

Suddenly he's through a door and into an indoor parking lot. It's disorienting and cold, the room so large that at first he thinks he's made it to the greenhouses. But then he sees the three cars, sitting lonely in their lined spaces. There's also a truck, a white van and a forklift.

Jimmy thinks back to the monitors showing Sutton's men out front with the police. The doors are closed now, probably to keep the police out.

Jimmy checks the cars and finds no keys, but in the truck, a deep blue Ford with wheels beginning to crack with age, the keys are plopped on the dashboard, a Home Depot mini-rewards card attached.

The engine turns over in one go, shuddering around him, and Jimmy feels some measure of safety for the first time in a long while, as if the truck were a suit of armor. He sits there idling, letting the cab grow warm, just taking a moment.

A single soldier steps into the garage with his gun raised, the barrel shifting back and forth until it settles on the truck. It's not Gutierrez, that much is clear, but for Jimmy, that's probably a bad thing. He ducks, his breath coming heavy, looking for a garage clicker or something. No good, there's nothing. Does someone in the control room usually let everyone out of the lot?

The soldier's close, fifteen yards or so, approaching from the side.

Screw it, Jimmy thinks, putting the truck in gear and slamming on the gas.

The tires spin, and the soldier shoots. The passenger-side window shatters, and Jimmy screams like a girl. The truck heaves forward, and Jimmy can feel the *ping* of bullet after bullet smashing into the cab. There's a *pop* and the truck lists. The soldier hit a tire. For a fleeting moment, Jimmy's big hands on the wheels, trying to get control of the truck, he finds himself impressed. It always pisses him off in movies when the bad guys don't shoot out the tires.

That's about all he has time to think, as the truck swerves straight for the massive metal doors. Jimmy closes his eyes. Why didn't he put on his seat belt?

There's a noise, a heavy grind, then a piercing shriek above his head, but no collision, and Jimmy peeks his eyes open to see that he's made it through the doors. There must have been sensors kicking on as he got close. He was moving fast, though, so the cab scraped across the bottom of the doors, but suddenly he's hobbling down a long empty drive, still in the Cave, with another huge door in front of him. The double doors must be a safety precaution, and Jimmy curses Mr. Kish for thinking of it.

The soldier keeps firing, but Jimmy doesn't take his eyes off the road this time. As he gets closer, the front doors to the Cave slide up from the ground. Behind him, he sees three soldiers now, sprinting down the long tunnel.

"Come on come on!" Jimmy shouts, banging the steering wheel. He can't squeak under the door yet, but he can't stop. He taps the breaks, sending shudders through the truck, the gate lifted high enough to see beyond the Cave.

It's morning outside, the sun shining bright against the snow-covered everything. The mountains are visible. The trees bent by heavy snow. The air is crisp and whips right into the tunnel and cab, freezing him up.

But it's not the cold air that catches his breath. It's the tank.

The barrel is facing right at him, a gaping hole ready to take down the doors or rip open his face. On top of the tank, on a small turret, is a soldier in a white hazmat suit. He's staring at Jimmy, confused. Then he looks behind the truck, probably watching his friends waving him down.

More shots ping into the back of the cab, shattering glass.

The gate hits the roof and Jimmy hurls the truck forward, swerving off the road and around the beast. On the other side of the tank are a half dozen soldiers—also hazmatted—and three cop cars. One of them has SHERIFF splayed across its side. The men are standing behind their open doors to protect themselves. Everything seems to stop when Jimmy comes into view, frozen in a moment before one cop draws his gun.

Jimmy watches, almost in disbelief, but of course they'd think he's doing something wrong, trying to bulldoze past them from the Cave. One officer's got a beard and a large, dark green wide-brimmed hat that matches his parka. Jimmy's seen him in Fenton plenty of times—the cop even yelled at him once—but doesn't know his name. The officer aims his gun and Jimmy swears he can see him close one eye to get a better bead, but then there's a shot and it's not from the cop.

The soldier on the tank fires his M240 at Jimmy's truck, the bullets coming so fast and hitting so hard that the tires completely give and Jimmy swerves right off the road and into a tree, smashing out every bit of glass remaining. The seat belt digs into his neck, cutting him, and his vision goes hazy.

Another shot and Jimmy ducks. Out of the driver's-side window he sees that the bearded cop's protecting him now, that the cop has shot the soldier on the tank's machine gun, knocking him from his perch.

"Come on," the cop shouts to Jimmy.

Jimmy stumbles out of the truck, still dazed from the wreck. His head aches, but he manages to use the truck's frame as cover, and slips his way in a wobbly dash to the police cars. An officer's been hit, lying flat on the dirty snow. Another's screaming into his walkie-talkie.

"Get in, get in!" yet another cop yells, and Jimmy does, right into the back. It's loud, bullets smacking into the car like punches, but the cruisers are built to withstand bullets—to a point. The car doors slam and two cops are in and the car's moving, reversing like mad.

"What's happening?" one of them screeches, the one in the passenger seat. He's younger, black, with a rookie-clean face and wide, terrified eyes. He's firing blindly out the window.

"Stop that," the bearded cop says. "Just reload and calm down."

Bullets thunk into the hood, a few whiz by, but inside it's quiet. The bearded cop spins the wheel and they fishtail fast down the road toward the highway and Fenton. Jimmy looks behind him through the glass. They've rounded a bend and the road's empty.

Beard is grim, his hands tight on the steering wheel. Rookie breathes hard, his hands tight on the gun.

"I'm sorry," Jimmy says, unable to think exactly what he's sorry for. But it's what came to his mind, an instinct after years of getting in trouble.

"You're from the Cave?" Beard asks, looking at Jimmy through the rearview mirror with eyes so blue they shine.

"Yeah, but I go to Westbrook."

The two cops exchange glances, nothing subtle about it.

"I don't have the virus," Jimmy says, raising his hands in the air. They hit a bump, swerve, keep on going.

"So, what, you're a teacher who *goes* to Westbrook?"

Jimmy looks down at himself, his aged body. "Oh, right, yeah. Um, no—I *had* the virus but I was cured. I'm a student there." He leans forward and the rookie cop fidgets with the gun. "Listen, lots of stuff happened at Westbrook. You probably know that by now. And the aqueduct—"

"We know about the aqueduct," Beard says grimly.

"Then what were you doing at the Cave?"

"They said they were National Guard," Beard replies, glancing at him in the rearview mirror. "They had documentation. They warned us about the outbreak. Who else would they be? We thought they were here to help. And they did, they helped us close the roads all around Fenton. But they've been giving us the run-around for hours about the Cave and then you come flying and they start shooting."

"The radios and cell towers are down," Rookie adds. "There's tanks at checkpoints on the highway in and out. But we weren't told what the outbreak is from. They didn't tell us anything." He looks past Jimmy out the window, back the way they came. "They're dead, Woods, aren't they?"

"Our boys back there? Probably," Woods replies, his voice stone. "Kid, what's your name?"

"Jimmy Diaz. My dad's Chris Diaz."

Woods slams on the breaks and pulls over. "What the fuck kind of game are you playing here, son?" he asks, turning in his seat. His mouth quivers he's so angry.

Jimmy's confused. "Officer Woods, I've seen you around Fenton for years. You caught me toilet papering Jenny Mila's house in seventh grade."

"I know Jimmy Diaz. I definitely know his old man. I don't know you."

"The virus. It's real. I don't have it anymore though. It made me older. It ages you until you die. But I got healed at *this* age so that's why I look this way."

Woods looks dubious; Rookie—his badge says his name is Hendricks—downright incredulous.

"Ya we've seen the virus, we know. But you expect me to believe you're Jimmy Diaz? The same boy who goes to Westbrook? Where does your daddy live?"

Jimmy snorts. "One twenty-eight Cedar Boulevard. He's always wearing a white cowboy hat and he owns half the developments in town and he's got that small lot just outside of Fenton, with the albino horse he says he'll stud. He calls it Wanker and tells everyone so. That's my dad."

"You're really Chris's son, huh?" Woods repeats, blinking a lot as if to make sure Jimmy's real.

"Listen, Officer Woods. I know this is strange. But this is really me. Those soldiers aren't good guys. We gotta get to the aqueduct to meet up with Odessa Cohle—she got infected and looks older like me. We have to get there *now*."

Woods puts the car back into gear, shaking his head slowly. "No, son, we're going to see your father."

Jimmy slams his big hands on the seat, freaking Hendricks out. "You're not listening to me! We *have* to get there. I'm really Jimmy Diaz, you have to believe me. We have to help Odessa. If we don't, the virus might spread to Fenton."

Those blue eyes stare for a moment, and it's clear Woods is debating what to say next. "Son, we're going to your father because the virus already has."

14

ARCOS'S CHAMBERS ARE, LIKE RANDT'S, ON THE TOP
floor of the building. Palu escorts us past plush sitting rooms filled
with comfy-looking chairs and small trees and burning gas fire
pits, like a manicured indoor campground. There's even grass,
thick and green and soft underfoot.

Along the far side of the room is a curving glass wall, bent
along the edge of the spherical building. The floor drops off into a
wide pool, an indoor/outdoor one, with water still and pristine. It
flows under the glass window and to a wooden deck outside,
where we can make out the shape of a figure standing with a towel
over his shoulders. He's smaller than most Keepers should be,
and is leaning over the railing taking in the view, not a care in
the world.

"I guess Brayden lived," Rob says.

He's right, of course. My mind is having trouble believing my
eyes. I guess I was just expecting him to be cut and torn and tor-
tured, bleeding all over some white bed somewhere. I shiver, equal
parts exhausted and uncertain. What am I supposed to do about
him? How does he expect me to act?

Palu motions to a door in the glass, not the invisible type Randt had, but one with a good old-fashioned door handle made of thousands of rubies. "Arcos will be here shortly," she says, ushering us through. "You may partake of the water."

"Thank you, Palu," Jo says. The Keeper seems to appreciate this, because her lips turn upward, almost a smile, before she takes a seat in a chair, staring, blank-faced, our way.

Brayden's watching me. His brown eyes are cautious, and below them are a pair of angry red lines, the remnants of the cuts Straoc left. What kind of pain was he in when he woke? *No,* I chastise myself, *more important things first.* I take Dad's hand and sit him down next to the pool and help him drink, then pour some water on his cuts.

"Dangerous what you did in there," I say to Dad. It's weird, taking care of him, washing his blood from his wounds.

He laughs. "What's this? My daughter lecturing me about safety?"

I stare him down. "I guess so."

"Maybe I deserve it," he replies, putting his arm around me. "While I'm not too pleased to see you in danger, I'm so glad you're here."

"You should've told me. Even yesterday, back in the Cave, you should've told me you were coming here."

He scratches his head, managing to look abashed. "I'm sorry, Mia. I am. I wanted to protect you." He pauses. "I wasn't *entirely* sure I'd be coming back."

I look away. I don't want him to see my face. I don't want him to see how much it hurts me that he was willing to leave me like that, knowing the risks. To distract myself I pool water in my hands and splash it on my face.

The water is cool and clean and, like before, immediately soothes me. Dad's wound is already closing, and down the line I can see Lisa twisting her torso back and forth, testing her ribs. Suddenly, Brayden's right behind me. I can feel it. I can see his bare feet in the periphery of my vision. He needs to cut his toenails.

I don't know what to say, because I don't know how I feel.

"Mia," Brayden begins, but then stops, his mouth opening and closing like a fish. Jo and Rob both look my way. Jo nods encouragingly, steadying me with her gaze.

"Sutton sent you after us, didn't he?" I ask. If I think Brayden's lying, I'm done with him.

"Yeah, he did," he says, not hesitating a beat.

"How'd he know to follow us? How'd he know to send you through the well?" Dad asks, his eyes strangely intense. A part of me is annoyed—this is my interrogation, but it's also the question I wondered next so I let it slide.

Brayden shrugs; his bare chest is smaller than I had imagined, less built. His six-pack looks like the product of a good metabolism, not workouts. He's skinny and dwarfed by the towel wrapped around his shoulders. "He said he could read the map too. He said you told him about the source."

Dad manages to appear shocked. What, did he not realize he told Sutton about this place? Even if he didn't tell Sutton how to get here, I figured it out; why couldn't Sutton? Dad shakes his head. Before he asks something else though, before I let this get away from me, I stand up and get in Brayden's face. Brayden retreats to the railing.

"Why are you here?" I ask, my voice leaving no room for confusion. It's angry and hurt and desperate for answers all at once.

"To get the source." Brayden doesn't blink. Again, no trace of a lie. He holds my gaze. The cold around me shifts. "Mia," he says, licking his lips, "I did what I had to do to save my family."

"Are they saved?" I ask, anger mixed with genuine curiosity. "Did your deal with Sutton pay off? Were our lives a fair trade?"

His gaze wavers, breaks. A part of me feels sympathy. His parents are most likely dead, aged to a husk of themselves by the virus, tied and bound in their basement at Furbish Manor by Sutton's men. But overriding it all is a growing burn. If Brayden hadn't betrayed us and let Sutton in, we'd not be stuck here. We'd be gathering water and figuring out a way to help everyone, his parents included.

"You realize," I continue, "that we can never trust you again?"

"I don't really expect you to. I'm not here to hurt you. I'm here because of my parents, and because Sutton has a gun. And now my body feels like it's been cut in half and put back together. I'll probably have nightmares forever because this water doesn't wipe away what I just went through. So I'll say I'm sorry and you can believe me or not, but as soon as I get a chance, I'm going to get the fuck out of here."

"And what, go back to Sutton?" Jo chimes in, her voice laced with disgust.

He shakes his head. "No, I'll lie to him. Say there's nothing down here. And then leave." He turns away from us, leans on the railing. "It's impossible, how everything has gone to shit."

It's like he just dismissed me. I'm breathing hard, I realize, and I take a moment to pull myself together. Dad stands up, and gingerly puts his hand on my shoulder. Jo turns away to give us some privacy, and joins Rob and Lisa farther down the balcony. I hear the wheeze in my dad's breath.

"You okay?" I ask, because I realize I don't know. It's crazy to think that Dad started this when he was my age, and now he's here, in the thick of it, with me.

But he doesn't answer. He's looking off into the distance, past Brayden, into the city.

Suddenly Brayden stiffens. "Guys . . ."

"What?" I ask, but see it clear enough. The others come too. Even Palu, standing a full head taller than any of us.

Across Capian we see smoke, black and thick, a column of it rising from the walls of a tower. There's no discernible fire, just an all-consuming smoke. It's so dark and thick that the empty black sky above us appears to be reaching down to swallow the building whole.

Lisa groans beside us. Her home is burning.

"You did this," Lisa mutters, her hands twisting hard against the railing. Rob opens his mouth to speak, but thinks better of it. Her face is numb, clearly in a state of shock. Lisa rounds on Palu. "*You* did this. You keep me here and use it to attack my father."

To her credit, Palu doesn't bat an eye. "I did not. That does not make sense, girl. Nor do I know who did."

"But I do," comes a voice behind us: Arcos steps outside. He's geared up, his bulky frame crammed inside the tight red suit he's wearing. Two spears are strapped to his back, parallel to each other and at an angle to his body. His face is painted blood red and he looks half terrifying, half ridiculous.

Behind him, through the glass, four Keepers wait. They're more heavily armed, with just one line of paint streaked across their pale faces. Palu stands ramrod straight, at attention.

"What's going on?" Dad asks. His voice is stronger, and his cheeks are flushed with life. The water's worked wonders on him.

Arcos's large eyes roam him up and down.

"Feileen's clan, they have decided they must move now to secure their place in the city. They have taken offense at the death of their leader. They move to take the source."

"And they blame my father?" Lisa asks.

Arcos raises an eyebrow. "Should they not?"

"You dare," she snarls, stepping forward, but Palu is there, a stiff arm pressing her back.

Arcos isn't pleased, but the fat Keeper's gaze drifts over his city. Distracted.

"Do not worry, young one. Your father is not the sole beneficiary of their distress. We too have fallen under their scrutiny." He points back over the railing and there they are, plain as day, hundreds of Keepers running fast through the maze of streets. They're wearing black, but their spears glitter in the gas lamps and glowlights like fireflies. Distant shouts float up to the balcony. Cries of alarm as they come nearer.

"My Keeper," Palu whispers.

"I sent emissaries to speak to their clan leaders, but they have no one Keeper in charge. Feileen's people fight amongst themselves. There has never been a need for a succession and they are not prepared. But what they do believe is that if they do not hurry, Keeper Randt or even I will take their place with a clan member of my own. There is still time to convince them that we are their allies, not their enemies."

"Allies against whom?" Rob asks.

"My father," Lisa says. Another building—a smaller one—is burning; this time the flames are visible climbing up its edges.

Arcos doesn't disagree, and it makes sense. Feileen and Randt have apparently always been at odds, and Arcos moderated. With Feileen gone, their clans could unite with Arcos to check Randt. But if Feileen's Keepers believe Randt and Arcos worked together, they'd come with weapons ready.

"This is not the course of events I had hoped for," Arcos says. "The remainder of Feileen's people will attempt to control the source. We must hurry there now."

Brayden leans over to me, his voice soft. "I have no idea what's going on."

Suddenly Arcos goes still and closes his eyes, but I can see movement underneath his painted red lids, the orbs rolling beneath the skin. "Your father calls for you." He opens his eyes, the wide pupils slimming down. He looks at Lisa. "He knows where you are. He can *feel* you. If we do not return you to him he will think I have taken you. With Feileen passed, he will want you to take her place. This has always been his wish. Now he will believe I have aligned with Feileen's Keepers." Arcos grunts, deep in thought. "Maybe I should prove him right."

"You cannot join Feileen's people," Lisa says, desperately. "You cannot attack my father."

"Tell me, Lisenthe," Arcos says, his voice curious. "What would you have me do?"

Lisa's tiny compared to him. I'm not sure if Arcos is really asking her opinion. Lisa runs a hand through her blue hair, something I haven't seen a Keeper do. She looks at Rob, then out into the streets where Feileen's clan members come ever closer.

"I do not need the source, I do not need to become like you and Father," she says finally. "But still we must go there."

Arcos considers. "Why's that?"

"Because I need to convince my father to allow a clan leader of Feileen's to join the Three. Not me. It is the only way to stop the fighting."

Arcos looks impressed. "Daughter of Randt but Keeper of herself. I like this one."

"Wait," I say. "What happens if you try to have someone else drink the source?"

Arcos stares me down with his enormous eyes, making me feel small and stupid. "The source is not some puddle for drinking. Not anybody can even take the source. But it does not even matter, as the Seven are alive, somewhere. This I know. This Randt knows. Even if no other Keeper but us know—it is enough. There can be only ten; it is all the source will allow." The streets fill with shouting as a group of Arcos's Keepers round a corner and smash into Feileen's. Arcos waves an arm and the Keeper guards inside rush to the deck. I think, at first, that they are here for us, but they don't even look our way. Instead, two of them pull a large slat of wood from the balcony, revealing a dark maw below us. One of them jumps in, feetfirst, and disappears. What, is it a slide? I guess we *are* at the top of a giant sphere—if this is an escape route, running down forty sets of stairs would be the slow way of doing it.

"Down we go, all of us," Arcos says. "We must be careful. The streets and the tunnels are filled with foes."

He jumps, his wobbling body keen on its feet, and then he's gone.

Jo's next, and in true diver style, she shrugs off her guard and goes face-first into the passage. Even with all that's going on, the guard grunts in respect. He jumps after her. We all do. One after the other, Palu presumably saving herself for last—a good captain.

I send Brayden in front of me. I imagine getting stuck and I want my feet to smash into him, not the other way around. I wait a beat for his black hair to disappear and then follow, and suddenly I'm in complete darkness, sliding quickly down a chute that's curving the entire time as it circles its way down the building's edge.

It doesn't feel like a ride. It feels like a trap. We fall for long enough that I start to lose my sense of time, of place, and imagine us tumbling down and down, below the city, forever.

15

WE LAND IN WATER, A DEEP POOL IN AN UNDERGROUND room, glowflowers planted all along the edges of the walls, lighting up the place. Dad pulls me and then Brayden out onto a slick ledge covered in moss. I'm cold, but no colder than any of the other thousands of times I've gotten out of a pool.

"Where are we?" I ask.

"With the gastrains," Arcos answers, squeezing water from his long hair. Behind me splashes Palu, and then we're all here. One of the Keeper guards is a stocky woman with tight braids down to the center of her back; she's ahead of us, cautiously tipping her head through a door and into a tunnel when suddenly she jerks her head back and a bright flash of silver hurls by, gushing wind into our little room like a full-body air-dryer.

Before I even have a chance to process what's happened, Arcos grabs Jo—the nearest Topsider to him—and shoves her toward the door.

"Go!" he shouts, and he follows. The stocky Keeper's already out of the room. Palu pushes me in the back and I turn on her.

"Hey, stop it. I'm going, all right?"

It's Rob, though, who understands what's happening. He's already at the door, frantically signaling us to follow. "Mia, we're running through the gastrain tunnels! If one comes and we're inside, we'll be ripped in half."

That's enough for us Topsiders, and we all hustle out the door and into a square tunnel that's dark and, like Arcos's building, has an immediately noticeable curve to the walls.

There are no train tracks. We run, all of us, as fast as we can for a few hundred yard; even with the water, my throat burns and my lungs ache. Dad's falling back, so I grab his hand and pull him with me.

Behind us, first, there's a noise. It's faint, like air through a vent. Then the wind picks up, a cold trickle that races by.

"It comes!" Lisa shouts, and all of the Keepers pick up their pace. They've been going slow for us.

The wind comes faster, physically pushing into me, a wall of air. I can't hear the gastrain, no *squeak* of metal or horn from a conductor, but it's right behind us.

Suddenly, the stocky Keeper sticks her head out from a door on the right about twenty yards up. I had lost track of her. She motions and everyone pushes even harder, Arcos managing his bulk, Dad sprinting like a pro, Lisa pushing Rob ahead with her hand in the small of his back. I'm second to last, Brayden behind me, and we're in.

The gastrain slams by. Brayden, eyes wide, the closest to the door, falls into me and I hold him because if I push him off he could fall backward, bump into the train and splatter.

"What kind of plan was that?" Rob asks, panting.

"No time, we go again!" Arcos shouts.

Again? I think, but I leap into the tunnel anyway, thinking of all the seconds already wasted. My body's gassed and desperate to stop; everyone's running ragged. This time, though, the air moves quicker, builds sooner.

"It's already here!" Jo says.

"Not much farther," Arcos replies, pointing up ahead. There, I can make out a platform, like the one we stood on when we first took the train. The ledge seems impossibly high from here, but we have to try. Either this works or we die.

Brayden gets there first and pulls himself up, then takes my hand and hauls me in. Palu leaps up with ease and so does another Keeper and they manage to get Arcos onto the platform after a few strong tugs. The wind's howling down the tunnel. One of the Keeper guards picks up Jo and throws her onto the platform. Lisa and Rob make it fine and then the gastrain comes, impossibly fast but slowing, apparently set to stop here.

"Dad!" I take his hand and it's warm and big and his cheeks are pale and I've never seen that face before. It gives me such a surge of strength that we get him halfway up the platform before the gastrain, like a bullet of steel encompassing the entire tunnel, slams into him.

The next thing I know I'm on my back, Dad beside me, totally fine. The gastrain has stopped in front of us and I can see blood smearing its front and side. I do a mental count, confused at what just happened, but come up one Keeper short. The one who threw Jo, I didn't even know his name. He must have pushed Dad up. And was hit.

I don't have time to even think about this, to ask Dad if he's okay or to get my bearings because the train doors open and inside, standing crammed into the space, are ten Keepers in black and white. They're armed with wicked-looking knives and spears and are clearly surprised to see us.

Palu recovers first, pulling out her ribbon weapon. She slashes at the door, whipping the edge of the ribbon toward them, pushing them even deeper into the car.

One of the Keepers in the train dips his hand into the bag of water at his hip and on Palu's next swing he grabs the ribbon, immediately slicing up his hand and arm, but he grits his teeth and holds on, using his other hand to yank the ribbon away. He falls to the ground, the pain too much, but now the others are free.

Arcos waves his hand and the black-and-white Keepers stagger, as if tripped by an invisible wire. He's doing something with the source, he's a Jedi. We're up and running, from a nearby set of stairs out into the streets, but not before we lose another Keeper to Feileen's troops.

There is chaos and noise. Feileen's Keepers move in the intersections. There's a haze of hot smoke drifting in the air. Behind us, bounding from the stairs, come six Keepers. We follow Arcos, but a part of me knows I can't go much farther.

A white hand grabs my arm, turning me, but then Dad is there, shouldering into Feileen's Keeper and knocking him off his feet. The Keeper lashes out and Dad stumbles to the ground. I stop, help him up but everyone—Jo and Rob and Arcos and the others—they all just run right by us.

One Keeper pulls up and whips his spear into the air. A figure, one of our dwindling group, falls to the ground. I can't tell who. They're too far away and the smoke too thick. I moan involuntarily, and the spear thrower spins to follow the noise. Behind me, the other Keeper—the one Dad tripped—gets to his knees.

We're alone between two Keepers. My muscles ache, and I'm breathing so hard my lungs sear in pain. I've nothing left. I search around frantically and see a stairwell, shooting down into the dark.

"This way," I grunt, dragging Dad to his feet. He's heavy. I hate that I have to carry my dad.

"Mia, leave me," he says, his voice ragged.

"Don't be stupid," I growl. And we stumble, deep into the darkness.

The Keepers are close. My eyes have adjusted to the faint light of the tunnels, enough to guide us, but not enough to spot them. I hear their footsteps, and the sounds of others down here. But we keep moving, turning when we can, trying to find safety. Dad's wheezing, and I notice blood dripping from his chest. My body goes cold.

"How bad?"

He rubs the blood between his fingers. "I'll live."

Great. Dad, the confidence booster.

It gets brighter, and suddenly we're in the Exchange. That much is clear. I'm not sure what district this is because the stalls are closed, shuttered by thin metal sheets, but at the very least it's like a maze. Easy to get lost in, but also easy to lose the Keepers behind us.

I take a left and see it, a small gap in one of the sheets, as if the stall owner closed up too quickly.

"We have to hide," I whisper to Dad, and he doesn't argue. He slides under, leaving a smear of blood behind. I need to cover our tracks. The stall ends up being full of books, so I grab one off the shelf; it's thin but weighs a ton, its cover made out of something like metal. But the pages within are soft and empty, like a journal, and I use them to try to wipe up Dad's trail of blood. It sort of works. Finally I lean back next to Dad, against a shelf. It smells like a bookstore, musty and full of dust, something I love. Except there's no comfort here.

Dad reaches out a bloody hand and puts it on my arm. "Good job, hon."

I swallow my fear, my queasiness at his blood. His skin's ashen, his lips pale and trembling. I can see now where the knife sliced him open, tearing apart the fat in a thin line from his nipple to his waist. It's parted, almost neatly, and I see his muscle stretched and tight below.

"Okay, Dad, okay," I say, trying to comfort myself as much as him. "It didn't go so deep. We can take care of this. We just need some water."

There's a noise in the alleyway, feet squeaking. I hold my breath, my eyes locked on Dad's. Then the feet keep going.

"Mia," he says, trying to sound normal, "do you know why I came down here?"

I don't say anything. I'm scared to.

"I had been sure of the source. Once you stare at the map long enough, there's no way you couldn't believe. So I always planned on trying to come, though ideally with some help. I don't fully under-stand what the source does, why Arcos can only sort of read minds." I know what he's saying. Randt's powers seem so absolute but when you really think about it, it's like he can only gather impressions of the future or people's thoughts. Why is that? "But I found something in the past few months that stuck with me: I think I found the key to the map. Remember how in the bottom corner of the map, in the last image, there's that miniature map, the map within a map?"

I nod. He had told us, when we first saw it, that there were some seventeen smaller versions of the map in that bottom corner. Close mirrors of itself. A potentially endless cycle. Dad's wheezing a little, clearly in pain, but he keeps going.

"Well, a year or so after we kicked Sutton out of the program for creating the virus, I was up late, I couldn't sleep, and you were off at a swim meet in Colorado Springs. So I went to the Cave and took out slides of the virus we kept for research. Sutton really is a genius. I mean, I could literally see how close the virus mimicked the water—it implanted itself into cells, even weak ones, and made them vital and healthy. It basically replicated the effect of the water except that the cells would then go into hyper mode, replicating too fast, growing old and burning out. The fact that the virus can spread makes it, in some ways, even better designed than the water. I mean, imagine if the water was a *good* virus and spread all over the world on its own, healing everything?"

He pauses, looks at me to see if I'm still paying attention, and I am. The virus and the water were never just opposites, but now they seem like brother and sister.

"The thing about that last image of the map, it's just the map in replica, over and over again, with only minor variations. Like what the virus does. But each map begins with the water from the well.

I wondered if I had it wrong, if the virus was not a bastardization of the water, but actually an inherent part, if they worked together. What if the water kept the virus in check, stopped it from killing people, but the virus was supposed to help the water spread?"

"How could it do that?"

"I'm not sure, but I just kept wondering why the well exists in only one place on Earth, and in the middle of nowhere? To just help the random person who found it? It doesn't make sense. Maybe I'm missing something, but I believe the map was put there to tell me: *go for the source, and you can get this water all the time, not just every seventeen years for ten days.*"

"So you think the source is like a tree made out of water? If you take some of it—a sapling—and plant it elsewhere, it grows. It becomes another source. Over and over again?"

"Right," he replies. "So when Sutton came, the only thing I could think was, *Get the source, bring it back and then nothing Sutton can do will hurt us. Then we'll have our own source.*"

It's strange listening to him talk like this, with such conviction. He sounds like a fanatic, taking small bits of evidence and turning it to his favor. I don't like it. Not at all. This weakness is not what we need right now. I want my dad to be my dad. To take care of the situation we're in. To act rationally. "Dad, stop talking. You're wasting energy. I have to get you some water."

He smiles, his lips ticking lazily upward. "Your hair."

I'm getting impatient. Maybe it's the loss of his blood that's making him talk this way. "No, Dad, stop talking. You stay here, just be quiet, and I'll be back, I promise."

He shakes his head. "No, your *hair.*"

I frown, touching my wet hair. Oh man, I'm an idiot. "You're a genius," I say, relief burning through me. I squeeze my hair tight over his wounds, getting a few drops out. It's less than I want, but I know it's something. I manage to force another couple onto his lips.

"Yum," he manages, and I laugh.

"Okay, that should buy us a little time." I stand up and scan the shelves, looking for something to cover his wound. A part of me envisions finding some thread to stitch it closed, but that's probably too ambitious.

We hear another noise outside, something falls to the ground. Then nothing. My heart is in my throat. Dad's breathing too loud. I imagine a Keeper walking by and hearing him. We sit and don't move for a moment, but there's no other sound. I don't relax, not really, but I can't just stay frozen.

I finally find a cloth on a table that smells relatively clean, and bend over Dad. He's sweating a lot, and his hair's sticky. He stinks, the smell of his sweat becoming unbearable.

"Dad," I begin, wanting to say something, but not knowing where to start. I hear footsteps and clamp up. They're quiet, slow, getting closer. I cast around for a weapon but a heavy book is all I can find. We're trapped.

A foot comes into view. It's small, tan.

"Mia?"

"Rob?!"

Brayden ducks under the door, a smile on his face. "I found you!"

My heart stops freaking out, and I cautiously wave him in, glad he's not a Keeper in black and white.

"No, come on. We have to catch up with the others."

"Listen to Brayden," Dad says, his voice stronger. He holds the cloth against his wound. "We have to find the others and get out of here. Can't do that hiding."

He's right. But I hate having to rely on someone I don't trust. "How'd you find us?" I ask, helping Dad to his feet.

"I couldn't find you. I thought you were dead. But then I couldn't find your body." He stops at a corner. "Then I saw the Keepers chase you down and followed them."

I grab his arm. "Brayden, I thought I saw someone get hurt."

"Jo," he replies, his voice grim. "Spear to the stomach."

"Is she okay?" I whisper frantically, suddenly so far away from where I need to be.

"I don't know. I'm sorry. I had a choice to make and I left to find you."

"Your friends are going to the source," Dad says behind us, between painful breaths. His eyes are squinted in pain, and his hand is on his chest. He's bent while he runs, his face dirty and ragged. He needs more water than my wet hair can give him. "That's where they'll find Randt, so we'll find her there."

"I should have helped. I shouldn't have left her."

"You're here," Dad says, taking my hand. "And because of that, so am I." He smiles gratefully and for a moment, everything seems worth it. The tunnels close in on us and we run and I'm afraid for my friend and for our lives. But still, everything seems worth it.

16

JIMMY

FENTON FLOATS BY, THE STREETS EMPTY. IT'S STILL early, but there's something abnormal to this level of quiet. Through the condensation on the window Jimmy sees the town like an abandoned Hollywood set.

"Who else has it?" he asks quietly. They're pulling off Main, past Pinewood Pancake House, where he used to work in the summers. Betty isn't behind the counter. No one is sitting in the booths.

Hendricks glances his way. "Not sure. Lots of people. We only started getting calls last night. People sick, reports of a mass of soldiers at the Cave. We went to investigate, but the soldiers were buttoned up. They just pulled classified rank on us and told us to help close the roads. That's why we confronted them at the Cave, to learn what's killing our people. You're our first clue, really."

"But where is everyone?"

"First people went to the clinic, but then it spread so fast that we had to drive around and shout on the megaphones to stay inside." Woods tugs at his beard. "I haven't slept in forty hours."

"We have to get Odessa," Jimmy says as they pull up in front of his house. It's a small thing with blue siding, a smoking redbrick chimney and a white door stamped with boot-print stains from where he and his dad always kick it open when it jams. The maple in the front yard is getting big, drooping its heavy branches across the old shingled roof. Jimmy sees all the jobs he has to do when the summer comes. He doesn't want to leave the car.

"I'm not going in," Hendricks says.

"That's fine," Woods replies, keeping the car idling and the heater running. "You say we need to get to the aqueduct to find Odessa? But it's blown up."

"The soldiers still got into the Cave that way. They must've cleared the debris or something."

"The thing is," Woods says, looking out over the neighborhood, "we have to do something about those soldiers. They killed my men. If what you say is true we need to get help. I can't just go searching through the forest for your friend right now."

Jimmy stares at him through the grating in the car.

"You don't get it. She has the water."

"What water?" Woods asks.

"The antidote. She has the cure!"

The two cops look at each other. Jimmy presses on, trying to force them into understanding. "She has it. And we have to find her so we can help!"

Woods takes a breath and pops his door. Once out, he opens Jimmy's and reaches out a hand. "I hear you, I do. But I can't have you just running through the woods with all this going on. It's dangerous. And, frankly, if you're really Jimmy Diaz, then you'll want to be here."

Jimmy doesn't want to see. Not really. He heard about Jo's dad and the way he died a shriveled old man. Jimmy isn't sure he can stand seeing that. He's not sure he can handle seeing his dad wasted away. He'd rather be out there, getting the water, *doing* something. Anything to not go in there. But Woods puts his hand on his neck, part comfort, part orders, and pushes him to the door.

His mother answers, her face covered with a painter's mask, her dark eyes bleary from crying. She's wearing jeans and a red turtleneck, and her hair's up in a bun. Did it always have gray streaks in it?

She pulls down her mask slowly, disbelief plain on her face.

"Mom, I'm sorry." He reaches for her but she takes a cautious step back. She looks at Woods, questioning.

"He had the virus," Woods confirms. "He says it's gone."

"How do you know?" she asks the cop, still not looking at Jimmy. He stands there, helpless. Everything is gone, for the moment, but his mother's fear.

"We don't, Patricia. But he came from the Cave, and the soldiers tried to stop him. He's your son. He belongs here."

Jimmy's mom stares at him, her brown eyes unsure. She lifts the mask back into place, then retreats into the darkness of the house.

Jimmy's body slumps. He has to lean against the door frame to hold himself up.

"What does that mean?" Woods asks.

"It means she doesn't know me."

Woods steps inside the house, flicks his flashlight on and points questioningly down a hallway. Jimmy nods, barely, and Woods grunts, covers his mouth with his hand, and gets moving. Seeing his house like this, dark and haunting, makes him feel like the place is already gone. His life is over, and has been ever since he contracted the illness.

It's a short hallway. Jimmy's room. The bathroom. Then his parents'.

His mom's in the corner, sitting on her rocking chair, a small lamp on behind her. There's barely enough light to see by, but she's reading. It's the Bible, which surprises Jimmy. She's never been the religious type. He didn't know they even had one.

"Mr. Diaz," Woods calls. "Chris?"

Jimmy hadn't looked until then. The bed was a king-size, not just because his dad needed it, but because it was the best. Now, though, Jimmy's dad's almost lost in the midst of shams and the flannel duvet. Jimmy has to suck in a breath. His father's face is sunken, a pale beard sprouting from his face, long enough to reach his chest. His mouth is open and his lips are chapped, but his eyes stare alertly at his son.

Jimmy takes a hesitant step forward. The floorboards creak beneath his foot. He remembers hearing that sound every morning when his dad woke up.

"Boy," his dad wheezes.

"It's me. It's me, Dad."

"You got this shit too?"

Jimmy cracks a smile at that, his vision blurred by tears.

"Yes, sir. But I beat it and so will you. I'll save you. You'll see."

"My boy can do anything. He can do everything."

Jimmy's heard that before. It's something his dad started saying when he was younger and excelling at sports. He'd repeat the words in the car and at the field before every game. *My boy can do any-thing. He can do everything. Go get 'em.*

Jimmy can barely speak. He can barely breathe.

Just then there's a loud noise, like a lawn mower at full steam. Out front they hear Hendricks slam the car door and shout something.

"Stay here," Woods says, and runs down the hall, unclipping his gun from the holster.

"That's not Jimmy, Chris," his mother says, her voice muted. She's still wearing the mask and doesn't look up from her reading.

"Mom," he says, pleading. "It's me. That virus that made Dad old, it made me old too!"

She looks up then, and for a long moment he thinks she's fine. Her eyes clear up and her thin eyebrows raise, sending lines across her pasty and veined forehead. She's in shock. She's never been like this before. There she is, watching her husband die and her son morph into a stranger.

"I heard the sirens," she whispers. "They said everyone was dead."

"I'm not! I made it."

"But you aren't you."

The front door bangs open, and Jimmy hears footsteps down the hall. He puts his body in front of his mom instinctively, ready for anything.

But it's Odessa, her red hair brilliant even in the thin light. Close on her heels are Woods and Hendricks, crowding the room. She doesn't say anything, just drops her bag and embraces Jimmy hard. He's never needed a hug more than in that moment.

"How'd you get here?" he whispers into her ear.

"The soldiers left rope ladders and snowmobiles at the aqueduct. Those things go fast."

Jimmy didn't know she could drive one, much less find her way here, but she did. The new Odessa. The most amazing woman he knows. He grabs one of the large water bottles from her backpack and brings it over to the bed.

"Dad," he says, opening the bottle. "This is the antidote. It will make you better."

His dad's never been one for medicine, so his wary expression doesn't surprise Jimmy.

"I'll go back to myself?" he asks, his voice so weak Jimmy can barely hear it.

He reaches out a big, clumsy hand and puts it on his dad's chest. He can feel his body wasting away.

"No, Dad. You'll stay this age, but you'll live."

His dad shakes his head. Jimmy pours a mouthful of the liquid into the cap and brings it close to his lips. "Come on, open up."

"No, Jimmy," he says, with surprising force, pushing him away. "Look at me. What am I now? Ninety? Ninety-five? I've got no strength. I can't move. I can't provide. I can't live like this."

"Dad, don't be dumb. You'll feel better."

"Listen to your father," his mom says in the corner. "He doesn't want it."

Something snaps in Jimmy, a flash of anger that burns across his vision. "This is *bullshit*. This water will save your life and heal everything that's wrong with you. So what, you'll be old, but you'll be alive and you'll be healthy. It's not like you'll be on a ventilator for the rest of your life. You take the water and get better!"

"Jimmy," his dad says, a fierce look across his brow. He's not used to being spoken to this way by his son. "Give your mother some and leave me alone."

Jimmy looks at Odessa, and then at the cap in his hand. It's not spilling. It's not shaking. He's not going to lose his father.

"Sorry, Dad. No can do." He holds his dad down and pours the capful quickly past his dad's lips, causing him to cough and sputter.

Then he hands the bottle over to his mom, who's watching with scared eyes.

"You're going to drink out of this and stop being crazy. We need your help. We need you alive. I want my mom back."

She takes the water, then begins to cry. Jimmy kisses her on the forehead and does the same to his dad. "Sorry, old man. I want you around to see your grandkids."

His dad's eyes are clearing up. His breathing's easier. Jimmy takes back the bottle from his mom and turns to the others.

"One down, everyone else to go."

17

OUT OF THE EXCHANGE, THE STREETS ARE FILLED WITH the echoes of Keepers. We don't see anyone, but they're close. The shouts are loud, like there's a violent protest in the next room. The walls of Capian loom close, and something I hadn't noticed before becomes apparent: the buildings near the edge of the city are smaller, only a few stories high, as if the Keepers didn't want to block the views of the more central buildings.

I wish we hadn't gotten separated. If we had Rob and Jo, we could just leave, just make for the gates. Dad, though, he wouldn't want to go. I can tell. He's anxious, desperate to get to the source. If not, he'd try to save me now, right? He with his daughter in this dangerous civil war, and instead of getting her to safety, he's running down a hazy street toward the sound of fighting. It's hard to remember that this is the culmination of his life's work. He'd rather be here risking his life. And mine.

Suddenly the small road we're on spills out into the huge boulevard that bisects Capian, the one we could make out from up atop the hill. This, clearly, is where all the Keepers went.

All along the boulevard are Keepers, thousands of them, giant pale figures screaming and fighting, cutting and pushing into each other. As I watch, a Keeper in Randt's colors of blue and yellow gets a knife to the gut. He just puts his hand in his water pouch, licks his fingers and keeps going. The water makes this fight endless and extra-violent. Either you're able to heal and then be hurt again, or you're hurt bad enough to die. There's no middle ground.

"You see Jo and Rob?" I ask.

"Um, there are like a million Keepers here," Brayden says.

"Look harder," I say. It's not like we have a choice.

The mini-aqueduct in the center of the boulevard splits the road in half and runs straight to the mountain, disappearing into a deep tunnel. Keepers fight near there in bunches, black-and-white Feileen supporters against red Arcos and yellow-and-blue Randt. There doesn't seem to be any alliance whatsoever, and each side is going at the other fiercely. There are even a few Keepers whose entire job seems to be to stand near the aqueduct and splash their clan members whenever they come near.

The wall that rings the top of the crater surrounding the city is bigger than the Hoover. It hurts my neck to look up that high. At its base is the tunnel, a gaping mouth in the wall, and the mini-aqueduct bisects it, as if the aqueduct taps into the veins of the source itself. Here's where the water comes from. This is where it originates.

"I've seen this," Dad says, his voice given over to awe. He's not looking at the tunnel, but at the mass of Keepers in the street.

"Where?" I ask. But I already know.

"The map," he says. "It's on the map. Black, blue, yellow, red in a circle."

"What's next?" I can almost see it. Almost remember it.

Dad scratches his head, as if trying to dislodge the memory. "A spear through a Keeper, through the eye. Then a dark hole with a tongue. Shoot, what was it, two doors, one open? And then the waterfall. A hand curled. A circle with ten points around it. A face, eyes closed, mouth open, tears maybe. Argh—I remember them, I'm just blanking on the order."

"What are they doing at the tunnel?" Brayden asks, pointing to the mountain.

"That's Randt," I say, somehow sure. From here, I can only really make out a group of blue-and-yellow-clad Keepers clogging the entrance to the mountain. But I'm sure he's there. They're protecting the entrance against a wave of checkerboard-wearing Feileen Keepers.

"I see Rob and Jo and Lisa," Dad says, and suddenly I do too. They're darting along the wall, a couple Keepers gaining on them. Jo's limping and with a sharp pain to my stomach I realize she's not going to make it.

There's a roar from the crowd of Keepers near the tunnel entrance as one, then many of them spot Lisa. A large contingent of yellow-and-blue Keepers dislodges itself from the tunnel and push their way toward their princess, just as a group of black Keepers surges toward them too.

"They want Lisa," Dad says.

"Why?" Brayden asks.

"Randt wants her to be one of the Three. Feileen's Keepers want their own, and need to stop Randt."

"We have to help them!" I shout, leaving our cover against the wall. Dad grabs my arm.

"No, Mia. You're not thinking straight. *Look* at them. We can't get there. No one's going to hurt Lisa. They need Lisa. If we go running into that mess we're caught too."

I pull loose from his grasp. He's surprised, his forehead creasing up. "They're my friends, Dad. We don't just leave them. We *have* to help."

Brayden opens his mouth to speak, and I don't want to hear him agreeing with my dad, so I don't give him a chance. I run right into the thick of things. I can hear them both calling my name, but I don't care. I'm a good hundred yards from Jo and Rob, and between me and them are dozens of fighting Keepers. I sprint, my energy fueled by desperation, swerving past lumbering figures left and right. A Keeper backs into me and I trip but I'm up again, moving fast. I can't even see where I'm going but I know they're near the tunnel, so I head that way as a marker.

I'm surrounded but alone.

And then I'm there, chaos everywhere, a crowd facing off against one another with Lisa, Jo and Rob right in the middle.

Dad pushes through next to me, puts his hands on his knees and huffs like an old man. "Mia, look!" he says, pointing to the tunnel. The remaining guards are all fighting with Feileen's Keepers. There's a clear gap to the tunnel.

"Dad, forget the source. We have to stay *alive*."

His face sputters and he points. I turn behind me and see the spear, arcing through the air, right at me. And then I'm knocked over by a blur of movement. My head smacks the ground, buzzing my ears and dimming my vision. It all happens so quickly.

Brayden's on top of me, his face red, breathing hard. "Are you okay?"

I nod, unable to speak. I'm on my back, and all around me I see feet moving and shuffling. I see Keepers, and somewhere in the crowd I see Rob's and Jo's legs. I swear I do.

"Mia?" Brayden asks, his voice close. He hasn't gotten up from me yet and for a second I don't want him to. It's not the warmth of his body or anything like that, it's the safety of him. I'm shielded from everything down here. I look the other way, see more Keepers, more fighting. And I see Dad, lying just like me, facing me, one eye open and the other eye gone. The spear hit him instead. Right through the eye. It pushes his head down at an awkward angle. There's surprisingly little blood. Just a piece of wood sticking out of his face.

"Get off me," I whisper desperately.

Brayden starts to shift but it's not fast enough. I push him away and crawl.

"Daddy," I whisper, my hands shaking. I touch his chest; it's warm but doesn't move. It's like he said of the map. A spear through the eye. But he had said it would be a *Keeper's* eye, not his. He knew but he didn't.

Brayden has me by the shoulders, trying to pull me away, and when I don't move he smothers me with his body, pushing me to the ground, and I lie there, staring into my dad's face while an entire troop of Randt's men run by, some of them jumping over us, like a herd of screaming albino deer rushing through.

Brayden's shouting something at me, but I can't hear him until he physically takes my cheeks in his hand and forces my face his way.

"We need to get him to water," he says, slowly, enunciating as if to a foreigner or an old man.

Yes, I think dumbly, reminded of Brayden in Arcos's pool. *We need to get him to water.*

The mini-aqueduct isn't too far away, lined with silver and gold. Brayden has two fists clenched into Dad's clothing and drags him along the ground. Now I see the blood, pouring from the back of his head, smearing across the ground. The spear's making it hard on Brayden, but I won't touch it. I can't. So I pick up Dad's feet. They're heavy, but there's no way I'm going to drop him.

By the time we manage to get to the aqueduct I can barely see. I have to fight down an urge to vomit. The aqueduct is about waist high and just as thick and Brayden jumps right onto it, pulling Dad up after him. Blood swirls bright, almost shining as it drains away. I wonder, fleetingly, whether this goes straight to the well in the cave.

I jump in, the water warm, and dunk Dad under, the water flowing around us, splashing over the side. Then pry open his mouth and drip some in.

"Should we pull out the spear?" I ask Brayden. I don't want to, but, like, what if the water closes the wound around the wood? What if we have to cut off the head and he's stuck with a spear shaft in his eye forever?

"That might make it worse," Brayden says. He's got Dad's head in his hands and is making sure that the water surrounds the exit wound. He looks at me and his brown eyes are the opposite of hopeful.

I touch Dad's throat, feeling for a pulse. My finger sinks deep into his flesh. Nothing.

"He's not coming back, is he?" I ask, trying to tamp down my panic. All around me there is fighting and movement but it doesn't really penetrate the bubble I'm in.

"I don't know," Brayden says, cupping handfuls of water over Dad's face, still trying.

"He'd hate this. He died next to the water. That's so stupid."

"Mia." I hear the strain in Brayden's voice, like the last thing he wants to do is say what he has to say. "We have to go. If the water's going to work, it'll work here. But it's not happening. He's dead. It's done."

Dad didn't mean to, but he prophesied his own death. If I had known it, I could have done something. What else did he say? What else did the map tell him that he didn't understand?

"A dark hole with a tongue, the waterfall," I mutter to myself, remembering what he said about the map. I stare at the tunnel, at the mini-aqueduct coming out of its center like a tongue. "The source."

"What?" Brayden asks.

"The source," I say, growing excited. "The source clearly gives Arcos and Randt more than the regular water does. And the map told of Dad's death. Maybe it tells us how to save him!"

"I don't know," Brayden replies, dubious. "I don't think the water's supposed to bring back the dead."

"You don't know that. You don't know that!" I scream. "Listen," I say, desperately trying to control myself. I need him to believe me; otherwise I'm all alone. "The standard water does amazing stuff—you should have seen what you looked like. But the source is a big deal, right? Dad came down here expressly for it—why? Because he knew that he wouldn't be able to help Westbrook and Fenton without it. If regular magical healing water isn't enough, then what can the source do?"

"But you're talking about bringing people back from the dead."

I look down at Dad, his body partly submerged, the water flowing around him and lazily carrying away his blood. We can't take him with us. We don't have time. I'll just have to hope he'll be here when I get back.

Brayden doesn't argue anymore. He takes my hand and I need more than that, so I pull him in and hug him fiercely. He's solid and real and comforting. For one second, I can ignore the Keepers fighting near where Jo and Rob are, can ignore my father's body lying next to me.

"Are you coming with me?" I ask.

"Always."

And then we're running, right alongside the aqueduct, slipping by the distracted guards and into the tunnel. A black hole with a tongue. A cave within a cave within a cave. Dad would've loved that.

18

THE LAST THING I SEE BEFORE ENTERING THE LONG tunnel is a glimpse of Jo and Rob sprinting out of an alley. It's like I'm on a moving train, watching out a window and then everything goes black.

We hurry along the tunnel, which has no lamps or glowflowers. The light recedes behind us, slimming to a pinprick. I run with my right hand along the aqueduct, tracing the wet rock, grateful for its reassuring presence. But after a fifty feet or so, I feel the aqueduct angle upward and lift into the air, where it merges with the ceiling. No more water at our fingertips.

It's getting cold in here, like a real cave should be. The walls are rough, unpolished. And it's almost totally dark. I'm beginning to lose my sense of direction and balance. My sense of reality. I wonder how much more the Keepers can see with their owl eyes. I hope that they feel as lost as I am.

"What if there won't be any light at all?" I ask.

"Why would that be? There's light everywhere else." His voice is soft, reassuring.

"They have huge eyes. They can see in the dark like we can't. They're *supposed* to see in the dark."

"Mia," he says. "We'll find it." A pause, a squeeze of my hand. "We don't have much choice, do we?"

I don't respond. It's clear I don't have to.

Darkness is a funny thing. It's terrifying until it isn't. Ever since I fell down the well as a child, I've been more than afraid of the dark; darkness feels like a physical being. A presence that could chase me anywhere. I used to carry night-lights to sleepovers, to swim meets. But here I am, running through the darkness, breathing it in, feeling it press against my eyeballs, and I'm somehow okay. There's a mountain over us, and I sense its weight, but there's no claustrophobia. Instead, I think I'm just numb. Dad's dead, and there are only two potential futures here: either the source helps, or it doesn't. The darkness is just an obstacle now, something to push through until I get to one of those futures.

If the source can't bring him back, I don't know how I'll get Dad back through the well, back to Fenton, where I can bury him next to my mom.

For a moment, I feel overcome. I want to go to my knees. And I would, but for the hand. If Brayden let me go, even for a moment, I'm not sure what I'd do. I'm not sure I'd keep on existing. I wiggle my finger experimentally to see how hard it would be to slip from his grasp, but he holds on tight. I wonder if he's thinking about his parents, tied and gagged and held in the basement of Furbish Manor? If they don't have the virus yet, if Sutton lied to him, they'll have it soon enough. Is he holding on to me for reassurance too?

I don't know how long we run. Time and darkness play games

with each other. But even though I've been trying to set a pace for us, I'm already feeling winded.

"Do you hear that?" Brayden asks, his voice a shock in the darkness. I do. I've been hearing it at the edge of my consciousness for a while now. A constant buzz in the background, pushing against my thoughts, slowly waking me up.

"What is it?" I ask, willing myself to filter the noise better. To understand its meaning.

"The source?" Brayden asks, a measure of excitement creeping in.

I wish we had Rob and his iPhone. "Dad said there's a waterfall somewhere . . ." And as soon as I say it, it makes sense: this is the noise of a waterfall.

"A waterfall," Brayden echoes. He pulls my hand forward, picking up the pace. "We're almost there."

"But Dad said there was something else before the waterfall." Just thinking about him makes me ache.

Brayden's not stupid; he hears the caution in my voice and already we slow. "What was it?"

"I don't remember," I say, the images flitting through my mind.

"Mia," Brayden says, coming to a stop, maybe hearing the strain in my voice. "I know I shouldn't say this. I know you don't believe me and don't trust me. And I know I haven't earned this, but I'm sorry about your father. I'm sorry about everything." I lock up, unable to move. I don't want to hear this, not now. I don't realize I'm crying until the tears drip from my face.

I look at Brayden and see the outline of his body, can see that he's nervous, that he's clenching his jaw.

"Wait," I say. "I can see you."

Up ahead there's a tiny pinprick of light and the tunnel takes shape before us. It feels like we're about to get launched out of a torpedo tube.

I wipe my face, and move past him, not ready to forgive. He says my name but I keep going. After a few hundred yards it's clear that the light is coming from an opening in the tunnel up ahead. The sound of the waterfall grows and it's hard not to get excited, which shames me some. I imagine my dad here in my place, thirty-four years after discovering the well, finally on the cusp of the source. If it couldn't be him, I know he'd be glad it's me.

The light begins to shift and reflect off of the tunnel's smooth surface and it's clear that it's a lot schwankier than I imagined. The rock doesn't look like it does back in Capian, where there's granite and marble and onyx carved and crafted, but here veins of what have to be precious gems and minerals spiral like comets together along the wall. Flashes of greens and blues, sparkles of gold and silver. They are so brilliant that they seem to move, as if the rock itself were liquid flowing all around us.

The tunnel ends abruptly, twenty feet off the ground of an enormous cavern, with stairs leading down to take us the rest of the way. Fires burn in tall cauldrons, and in hundreds of torches lining the walls. More eye-catching, way more breathtaking, way more magnificent than anything we've seen so far, is the waterfall.

It falls from a hundred feet up, just as wide, a huge sheet of water pouring angrily into a pool below. A mist sprays out, shimmering. The room smells wet. I can almost feel the spray from here. In some ways I'm disappointed. A waterfall is so beautiful, but also familiar. The end goal of a hike or a weekend drive, not of a trip to another world. Where does it come from? Why don't Keepers come here all the time? I guess it doesn't matter, as long as I can use it to save my dad.

"We didn't bring anything to carry the source water out with," Brayden moans.

For a second I panic, but then remember the pockets. One of mine has a hole in it from the knife. The other is probably coated with poisonous berry juice. Not a risk I'm willing to take. "You have waterproof pockets," I say, pointing them out. "Mine are torn, so you get to carry it."

"You broke your pockets?" His eyes twinkle, the scar on his chin flashes white.

I smile and it feels good.

Brayden bounds down the steps and it's a strange sight to see. Just hours ago he was cut open and left for dead. Now he's running.

I'm kinda surprised there isn't an altar or something like that. This is where the Three go, right? This is the Holy of Holies for the Keepers. What do Randt and Arcos *do* here? Do they burn incense and chant? Do they make offerings? Or do they just sit by the edge of the pool and drink water and hang out?

I walk the steps slowly, taking it all in. The waterfall gets louder with each step, the white churning water mesmerizing. What was it that Dad said was painted on the map before the waterfall?

Brayden's almost to the waterfall when it hits me.

There's nothing living here.

Everywhere we've seen this water there's been some sort of

surrounding ecosystem. As if the water can't not create life. Back at the well Topside, as soon as the water began to flow again, there were trees and plants sprouting right up. Here, though, everything is lit by gas lamps. Why aren't there any trees, any glowflowers? Why is there no life? Why did the mini-aqueduct disappear into the ceiling of the tunnel back there and not just take its water straight from here?

"Brayden, stop!" I shout, but it's too loud. It's too late.

He dips his hand in the water and raises his cupped palm, water dripping between his fingers, in what feels like slow motion. He glances my way and sees me screaming. Startled, he drops the water. Wipes his hand on his pants.

"What?" he says, standing up and looking around, wondering where the threat is.

I hurry down the steps, fighting the urge to close my eyes against the mist in the air. I hold my breath, cover my mouth and grab him away.

"Mia, stop! What is it?"

"That's not the source!" I say, pointing accusatorily at the water.

"What do you mean? How can it not be? Look around, this place is amazing, that waterfall is from the map, everything fits."

"Almost everything," I say, waving my hand around. "But where's the plant life? Where's the magic green thumb? Why is there a waterfall but they are using torches and not glowflowers to light the place?"

Brayden's skeptical. "Mia. We don't have time for this. Where else can it be?" He turns back to the water, but I grab his hand. He looks at me, annoyed. "Just let me try it, Mia. Worst-case scenario, you're right and this is just regular water and whatever, nothing happens."

"Something's not right," I say, still holding tight to his hand. He tries to break my grip, but when he pulls, his hand is weak. We both look down, and somehow, I already know what I'll see.

His hand, the one he dipped into the water: it's old. As in, it's thin and lined with wrinkles and wormy veins and covered with splotches of red and purple, bruises already forming under the skin. His fingernails are longer, curled and yellowed. They remind me of Jo's dad, lying dead in the hallway.

My mind flashes red, and for a second I'm so helpless and pitiful my legs wobble. Now's not the time for that. I pull up Brayden's sleeve. The aging only pushes up to his wrist; above, the rest of his arm looks sturdy and normal. But even as we watch, the healthy skin slowly dries and goes pasty, a millimeter at a time.

Brayden stares at his arm in horror. "I'm aging! It's like the virus! What's going on?"

I look at the water, so crystalline and perfect. Beneath its surface you can see straight to the rock, to the dazzling colors swirling there, a Venus flytrap.

"It's a trick to protect the source."

"But where's the source?" he says, dazed. "I need some water. I need some help!"

"I don't know," I reply, trying to sound calm. There's nothing here other than the death water, waterfall, torches, cauldrons. The mini-aqueduct is way back at the beginning of the tunnel. "But dad's right—the virus *is* related to the water." Another thought occurs to me, this one even worse. "Maybe the source is for the virus, not the water."

"Why would you even say that? I need help!" Brayden says, his voice shrill. He's holding his wrist, as if he could physically keep back the aging process, and he's sweating, his face flecked with fear.

I turn toward the steps and start back up. "You're right—we can get to the water. Come on."

He doesn't move. It's like he *can't*, like he's worried if he takes a step he'll accelerate the aging. "Mia, this *is* the entrance to the source. It's here somewhere. We can't risk going back; the Keepers might just be standing there waiting to take us prisoner. We need to find the source."

He's right, I know it, but if we went back I'd know where to find water. Here, I know nothing.

"Well, where is it?" I ask, exasperated.

"What about the map?" he says. "You remember the waterfall. Do you remember anything else?"

"I don't," I say, cursing myself for not having memorized it all. And for not bringing Rob and his OtterBox with me.

"Well, the good water comes from somewhere, right?" he asks, walking around the edge of the pool, peering at the waterfall. I don't see any steps, any way to get up there. What, am I supposed to climb slippery rocks covered in virus water?

I try to remember the map, but the shape of my dad lying dead, a spear sticking out of his eye, keeps popping into my mind. *Stop it, Mia. He'd want you to be here. He'd want you to figure it out. You can't let him down, you can't let Brayden die. If only we were back at the Cave, where they have the images magnified, zoomed in and we could figure . . .*

"Wait," I say, the thought flitting in and out of my mind. The zoom back at the Cave . . . "Brayden, wasn't there something crazy about the last image?"

"Yeah," he replies, remembering immediately, his face flashing hope for the first time since he touched the water. "It was a miniature replica of the entire map, a map within a map. They said there were, like, seventeen versions or something. Except that each map was a *little* different. The moon was shaped different. Remember?"

I'm starting to get excited, to feel the adrenaline pump through my body. "How'd we get here, huh? We went through the well into a new world. And here we are, at the waterfall. Something that takes away life. So how do we get to the source?"

"Through the killer waterfall?" Brayden says, clearly dubious.

"That's right," I reply, hurrying to the pool's edge. "Or at least, through something here." I look at the waterfall where it pours right into the pool. It's so strong and flowing so fast, you can't see behind it. I can't make out a well, either.

I take a step toward the water.

"Mia, what're you doing?" Brayden shouts. I can see from here that the aging is up to his elbow.

"It makes sense," I reply, trying to psych myself up enough to do this.

"No it doesn't," he says, with more conviction than I've mustered. But he's wrong.

"If you want the source," I say "you have to take it."

"Look what it's done to me," he cries, taking a step my way. "You'll age up immediately. You'll die."

When I don't say anything he hurries my way, but I take another step toward the water and he stops. Like I'm holding a grenade and any movement on his part will set it off.

I don't know if this will work. And if it doesn't, everything will end quickly. So I keep staring at him, needing him right now. His face is so racked with concern that I almost feel bad. His hair is shading gray and his body is beginning to shake but his eyes don't leave me. I think of my dad, of him floating in the water, of him sacrificing himself for me. It's not a great feeling, but it gives me the strength to turn and dive deep into the pool.

I hear Brayden call my name, muted and distant and gone.

19

JIMMY

JIMMY STANDS OUTSIDE HIS OWN HOUSE WITH Hendricks and Woods and Odessa. The day's bright, sun reflecting off of the snow, turning top layers to ice, sending icicles dripping on all the houses down the block. He tries not to think about his healthy ninety-five-year-old dad in there. About how selfish he was buying his dad another year or two. He sucks in the fresh air, feeling it chill his lungs, trying to focus. He's warmer now, at least, actually dressed in his own clothing. Odessa is wearing some of his mom's stuff—a big green parka and her ski pants.

Woods is waiting on him to make a decision for some reason. He's the cop, Jimmy thinks, he should be running the show.

"We need volunteers," Odessa finally says, tired of the delay. "We have to go door-to-door and distribute the water."

"The firehouse?" Hendricks suggests. "Chief Brosh called in all the volunteer firefighters."

"Good." Woods nods. "And I'll get to First Baptist, and then Saint Ann's. I know there's a crowd there."

"What about the quarantine? The roadblocks the soldiers got you to set up. Are they still in place?" Jimmy asks.

"Deputy Wilkshire is down off of County Road 48. Thompson's

over on 210." Woods pauses, his voiced pained. "They didn't set up their block with soldiers, they're probably still out there watching the roads. I could have 'em back here in twenty minutes to help."

"We still *want* the quarantine in place," Odessa says. "Until we hand out this water. Remember, this can't spread beyond town."

Hendricks shudders. "Oh, God, she's right."

"Of course she's right," Woods replies. He reaches for a couple bottles from Odessa's bag and tosses them to his partner. Odessa takes Jimmy's arm and pulls him toward the snowmobile.

"Where you two think you're going?" Woods asks. Odessa hops into the driver's seat, with Jimmy behind her, his arms wrapped around her waist.

"To Westbrook," Jimmy calls.

"No way. We need to stick together."

"Woods," Jimmy says. "We've got to. The more people we hit, the safer Fenton gets. You take the town, we'll take the school. We know it better and that's ground zero."

"You'll get hurt," he says. Hendricks is already in the car.

Odessa shakes a bottle of water in the air. "Not with this." She revs the engine and eases forward. "Good luck," Jimmy calls to Woods, who seems stuck watching them leave. Hendricks slams on the horn and Woods snaps to it. A few seconds later Jimmy sees the cruiser flash its lights before zooming around the corner.

The wind is cold, sharp enough to bite. The last time Jimmy was on a snowmobile he was captured by Sutton's soldiers and taken to Furbish Manor, the base of operations for the maniac. It also happens to be Brayden's parents' house.

"You think they're still guarding the school?" Odessa shouts over the noise of the engine. They're moving fast, taking the frozen creek up toward the lake that borders the school, the same one they skated over to escape the quarantine just a few days ago.

"Maybe," Jimmy says in her ear. Sutton put the soldiers there to stop Mia from getting out. To make sure he could use her to get into the Cave. Once Mia fled, there'd have been no reason to leave people there at all. Except to keep the virus in.

"Let's play it safe then," Odessa says, getting them within half a mile before cutting the engines. "Too loud." She points at the snowmobile.

Jimmy gestures to the bell tower on campus and the spotlight affixed there. It's not sweeping the ground, but it's on. Maybe it means someone's there, but the sun's too high in the sky to bother using it.

Jimmy carries the water and they move quickly through the snow. He finds himself surprised again at how well his new body works, how fast he can move, and with how much ease. Odessa keeps pace, and he wonders why she never played any sports. The water brought her to peak physical fitness but she's clearly got endurance. They plow through the snow together, getting warm, unzipping their jackets and wiping snot from their noses. He realizes something with some reluctance: they might not find any guards at Westbrook because there might not be anyone left to guard.

The wall that surrounds the school greets them suddenly, a thick layer of defense just fifty yards away. He finds himself not entirely ready for this.

"Should we skirt it until we get to the lake? Then enter that way? Or try to sneak through at the front gate?"

Odessa shakes her head and keeps going, all the way to the wall. It's tall, about twelve feet high. It's redbrick covered in heavy snow, and its surface is spotted by slick icy runoff.

"We can climb it," she says between deep breaths.

Jimmy looks up and down the wall. There are no trees close enough to climb, and every tree is covered in snow anyway.

"I don't know, Dess."

"Give me the water," she says, and he does. She doesn't wait a moment, just tosses the bottles over the wall. They barely make a sound on the other side. He hopes they didn't burst open. "Now boost me up."

It goes easier than he expected. He lifts her and she knocks the snow off the wall, peers over and then sits, Humpty Dumpty–style, facing him, her legs dangling.

"What are you doing?" he whispers.

"Grab my legs."

"I'll break them," he says, shaking his head.

"No, you won't. Grab them and use me to climb up."

"You're crazy," he says.

She smiles. "You like it that way."

Jimmy feels a flash of warmth and jumps, grabs her legs and then she helps to pull him up onto the wall with her. For a moment they sit there, butts cold, breath like smoke, and all Jimmy wants to do is laugh. Odessa points to the ground, so he jumps, then helps her down. She grabs a bottle, takes a swig and hands it to him. The rush of the water is too good to ignore. He feels like doing jumping jacks.

They cross to the dorms, and when Jimmy crouches in the snow he can see his own room on the third floor, the lights still on.

He doesn't see any soldiers. He doesn't see anybody in the windows. He's always taken for granted the music from the hallway or the laughter of his friends or the simple feeling of *stuff to do* that's always on campus.

They stay low, but no one's near. They don't have a key card but a window's cracked a few rooms down. "That's Todd's, isn't it?" Odessa asks. He nods. Todd and Rory smoked cigarettes out their window all the time.

Jimmy looks in. Just a dorm room: dirty bed, lacrosse stick and Muhammad Ali poster. "He's not there."

They sneak in, climbing into the window significantly easier than scaling the wall. Jimmy creaks open the door to an empty hallway.

"Where is everyone?"

"Didn't Sutton say something back at the Cave about them barricading themselves somewhere?" Odessa asks, peeking into another door.

They move through the hallways, opening doors, and every room's empty. All of his friends' rooms, their lights on or off, Xboxes loaded in some, beds made in others.

Jimmy feels a growing sense of panic. He had expected the worst, steeled himself for broken bodies, aged to death. Or evidence of foiled escape attempts. Or soldiers everywhere with their guns and flashlights. But this emptiness grates deep on his nerves, the unknown as bad as anything.

It isn't until they reach the Castle that something strange happens.

The Castle's the name for a part of the dorm that rises up in one section for an extra three floors. Only seniors are allowed to live there, and the only way up is a spiral staircase that runs right through the middle of this wing. Jimmy's had his eye on the top room, the "penthouse," for ages. He's been to enough parties up there to know how good life is in the Castle. He's been to enough parties up there to know that the mattresses now barricading the stairwell aren't the norm. There's more than mattresses. He sees a few desks and chairs and even a couch, all pushed into the tight space, blocking anyone from going up. He can the bannisters overhead. Someone could still hear him.

"Hello?" he shouts, his voice echoing up the stairs.

Odessa hits him in the arm and shushes him.

"I'm sorry," a voice calls down. It's a girl's, and it's familiar. "We're not changing the rules. No exceptions."

"Amber?" Odessa asks up the stairwell.

Of course, Jimmy thinks, *it would be Amber who organized this. Student body president. Control freak.*

"Who's that?" she calls down.

"Odessa and Jimmy."

Amber's face appears over a ledge three stories up. Her black hair falls straight down, making it hard to figure out her expression.

"You're sick," she says after a while. "You're aging up."

"Not anymore," Jimmy replies. He holds up a bottle of water for her to see. "We've got the antidote. We've come to help you."

She snorts. "You're a little late for that."

Another head peers over the edge, then another. Brent and Casey. His teammates. And then there's Sally Weathers and Lydia Yu.

"You disappeared," someone says.

"They're townies," Sally adds.

"Oh, my God," Odessa moans. "Enough of that bullshit. We escaped and got the virus anyway but found an antidote and came back here to help. Is everyone up there? Where are all the soldiers?"

"They left," Amber says, her voice closer. She's come down three flights and is now at the head of the barricade. She's in sweats, her eyes baggy and tired, her face a mess. She's her age though. Uninfected.

Jimmy and Odessa share a glance. The soldiers *did* leave after Mia fled.

"Then let us up!" Jimmy yells. "You're free now and we need your help. We have to get this water to everyone possible."

"I thought you said it was the antidote. Not water."

Jimmy shrugs. "Same thing."

"Is everyone up there?" Odessa asks.

"No." Amber shakes her head, unable to look them in the eyes. She's not moving to undo the barricade. They're safe here, Jimmy realizes. Why would they leave?

"After the soldiers left," she continues, "we found the teachers dead in the infirmary. The sick students volunteered to stay away from the healthy. They went to Dylan."

Jimmy pictures the school's auditorium: hundreds of aged, desiccated bodies slumped in the seats. His stomach curls. They went there to die.

"You need to drink this water," he says. Amber shakes her head, sucks in a snotty breath and hugs herself. The others watch quietly from above her. There's an air of reverence; she must have organized this place and saved their lives. She's their leader now.

"After a while, when someone else got sick, they didn't stick around. They got in their car and left. They just drove off. We watched them from the windows."

Odessa gasps. "Did the soldiers stop them?"

"I don't know."

Suddenly, there's a noise down the hall.

"Don't move!" shouts a voice, and Jimmy whirls to see Gutierrez, gun raised at them, bag hanging from his back filled with water bottles.

"Gutierrez," Odessa cries, hands raised. "You came!" She sounds almost happy. And he looks almost happy, lowering the gun with a tentative smile.

"I told you I would," he says.

"You take care of Furbish first?"

Gutierrez's eyes flick to the ground. "They're gone," he says. "They're all gone. Some were dead. But the others took the trucks and the snowmobiles and the suits. They're just gone."

"Why would they do that?" Odessa asks. "They knew about the water, right?"

Gutierrez shakes his head, looking sheepish. "Sutton didn't tell everyone."

Fucking typical, Jimmy thinks.

"What's going on?" Amber asks. She peers through the railing and sees the soldier. "You're with them!" she shouts, recoiling, her eyes incredulous and betrayed, and then she runs up the steps.

Something falls and Jimmy just barely manages to pull Odessa out of the way. It's a bottle of Absolut, and it smashes on the ground, glass flying everywhere. A lamp follows right after. They scurry out of the way, and Gutierrez raises his rifle to try to get a shot off.

"No!" Odessa yells, pushing down the barrel. "They don't understand. They aren't the enemy."

"Well, neither am I," he replies, peevish.

She looks at his gun with eyebrows raised. He lowers it, glowering.

"What do we do now?" Jimmy asks.

"Leave a bottle, Jimmy," Odessa says. But he knew that. He meant about the ones who left, who got away.

"Let's hope they die," Gutierrez mutters.

"What?" Odessa says, shocked.

"Yeah," the soldier replies, his eyes fierce. "Let's hope those kids who got away and the soldiers in their Humvees age to death before they get anywhere or run into anyone and give them the virus. I bet they break the roadblocks—I bet they're on their way to the nearest real hospital or town or they're just running for their fucking lives."

"Spreading the virus," Jimmy whispers. He's thinking of the richies' parents, how they'd come with private jets and take their sweethearts back to their private doctors across the country and the world.

"Let's hope they all die way before that happens."

Jimmy imagines himself driving down the highway, completely unaware of what's going on here at Westbrook. He sees an army truck smash into a tree. He knows he'd pull over and help. That he'd put his finger to the old, wrinkled body's neck. That he'd breathe in the infected air. That he'd catch it.

He imagines the virus even now sifting down the arteries of the country. The interstates and the cities. From Denver to everywhere.

"We're too late," he says, his mind reeling.

"Hey Amber," Odessa calls up the stairs, tossing a bottle toward the barricade. "Make sure everyone drinks a little of this water." She turns and heads back the way they came, motioning for Jimmy to follow her. "We save who we can. They're all that's left."

20

THE WATER'S COLD, A STARK CONTRAST TO THE HEALING type. It presses against me and reminds me of swimming under ice. I undulate my body like I would in a race, trying to stay beneath as long as possible. When I finally break the surface and start to swim—freestyle—I immediately feel an ache twist through me. I know what it feels like to get tired. I know what it feels like to push myself so hard that the edge of my vision goes black. I know what it takes when I'm close to the finish mark, when I have to skip the breath and keep my head underwater to gain those extra milliseconds of speed. I can remember nearly passing out a half dozen times after a race, holding weakly on to the plastic blue lane dividers, letting chlorinated water fill my mouth and spitting it slowly out. But the tired I feel so suddenly, it's different. The pool's small, maybe thirty yards, the kind of distance I should laugh at. My arms are sluggish, my bones squeak in my body. I can feel my eyes dim. And when I turn my head to breathe, my lungs can't get enough, can barely get any air, so I go back under breathless, and it takes my entire will to keep the rhythm and not pull up to paddle like a dog.

The coldness spreads and I can't feel my feet. My heart races, part fear, part desperation, pushing against my chest, but suddenly there's something else pushing on me, holding me down, and it takes me a moment to realize that it's water gushing onto my arms, then my head, then my back, the waterfall shoving me under and trying to drown me. I switch to breaststroke, frantically aiming for the surface. For a moment I can only see the churning haze of foam over my head. But then I break the surface and gulp air, the sound of the water pouring right past my head so loud I'm deaf.

It's dark behind the falls, almost black, but I can see something up ahead, a hole in the wall and some sort of light coming from beyond it. There are marble steps up from the pool and a thin tunnel before me. I was right. I knew I was right. But as I move toward the steps, those final easy strokes are like agony, and I see my arms for the first time since I've jumped in. They're tiny, shriveled, the muscles hanging small and loose from my arms, the skin like a plastic bag. I grit my teeth and push forward, slogging through the water to get to the stairs.

I shouldn't have gritted my teeth, because a tooth shatters like porcelain, cutting up my mouth. But I don't have time to gag, to do anything but keep on. I might have been right about going through the waterfall, but Brayden was right about the water and my body's quickly disintegrating. I climb the steps shakily, my feet flat and callused and wrinkled beyond belief. I can hear Brayden calling my name, a small sound sifting through the waterfall, but I don't have the energy to call back. I feel my skin shift, as if no longer fully attached to my body. My hair turns brittle and grows quickly down my shoulders, as gray as anything.

I'm out of the water but the aging's not stopping. Just like it didn't stop with Brayden, and he only dipped into the water for a second. I try to hurry forward but my legs are like jelly and I fall to my knees, blinded by pain. I think I shattered my kneecap. My hip. I don't know but I can't stand up. If I stay here I'll die, I know this, so I moan, and put my hands onto the stone and drag myself forward, pulling my splintered bones farther apart inside me.

Five, ten feet of agony. Ahead, at the end of the tunnel, the light grows stronger. For a moment I can't help but think of it as the end. But that's stupid. Here, the light means something more.

"The source," I whisper, and out of nowhere a drop of water hits me in my face, sending shockwaves through my body. For a moment I convulse, like I'm having a seizure, and I lose all control of myself, my limbs flailing about, my knee screaming in agony. I clench my eyes shut and will the pain away and then, as soon as it's begun, the shaking stops and I'm calm, breathing deep, feeling better.

My eyes clear, so much so that I had no idea how bad they were, like I had glaucoma, like I was ninety. I'm out of the cave and in a vast glowing field of flowers. Thousands of them. Different and the same as those I've seen before. Like magical wildflowers off the interstate. They come right up to my feet but stop at the edge of the tunnel leading toward the waterfall. There's something strange about the field. It ripples and sways and grows, as if the field were breathing.

Another drop hits me, this time on my arm, and the skin immediately firms up and heals.

The drops fall languidly, and when one lands on the ground, it sprouts a flower like in a time-lapse video we've seen in biology, an enhanced-speed version of a plant's life. It grows to my knees and bursts a flash of glowflower light along its petals and suddenly I realize what's going on: water is landing all around me and creating new flowers instantaneously. Another drop hits me, and then another, coming from above, and my body continues to heal. Not like Odessa and Jimmy, who were given water and then remained stuck in the bodies of thirty-year-olds. Instead, this water's reversing the effect. I can feel my tooth sliding back into place. My knee knitting together under the skin. I raise my face to the sky, unable to contain a giddy laugh as more drops hit. And then I see it. How could I not have?

There, some fifty yard away and cascading *upward* from the ground and into the endless black of the ceiling above is the fountain. My breath hitches. The water swirls and twists like a lazy, beautiful tornado, drifting back and forth above my head, but anchored to one spot on the ground. The tornado's spotlit by the thousands of glowflowers in the field. The water is mesmerizing, shadowed and glittering like it's made of diamonds and every few seconds a drop of water hits a glowflower at just the right angle to flash a rainbow of color. An ache burns through me. I wish Dad could see this. Right now, right here, I know that I'm witnessing the greatest thing I'll ever see. It's strange to recognize that at the moment it's happening. To recognize the beauty and to be all alone.

Maybe it's supposed to be this way.

There's no path, just endlessly growing flowers, so I run with my knees high through the field toward the vortex of water. The flowers rub against me like cotton candy. As I get closer to the fountain the water gets louder. The earth vibrates beneath my feet and this close there's a mist, no longer just drops. The water sinks into me and I feel a sense of euphoria. I can see why no one's allowed here;

I'm having a hard time focusing. If not for the memory of Brayden calling me through the waterfall, I'd want to lie down here forever. I bet I could, here, with the water dropping on me. Live forever.

The cyclone of water is big, maybe twenty feet in diameter, and now that I'm close enough I realize I can't tell where it's coming from. The wall of water making up the cyclone is so thick that it's hard to see beyond it. There could be a hole, or a pool, or it could be spinning directly up from the ground. I have no idea. It's hard to understand the strange logistics. I look around to get my bearings and realize that I don't understand where this place is in relation to the city and the wall and the mountain and everything. Back on Randt's tower, we could see the mountain, and I just assumed the source was there, at the top. But I haven't climbed at all, so I must be in the center of the mountain. Yet still, this looks like open space, with the same darkness above me as in Capian—it's as if I'm not inside a mountain at all. I might as well be standing on the edge of a vast prairie, and behind me is a cliff face, jutting straight up from the earth, keeping this place from the Keepers. Inside that cliff is the waterfall, a trap to protect the source.

The water goes up into the black as far as I can see. Where does it go, I wonder, staring up at the tornado. The drops that land don't seem to gather and drain anywhere, they just sprout new flowers. But the mini-aqueduct of water back in Capian—the one my dad's currently lying in—seems to tap directly into the mountain, as if draining a fruit. Maybe, somehow, enough of the water drains below me and into some underground water system. But this place, the source, what am I even supposed to do here?

I circle the edge of the cyclone, looking for some clue, but there's nothing beyond but an endless field. I've gone around twice before I notice it, a lump in the flowers, right back near the tunnel that led me to the field. I must have missed it when I crawled in half blind. I hurry over and tear off the greenery, my hands ripping at strong and sticky vines and moss and flowers that have overgrown a stone structure, what I think is an altar. But after I clear it off, I know different. I'm breathing hard, hands aching, but that heals up after a couple drops and I'm staring at a flat rock, smooth and painted. There are ten cups slotted in a circle into the rock, each a different color, carved of a different stone. One slot has a cup, but it's glass and plain and entirely different than the others. I can't find one that's onyx or obsidian or some other form of black mineral. Maybe Feileen's cup just faded away. The other nine are probably for the remaining Keepers who have had the source. Maybe this is how and why Arcos and Randt so fervently believe the seven Keepers that went Topside are still alive. Maybe the cup fades if you die. And theirs never did.

The cups encircle a drawing of what looks like the earth, a spherical ball of blue and green, though the green doesn't match up to North America or Africa or any other landmass we'd see on any globe. From the top and bottom of the sphere, like the axis of a globe, is a blue-and-white spiral. I look up at the tornado, see it disappearing into the black nothingness above and am sure that's what the spiral is. The axis of the earth. But what does it mean?

I don't have time to rack my brains. There are cups and this is the source so I grab the glass one, surprisingly heavy, and start back through the fields. I try not to think about Feileen using this; I have no idea how to get my own, or how blasphemous touching someone else's cup is. But I'm not struck by lightning and the cup's heft feels good in my hand so I go for it.

This source, this font, gushes straight up, and I find myself remembering the strange physics of this place, and how I swam through the well in the Cave to get here, down down down until I surfaced *up* on a lake. As I get close, the wall of water is so thick and impenetrable that the cup in my hand seems ridiculous. I could hold it up in the air and hope to gather drops, but that would take forever. The mist comes off in waves, shimmering around me, and I slowly reach out the cup and bring it to the water, but as soon as the cup touches the water, the force of the spray shoots it out of my hand and up, way up, so high and far I can't see it. I let out a loose laugh. I'm somehow absolutely certain the same thing would happen if I tried again. I spin once in a circle, searching for some sign, something to show me how to actually take the source.

Okay, think, Mia. What did Dad say? I can't remember. The Keeper with the spear, the circle, a hand. I don't know. I'm at the edge of all of this, the entire reason for being here, the entire reason my dad is dead and I can't do a thing. I can't even gather the water.

What do you want with me? I imagine myself shouting to the cyclone, my voice ragged and useless, but for some reason I just whisper. As if in response, a drop hits my face and, blinking away the water, I swear I see something. A space in the cyclone. I squint, but it's gone. *What was that?* I look around me and then bend down and pluck a flower from the ground. Its bright, glowing petals are covered in dew and I wipe them against my eyelids. They feel cool and as soon as I open my eyes I can see the water in front of me shimmer. I realize that the cyclone isn't a firm wall of water, but rather it bends and twists like tall sheets of laundry in the wind, sheets that sway and shift and open small gaps between and beyond themselves. I blink, the shimmer fading, but not before I see something shine in a gap in the water.

I think *wormhole* or *aliens* or maybe both. The Keepers are probably human descendants, right? It's clear from the painting of the globe that the Topside is way more connected to this place than I realized. Even the way Randt and Arcos use the source proves it.

But I shake away my thoughts. I have to get water back to Brayden, to Dad. Maybe that's what the water does—it brings you back. The water here rejuvenated me, it didn't just halt the virus's progress like in the Cave. Maybe it really can bring Dad back too. Maybe he'll wake up in that aqueduct and know that everything he's spent his life on was worth it.

"Shit," I mutter. I can't see the gaps anymore, or the light inside the cyclone. I could soak myself to carry the liquid. *You can't really be thinking this.* But I am, and my hand is already moving again to try it.

I hold my breath and touch the water, imagining my hand being shot into the air like a fire hose going off in my palm. But unlike with the cup that doesn't happen. The water separates and flows around my hands, dripping gently *upward* through and around my fingers, floating around them like I'm in outer space, with no gravity. The light within the whirling cyclone shines again and I step forward. My leg splits the curtain of water and then my body and

I'm soaked and hot and I feel a pressure at the base of my shoes that wants to eject me to the sky, but that isn't what happens.

What happens is that the curtain closes around me and it goes so dark I'm afraid I've disappeared. And then I hear my father calling my name.

21

HIS VOICE IS FAR AWAY, MUTED AND ECHOING.

"Dad?" I yell. Jo or Rob must have healed him somehow back at the battle and he's followed me here. "I'm here, in the source. I'm *in* the cyclone." But my voice sounds odd. Smaller, nasally.

I realize, suddenly, that I'm not in complete darkness. Above me, larger than a star but smaller than the moon, is a circle of light. It's blindingly bright but illuminates nothing. And I've seen it before. My stomach curls. I'll never forget that light. What's it doing here? I try to look down but my head slams into a hunk of rock, hurting so bad I want to throw up. A drop of warm liquid drips down my face, not water now, but blood from a gash on my forehead. I'm dizzy but when I try to sit down I realize I can't move, can't lift my arms or anything. I'm stuck, rock surrounding my body, like I'm in a tube of concrete. I shiver, suddenly cold. I know what this is. It's impossible, but still, I know. What isn't possible down here? How can I disbelieve something that I *remember*? This is it, my first memory. I remember the well.

I take a few deep breaths. *Calm down, Mia.* I bend my head forward again, slower this time, until my forehead comes in contact with the cold stone a few inches away. Below me, I can tell that I'm wearing a green dress, one with white flowers. It used to be my favorite.

There's a sound above me, a clatter, and some dust scatters onto my face. I blink away the grit and see something solid coming my way. I try to duck but can't. I can't do anything. I close my eyes and take another breath; I know from swimming that if you breathe too much, too deep, you can pass out. Hyperventilation. But I can't help it. This is my nightmare.

The object above me drops down, then stops, dangling above my head. It takes a moment for my eyes to adjust, but I already know it's a Pink Power Ranger lunch box. *My* Pink Power Ranger lunch box. I want to scream, because there's no more doubt.

I'm in the well. My well. I am me, *Baby Mia, who fell down the well.*

The newspapers all wrote about the lunch box. But no one reported on how my hands were restricted, and how I couldn't eat the food. No one knew I didn't eat the food. They lowered the lunch box down by rope and pulled it up again, full. Then tried another time, with a string attached to open the box. They thought this had worked, because the lunch box was empty when they pulled it up. Instead, I had stayed down there for hours with a peanut butter and jelly sandwich lodged behind my head like a thin pillow. When they managed to break through to me via a parallel tunnel, the sandwich disappeared into the dirt, eaten by the earth.

I watch the lunch box get raised and take a moment to get myself together. Why am I here? I'm in my own body, my childhood body. The only difference is that I know what's about to happen.

Does that matter? I wonder. Or am I fated to watch my past with no faculty for action, like Ebenezer Scrooge?

Right on cue, the next lunch box is lowered. I'm reliving the moment, but maybe I can actually do something. My dad yells down to me but I can't understand him. I lean my head back and this time when the lunch box opens, the sandwich falls and hits my forehead. It's about to slide down behind me into nothingness but I snatch at it with my teeth and catch it. It's wrapped in plastic and the sandwich gives between my jaws but I don't care. Elation surges through me. I *can* move. I can make a difference here. It takes a few painful minutes, but I manage to shove the sandwich against my shoulder and pull the plastic off. I can't believe I caught it! It smells like our kitchen and the longing I felt when my mother used to put me on the bus.

My mother. She's alive right now. She's alive here.

"Mom!" I scream, but my voice is still shrill and tiny and I can almost imagine it bouncing right back at me.

I stop to listen for a moment and hear the grumble of equipment, still distant. I remember that feeling, the terror of the wall caving in, of the noise of the digger which had already been so loud becoming suddenly ear-shattering. I peed down my legs. The news didn't report that either. I'm not sure I even remembered that until right now. Even when I saw that my rescuer was Wilkins, the Santa Claus–looking man from the aqueduct, I screamed *no* at him, didn't want him to move me, to feel the hot urine that had soaked my dress and legs. Now, stuck here, I feel the cuts and bruises of the fall, of the rock scraping into my legs as I tumbled. I feel the warm blood oozing from my wounds. The fractures splayed along my bones and in my nose. The water isn't shielding me anymore. The pain is becoming unbearable.

"Let me out of here," I yell up the hole, and my bruised ribs explode in protest. No one can hear me. They didn't then and they won't now. Not Dad, not Mom. "Please," I try again, speaking through the pain into the darkness, straight to whatever sent me here. "Let me go and I won't take any. I didn't know you'd bring me here. I won't touch the source. Please."

There's nothing. Just the growl of the digger and the light above me.

The lunch box begins to rise, jerked up bit by bit as my father—or someone—tugs at the rope, hand over hand. I watch it lift, blocking the light, spinning in circles, bouncing against the well's edge. Something falls out of the box and I flinch, but then it swirls lazily in the air and slowly down, a sheet of paper folded in half. My mom used to do that: send me to school with my lunch and a note folded in half. The notes were usually pink and consisted of a heart or a smiley face drawn at the top. I loved them.

The paper lands on my shoulder, halfway unfolded. I push down an end of the paper with my chin and stare at the sheet, squinting, trying to read it, trying to suppress the jumble of emotions—joy, fear, excitement—the pain amplifying it all. But I can't make anything out in the darkness. The reporters used to ask me what I remembered, and I never used to say my mother. Ever since she died, she's been slowly disappearing from my memory. Like forgotten treasures stored in the attic, I owned my memories of her but didn't use them. She sent me a note and I never knew.

Suddenly I can see her, standing with my father on our porch watching the diggers at the well. Her head on his shoulder, his dirt-covered arms around her waist. She sits on my bed, listening to the *clank* of shovels. She walks out in the middle of the night, when the generator is blaring and floodlights blinding and she puts her hand on the controls of the drill and everyone stops while she walks to the hole and gets on her knees and wishes me good night. My mother packs my lunch for me, a peanut butter and jelly sandwich and writes a note and lowers it into the well. Did she really add a note, or is that just here, in the source, in this nightmare? Why give it to me if I can't read it? Why torture me so?

I begin to cry, which is a mistake. My body heaves and scrapes and the pain makes me cry out louder.

Then, suddenly, there's a bright light. I blink, blinded for a moment, and stare up the hole. Usually I could see the sky above the well, a bright blue, but now the sun's actually hitting my face, which I don't remember ever happening. Some part of me knows that it must be noon. I look down, tilting my head to the left, pressing as hard as I can against the rock. I squint uncomfortably at the paper. There's enough light now to read the words. It's her handwriting, it's really hers.

Mia,

> *I know you can't read this, but it makes me feel*
> *better writing, so I'm going to do it anyway. It's been*
> *over twenty-four hours now and I'm losing my mind*
> *with you down there. I'm lying in your bed right*

now, writing this. How silly is that? I want you to know that your daddy has been out there trying to get you the whole time. He hasn't slept. He hasn't eaten. He's too worried about his baby Mia. Just like me. I wish I was down there instead of you. I wish it were me. And I hope that you see this letter, even if you can't read it, and know that I wrote it, know that your mommy is thinking of you. See those stains? Those are tears—Mommy's crying, but that's okay. These are magic tears that will help you come home. They will help you forever. Come home, Mia. We're waiting.

Love, Mom

My heaves subside but the tears keep coming, pouring down my cheeks. It's uncontrollable, the pain of missing her sears my face, my stomach, my chest. Not even when she died and I watched her casket lower into the ground did I feel like this.

But something pierces my grief. As a four-year-old kid, I wouldn't have been able to read the words. This note was for her, then. But it's also for me, now. The source didn't just send me here for fun, and the one thing out of place in my memory of the well is the note. *Mom, I read the letter. I read it anyway.* The sun's path continues on its arc overhead and the darkness returns to the hole, but I'm not scared anymore. *Magic tears,* she said. I close my eyes and feel my eyelashes stick together. I let my tongue taste the cold air, then run it across my lips, drinking in the salt from my tears, the pain of my body and of her death.

This is the source. More than water. Something entirely my own.

I blink and am back in the eye of the cyclone. My arms and legs are free. There's no sound, as if I'm in a vacuum. Beneath me is a thin layer of water, and below that, maybe stone—it feels like stone. It's hard to tell through the dark water. I'm out of the well, but still inside the source. The cyclone spins around me, a shimmering blue cylinder shifting back and forth like a charmed snake. It is the most beautiful thing I've ever seen, and the mist instantly revives me and melts away the pain of the well.

I breathe in the air and feel a tingling, like an electric current. My mother wrote me a note thirteen years ago and brought me back. She gave me life. Far above me the eye of the cyclone is as blue as a clear day, the same thing I remember in the well, the first thing I remember at all. I don't know if I would have been stuck in the well if I hadn't read that note, if that was some kind of test, or if tasting those tears somehow counted as "drinking" the source. But a part of me knows that just as I'm now in the source, the source is now in me.

22

JO

JO WATCHES MR. KISH STUMBLE AND MIA STOP RUNNING, and then wakes up.

She must have blacked out, because she isn't on the streets anymore or with Arcos. Instead, she sees Rob and Lisa kneeling over her, their faces blurred. They're in a dark, tiny room. She can't really move. Jo remembers fleeing Arcos's tower, and getting separated from Mia and turning back and then nothing.

Nothing and the giant spear sticking out of her gut.

"Are you okay?" Rob asks. Jo realizes, vaguely, that he's speaking to Lisa. They must not think she's awake.

"Yes." Lisa pauses. "Are you?"

"I'm fine, yeah."

For a long moment they look at each other, and Jo watches, unable to speak up.

"We have to pull it out," Lisa says in a whisper. Why is she whispering? There's no one else here.

"You could kill her that way," Rob says. "Why can't we just put her in the water and *then* pull it out?"

Jo tries to say something but can't; the pain's like a vise on her mouth. Every breath, every movement tears open her insides. Like she swallowed an arrowhead and it's now making its way through her gut. She moans and Lisa puts a hand on her head. The hand's warm, it feels so good. Jo tries to tell her so.

"No, Rob." Lisa says, "I know about this. If you give her water now, she will heal around the spear and then you would have to hurt her again to take it out."

"Fine," he says, and Jo realizes that he's sweating like crazy. She's not hot at all. She feels almost nothing except the pain. "But how do we get it out?"

"It is very not good that Jo has awakened," Lisa says, glancing down at Jo.

Rob's face seems to tighten, the skin along his jaw going rigid. Jo's seen that face before. He makes it when he has to do something he doesn't want to.

"Jo," he finally says, his voice hushed, "this is going to hurt. Then it's going to feel better, okay? You have to trust us."

Jo makes out his words, but they come through a haze, echoing and fading and hard to understand.

Lisa physically turns Jo's head sideways and her vision flares, almost goes black.

"I will take the spear, you hold her."

"That's stupid," Rob says. "We should cut it to make it smaller. It will be easier to get out."

"Hold her," Lisa commands.

"Please," Jo manages to croak. But they don't listen. Someone grips her shoulder, locking her in place. And then she feels a tug, small at first, the spear inching along inside her.

"One—" Rob begins to count. But Lisa yanks right away, her

long Keeper hands pulling hard and sure on the spear, bringing it straight out of Jo's body. The feel of the wood as it slid against her innards was enough to make her vomit, and she curls on herself and spits up blood.

"You didn't wait for three," Rob complains.

Jo feels their hands pick her up and place her down into a puddle of warm water. The blackness at the edge of her vision fades, then so does the pain. She opens her mouth and drinks some water on reflex, and it feels like the water mixes with her blood and disperses all around her body. She coughs, and it only hurts a little. Her breathing's slow and steady and soon she feels okay enough so to sit up.

"Easy, Jo," Lisa says, holding her down, the Keeper's plum eyes studying her. Jo cranes her neck and sees the entry wound, a two-inch circle in her gut. It's still there, and still bleeding.

"I thought I was better," she says, surprised at how strong her voice is. Her friends sit back, relieved. Lisa's blue hair isn't so spiky right now; she must have gotten wet in the pool. The room's steamy, the walls are close.

"You will be. The water first heals the inside, then helps your body on the outside. This type of injury will take time."

"We don't have time," Rob says.

"Do I not know that?" Lisa snaps, flicking her blue hair out of her eyes. More than ever before, Jo decides she likes her.

"Where are we?"

"In the private pool of a clanmate of Arcos. After you were hit, there was much chaos. We had to save you so we broke into the first place we found. We left Arcos behind."

"Where's Mia?" Jo asks. She remembers something, seeing her somewhere.

Rob and Lisa exchange a look. "We don't know," Rob says.

"We have to find her."

"We will, but first we have to find my father," Lisa says. "We have to stop the fighting."

"But, Lisa," Jo says, her mind beginning to work clearly. "Mia could be hurt. She doesn't know this place."

"Forgive me for pointing your wrong," Lisa says, her voice ice. "But Keepers are dying because Feileen's clan wants the source. My father apparently fights because he wants *me* to be of the Three. Either way, a new Keeper must have the source to end the dying, and to help I need to find my father and convince him to let Feileen have their own member of the Three. We must fix this first, then Mia."

"She's right, Jo," Rob says. Jo would roll her eyes if she could. Of course he's taking Lisa's side. "Mr. Kish wants the source too, and Mia will be with him."

"Wait," Jo says, suddenly remembering. "What about Brayden?"

Rob looks like he just swallowed a Sour Patch Kid. "He disappeared."

"What do you mean? With Mia?"

Rob shakes his head. "He was running next to me then he wasn't."

"I never trusted him."

"Enough," Lisa interrupts. "You are healed of a sort, friend Jo. So we must hurry."

"Will I be able to walk?" Jo asks, touching tentatively around the wound. She gasps. It feels like she's prodding a burn.

Lisa pushes her back under the water. "We leave in three hundred heartbeats." Then the young Keeper takes the bloody spear and cleans it in the water, like that's something she's done a dozen times.

The room is almost completely filled by the pool. There're a few gas lamps but only one is lit. The entire room is painted in stars, surprisingly realistic. This is like the romantic Jacuzzi of a honeymoon suite, minus a window or a balcony.

Rob's chewing the inside of his cheek, worrying about something, though Jo assumes the "something" is everything. His face is paler than usual, and there are bags under his eyes, which she didn't think was really possible with the water lying around.

Lisa, on the other hand, is vibrant. Her eyes are tense, capable, like all those years stuck in a penthouse training for an imaginary life have paid off. For the first time, Jo imagines her at Westbrook. Lisa's skin is as light as any of Westbrook's East Coast girls, pre-bronzer; she'd probably start a trend of plastic surgery induced eye-widening.

Outside, somewhere, there's a noise, the dull echo of thousands of voices screaming at once.

"What's that?" Jo asks.

"That is, my friend, our way home."

Jo leans heavily on Rob while Lisa leads the way, but with every step she feels stronger, the ache in her side more superficial. Lisa had cut a swatch of Jo's shirt off, so that now her midriff is showing. Jo keeps checking her stomach, watching the hole fill in, like an inverted scab.

Two Keepers stand at the exit of the building, watching the streets outside like a couple might watch a parade. They are extremely thin, almost gaunt, and draped in gray cloth that hangs to their feet. Something about them seems different. They lean against each other, their large eyes curious, and they blink in slow, languid time.

One of them, the female, says something to Lisa in their language.

"She says they have waited a very long time to see a Topsider," Lisa says, translating. The woman speaks again, and Lisa grins. "She says that you are weak and ugly, and she does not understand how you have survived so long."

Rob laughs. "I will never forget the day Jo's called ugly. Oh what a day."

Jo, though, finally gets what's different about these Keepers. They remind her of her grandparents.

"Lisa," she says. "How old are they?"

Lisa doesn't have to ask. "Many, many cycles. The Keepers from the beginning, most stay inside, in their pools." She gives a look that seems part sadness, part disgust, part pity. "They do not move. They do not eat. This, seeing them here, is very rare. My father would be this way, if not for the source."

Outside, a troop of Keepers in Arcos's red bound by. The two elders step out the door, as if to follow them, but instead just begin walking down the street, like they are out for a stroll.

"Where are they going?" Jo asks.

Lisa squeezes her arm. "To watch their world get torn apart."

. . .

They move through side streets, running progressively faster as Jo heals more.

"There are too many Keepers on the streets," Lisa says, after stopping them to let a few Keepers in Feileen's white and black run by. "We need another way to get to my father."

Lisa veers toward the outer edge of the city, and brings them into a three-foot-wide alley that runs parallel to the wall. There are no torches here, so they run in the dark, glimpses of Lisa's white skin their only guide. Sometimes they hit a break in the buildings, and a flash of light enters the alley, and just as soon they're covered in darkness. Jo accidentally bumps the wall, scraping her arm, but she doesn't really mind. This is the type of place, she realizes, where she needs to keep a grip on reality.

Ahead of them, another gap in the buildings. They run through, Jo grateful for any brightness, but they hear a shout. A trio of Keepers swerves their way. Without saying a word, Lisa picks up the pace. Jo tries to match it, but she's not herself yet and she quickly falls behind. Her stomach begins to tear, and she can feel the warm blood of her insides leaking down her leg.

She can hear the Keepers behind her now. Risking a glance over her shoulder, she thinks she sees someone. The glint of an eye. Big shapes in the dark. She hears their feet and their grunts and she keeps thinking this is like a nightmare, being chased in the dark, unable to see, running out of options. She presses a hand to her wound and tries to ignore the burn.

They pass another gap between buildings, and in the light she sees them: the three Keepers in black and white, each carrying a short, crystal knife; their blades look like icicles.

Lisa and Rob are far ahead of her now. She sees them disappear into the next alley. Jo doesn't stop, but when she hits the darkness again she feels alone. She has no idea how far they have to go.

"Rob!" she shouts.

Suddenly she's snatched up, two big arms snaking around her and lifting her off the ground. She screams and bites on reflex, then is disgusted to feel muscle and skin give way between her teeth, like the first bite of a chicken leg. Blood, coppery and warm, hits her tongue and she gags. The Keeper holding Jo screams in pain and drops her. His body is just a shadow, but Jo can still make out his arms sweeping down to strike down at her.

A spear thunks through the Keeper's chest.

Rob's there, pulling Jo to her feet.

"Go, Rob," Lisa says in the dark, her voice very close.

"No."

"I said go," she yells. Jo listens to Lisa and grabs Rob. Lisa's shouting in her native tongue, screaming at the Keepers, maybe telling them who she is. Maybe a war cry. Who knows.

"We have to help Lisa," Rob says, his voice desperate. It's dark still and she can only see his outline, but even that twitches with energy and fear.

"With what?" Jo shouts. "She's doing this for us. Now, run!"

He goes, resigned and reluctant. Jo manages to keep up with him. She spits out the Keeper's blood as they run.

They hurry on, and suddenly the alley exits into the main boulevard that separates the city.

Down the street, far down toward the entrance to the city, there are thousands of Keepers facing off against one another, reds and yellows and blues and all. They swirl in a blur of vibrant colors and pale skin.

"Crazy," Rob says at her side.

Straight ahead along the curve of the city wall is the tunnel. Twenty or more Keepers, all in Randt's yellow and blue, stand in a semicircular formation around the entrance. They're being pressed hard by the black of Feileen's Keepers, who are trying desperately to get to the source. Jo even thinks she sees the twins from the Exchange, their bodies twisting and turning, their ribbons prettier than any weapon should be.

"They're losing," Jo says, watching Randt's Keepers fall one by one. Oddly, though, they aren't retreating into the tunnel. They're holding their ground.

"That's good, right?" Rob replies, giving it only a glance. His attention is backward, to the dark, and Lisa. He's fidgeting, and Jo can tell he's an inch away from diving back in.

"Rob," Jo says, squeezing his arm, "she'll be okay."

Just then a small group of Keepers from a distant street hurries toward the tunnel. There are five of them, including Randt, who stands out even among his own, his clothing finer, his stature regal.

"Come on," Rob says, and hurries in the Keepers' direction.

"What are you doing?" Jo asks, catching up to him.

"Randt'll save Lisa," he says, his face determined. Jo feels a twinge of guilt—when she was injured, Lisa and Rob helped, but sticking around here is the furthest thing from her mind.

From the alley behind them, they hear a cry.

Everyone freezes, except for Randt. He knows that voice, it's like a beacon. In a blur he moves, pushing aside his own men like they are nothing.

Lisa stumbles out of the alley, an icicle blade in her back. Behind her are two Keepers, one bleeding from a wound to his neck. Jo stands helpless, watching them catch up to Lisa. Even Randt won't get there in time.

But then a strange thing happens. Randt raises his arm and barks a command. The faces of the Keepers on Lisa's trail go red and their bodies halt, paralyzed. Randt lowers his hand to the ground and they both fall to their knees. He's controlling them, Jo realizes. He can do that? Is that what the source can do, she wonders, unable to look away. Randt hasn't stopped running. He catches Lisa, puts her gently on the ground, and then moves to the terrified Keepers.

Rob pulls Jo along until they're kneeling at Lisa's side. She's breathing, but in quick short breaths. Rob freaking out, trying to stop Lisa's blood from flowing, but Jo's not worried; there's water nearby. Healing is only a drop away.

Randt puts a hand on each of the Keepers' chests. They're straining against some invisible forces, the tendons of their necks raised and their bodies shivering. Randt whispers a few words, and the one with the neck wound begins to gush blood; it spills out of him and onto the ground. The other's eyes roll back into his head, becoming two enormous egg whites, then they're gone; just like that.

"What did he do?" Jo asks through clenched teeth, not really expecting an answer. Her wound reopened and she's starting to feel light-headed.

Randt leans over his daughter, and with no hesitation, he yanks out the knife. Rob moves to cradle Lisa's head as she screams. Randt stares at him for a beat, then continues with calm precision, putting his hand on her wound and whispering, his eyes closed. His men stand in a circle around them, pressing in, and Jo realizes she isn't hearing any fighting. Randt's men are keeping the fighting out. Randt continues whispering, his hand covered in blood, and Jo's getting confused. Where's the water? Why isn't he just putting water on her?

Lisa stops screaming, jerks her head up and realizes where she is. Her blue hair is matted with blood, but otherwise she seems fine. She scrambles away from her father, huddling with Rob and Jo.

Randt holds his hands up, both red with her blood. "Daughter of mine. I thought you were taken from me."

"What did you do, Father?" she asks, her voice mournful. She flicks her chin toward the fighting down the street.

Randt's expression is cool. He stands up, wiping blood from his hands onto his clothing. "I suppose, then, that Arcos let you go. Good. It matters very little, because Arcos is trying to join Feileen's clan to create the same balance as before, even while they attack him. Stuck in his past, the idiot. We must end this; you must join me."

"Not me, Father. It *should* be a Keeper of Feileen's."

His eyes shift to Rob, then to Jo. "Your friends here, they have seen something. A map. But they do not understand what it is for.

218

They think it is about them. That it is about here." He shakes his head. "No, it is about something we lost long ago. Our time is now, the map beckons, and we must go Topside before the cycle ends. The Seven want us to follow. Feileen's clan, with Arcos's support, would never let me leave Capian. They would have all Keepers remain here, locked away. So I cannot allow a member of her clan to follow in her footsteps. I need you, daughter, I need you to be one of the Three. We would be safe then; Arcos is too kind, too cautious, he will never move against you the way I had to against Feileen."

"Wait," Rob interrupts her. "*You* killed Feileen?"

Randt's lips purse, annoyed. He ignores Rob. "I will take you, daughter of mine, and you will drink of the source. And Arcos will stop fighting because he would never support dethroning a member of the Three—it is too dangerous for himself. And then when I go Topside, you will rule here in my stead."

"You really did kill Feileen, did you not? This was your plan, to kill her and have me drink and then you would control most of the city? But first you wanted the map, and then I disappeared and Feileen's people fought back and you did not have enough time. And so our clans fight and die for nothing." Lisa says, disgust plain in her voice.

Randt takes a deep breath, the closest to regret Jo has yet seen him. "If we had moved quickly, there would have been no bloodshed." He pauses, looks at Jo and Rob. "I was waiting for the gates to open, and when they did, I was not expecting Topsiders to come with the knowledge of the map. It changed priorities."

"And the fighting will stop if I am of the Three?" she asks.

He pauses, thoughtful. "Feileen's people cannot overcome both Arcos and our clan. They must see this. It is the only way."

"What if they try to kill her?" Jo asks.

Randt almost snarls, he's so angry. "Do you think I cannot protect my own daughter? Do you think that any Keeper can stand to the Three acting in unison?"

Jo keeps her mouth shut.

Lisa looks at Rob, which startles Jo a little. They've gotten close very quickly.

"Do it, Lisa," Rob says. "They'd be lucky to have you as a leader."

Randt's bemused. "You are so very helpful, little one."

Rob pulls his OtterBox out of his pocket and powers it on, an act which drains even more of the battery. A jolt runs through Jo at seeing it.

"You think I'm helpful now—what do you think about me giving you a copy of the map you want so badly?"

"Rob, no," Jo moans. "We have no leverage without it."

Rob gives her a smirk, his puffy, tired eyes filled with a self-confidence Jo hasn't really seen since back at Westbrook.

"Randt, check it." He holds the phone up, on the home screen. There's almost no battery left. "On this thing is your map. If you let all of us go, I'll help you work it."

Randt's intrigued, and so are the other Keepers in the circle. The Topside technology is a hint of the world they only hear rumors about. Jo watches the awe in their eyes and realizes that this is only strengthening the case for them to go Topside. What they see, they want.

"I am not simple, Rob," Randt says, finally, with a dismissive shrug. "I will just take that from you and figure it out on my own."

"True," Rob says, giving the phone over to Randt. It looks so tiny in his massive hand. "But it's almost out of power. And while you might figure out how to make it work, it would be much easier if you had someone showing you the lay of the land. Like, think about it—would you even know how to make this *thing* work?

"Let us go—Mia and Brayden and Mr. Kish too—and I'll help you out up top."

Randt's eyes light up. "That is all? You would like to be my guide in exchange for your life? In this case, I accept, young Rob." He grabs Lisa by the elbow; she's too small to fight back against her dad. "Now, for everyone's safety, we must go to the source."

"But Mia's in the city," Jo pipes up. "We have to find her."

"First the source, then your friends," Randt says firmly, drawing a long, curved blade and resting it easily on his shoulder. He motions for Lisa to move, for them all to move. "As soon as my daughter drinks of the source, then we shall have another set of Three and the fighting will have to end. Now, come." His Keepers hold a protective ring around them as they move to the tunnel. "And please do ask my daughter how quickly I can take your arms from your body if you do otherwise than what I say." Drawn up to his full height now, all seven imposing feet, he stares hard at them and cries something in his native tongue. His whole army shouts a reply in return. They're ready to protect the source, and they'll need to. Beyond Randt's Keepers are Feileen's and Arcos's, joined now, coming fast. Jo's arms tingle despite herself. They enter the darkness of the tunnel, counting on the protection of the crazy man who keeps threatening to kill them.

Randt jogs and they follow. The mini-aqueduct vanishes into the ceiling of the tunnel and after twenty minutes or so they step into a wide room with a beautiful waterfall and swirling rock walls. Jo sees Brayden first, lying at the foot of the stairs curled in a ball, his arms tucked tight into his chest. Brayden's hair is thin and gray, his body small. She has trouble recognizing him, but for his Topside face.

"Where's Mia?" Jo asks, squatting next to him, taking him by the arms.

His eyes daze at her, his face a mess of wrinkles. Jo shivers. She's seen this before. She'll never forget it. He looks like her father did just before he died.

"Yes," Randt asks, his voice sharp. "Where is she? Where is the missing child?"

"What happened to him?" Lisa asks.

"You don't know?" Jo says, a bite to her voice. "You haven't seen this?"

Lisa just shakes her head, too stunned to speak.

"It's the virus," Rob says.

Randt looks at him. "The illness that afflicts your Topside finds its source here, yes."

Jo looks around at the waterfall and the pool rippling near her feet. "But . . . but where is she?"

Brayden seems to hear this because he points right at the waterfall.

Lisa steps toward the water, but Randt grabs her and pulls her back. "No, no, this is not the source. Do not touch it."

He bends close to Brayden, his face an inch away, close enough that Brayden flinches. Jo's right there too. She can see the veins beneath his skin.

"She is not dust? She went through the fall?"

Brayden doesn't answer.

Randt closes his eyes and Jo sees them move beneath his lids, searching left and right in the dark. Suddenly, he goes stiff and angry. "She did!"

And without another word Randt jumps into the water and splashes toward the waterfall. Lisa moves to follow, but he seems to sense this and he turns pointing a stiff finger at her. The water's not aging his body; the source must be protecting him.

"If for once, girl, you listen to your father, then let it be now. Do not touch this water. Not without me."

And then he's gone, into the waterfall, his outline fading quickly in the white foam.

"What now?" Rob says.

"We need to get some water to Brayden," Jo says, rubbing her thumb lightly across the thin skin of his forehead. His eyes flutter, and he moans.

"My father is responsible for all of this," Lisa says quietly. "I have seen his paintings of the Topside. He has taught me always to think of it as our future. But now he has hurt his clan. He has ended Feileen. He has caused this war. He is my father, and they will remember him as the great betrayer."

"Not if he gets his way," Rob says, muttering.

Lisa stands with clenched fists, heaving. But then her fingers unwind and begin to shake. She runs them through her blue hair in worry and whispers, "*Oh, Father.*" She slumps to the floor, keeping her eyes on the waterfall, waiting for him to return.

Jo stares at Lisa. Randt's not the dad she thought he was. He'll never be. Jo aches for her. She knows what it's like to lose a dad.

23

THE SOURCE SPINS ITS LAZY PRETTY CIRCLES AROUND me, like a charmed snake. I breathe in humidified air and close my eyes. I want to go back to the well. I want to be pulled to safety and see my mom. But something strange happens when I close my eyes. I can feel a pulse. Or maybe I can hear it. Whatever I'm sensing, something close by is beating, rhythmic and slow, and reminds me of my own beating heart.

I try to keep my thoughts on my mom, like a fleeting dream you can return to, but she's fading. The warm air saps my energy, making it difficult to stand. My shirt clings to me, tight and wet. I shake my head clear, but the sound won't go away. It's insistent. After swim practice, we had to measure our pulse. Maybe the source is amplifying mine. I put my finger to my neck, but can't feel a thing. I must be rusty, because I'm definitely not dead like . . .

Dad.

It hits me. *What am I doing? How long have I been here? Dad, Brayden. Am I stuck here, inside the source?* I think of Jo, the spear through her gut. I need water, and I need it now.

I step toward the edge. The cyclone is spinning so fast I can't think. But before I can even raise my hand, the wall parts, leaving a small hole just big enough for me to walk through. The field is the same, the flowers swaying and flashing like fans at a concert, their cellphones in the air. I can hear the noise, the beating, even louder now. My hackles raise.

"Hello?" I shout, stepping into the field. Suddenly, the beating grows faster and closer and then a huge Keeper comes bursting from the tunnel. His eyes are wide and enraged, his mouth open, and he yells, spittle flying from his lips. I realize it's Randt about the same time he lands on me, driving me deep into the greenery, so that the only thing I can see is his red face.

"What have you done?" he roars.

I scream, trying to get away but his huge hands grab my throat and flex, cutting off my air and my vision quickly begins to fade to black. I want to cry for help. I want to cry in pain. But I can't do anything. He's enormous, he's impossible.

"Answer me!"

Finally he lets me go. My throat burns and aches and I gasp for air. But even as I lie there, curled, the bruises on my arms begin to disappear and the pain in my neck subsides.

"You went into the source. I can *feel* it. How could you?"

He can feel me, I realize. And I can feel him. That beating I've been hearing . . . It's his heart. He watches me, his chest heaving, as I figure it out. Now that I know what to look for, I can feel other sounds, other beatings, glimpses of shapes and movement at the edge of my vision.

"What's happening to me?" I ask, holding up my hand and half expecting to see it waver in and out of existence. We're neck deep in the fields, and I can't see much farther than his shadow.

"Do not pretend, Topsider," Randt says, his voice under control now and angry as spit. "Your father came here for this, *you* came here for this. But there can only be ten, and yet you have drunk. The final place was for Lisenthe! You stole it from her."

"But I thought Feileen—"

"The source was meant for my daughter. For one of my clan. For the Keepers."

"I need to save Brayden. I need to save Dad. And Fenton. And—"

"The source will not help you or your city," he says, his voice rising again. "I have seen the rise and fall of Topsiders every cycle and it will not help. It is futile." He comes at me in two great steps. I can't move quick enough to get out of his reach. He grabs my hair and tosses me into the air, ripping a huge chunk out, searing my head. I can feel the blood already pooling before I hit the ground, right next to the source. It feels menacing now, an actual tornado spinning right behind me, blowing a gust of moisture into my face. Even in the pain, my scalp tingles and begins to heal.

"We are the watchers of life and we control the source," Randt says, shaking the handful of my hair into the air where it dissipates into the field. The glowflowers shine, lighting up his enormous figure from below, making him seem even bigger. "You have broken that now. If there can be only Ten, then you must be removed."

I struggle to my feet. The fact that Randt's here means that he's been through the waterfall. Is Brayden dead, now? Are all of my friends gone? Am I stuck here all alone? I stand up, my throat, my scalp raw.

"You can't kill me. I had the source."

Randt keeps coming, so I start walking backward. "Feileen was difficult. I had to cut her legs so she could not move, gag her mouth she could not speak, cut out her heart so she could not feel. But you, you know nothing. You *are* nothing. I can kill you with nothing."

I try to shake the terror from my limbs. He killed Feileen. He mutilated her. No wonder her clan is up in arms.

"But wait, what about Arcos? He's gotta know. Killing me isn't going to change that."

"Either Arcos chooses to ignore what he knows or he does not. He is an old friend and a new enemy. You are neither."

And then he strikes, blindingly fast, charging into me and knocking me down. He punches me so hard I can feel my face cave in. He punches me again, but I'm already numb. I hear the beating, loud and insistent, his heart right there above me, pushing heavy against his chest. I can't see out of one eye. The source is right next to us, shedding enough mist to feel like a rainstorm. I feel Randt's hand go into my face, feel the contours of his thumb hook into my bad eye and raise up my head. The pain slams through me, unlike anything I've ever experienced. But even still, I feel my body trying to knit itself back together, except this time, I'm losing the battle of speed and time. He's hurting me faster than my body can repair itself. I'm helpless. He smashes me back down. I stop struggling and lie there, tired of it all, and let his fist rise and fall and rise and fall. In a detached way I know I'm going to die. I feel his hand push into me as he punches. Up and down and up and down. But the rhythm is jarring. It doesn't match the beating of his heart. I can't help it. I just want it to stop.

Without thinking I raise my hand to adjust the heartbeat, just a tiny bit. I just want the sound to align. And the hitting stops.

Through my one good eye, through the smear of blood all over my face, I see Randt sit up and grab his chest. The beating slows now. I feel my face re-forming, my eye shifting back into place, like a marble in my head. The vision in my eye returns, blurry then clear. Pain sifts into focus, a dull throb as my bones reknit. Randt grimaces and reaches for me. At first it seems like he's going to hit me again and I flinch, but instead he's just looking at me, his fingers crooked. I can feel him trying to *reach* out to me, like I just accidentally did to him.

But nothing happens. The beating of his heart, once so loud, barely thuds. I sit up, watching him warily. He grunts, spits blood. It's a stark contrast to his white skin. "You should not know to do this. How can you know?"

"I don't understand."

He laughs at the irony, teeth red.

"I'm sorry," I say. I'm not sure I mean it, and I'm not sure what I did. But he looks hurt, so wretched.

Randt takes a ragged breath.

I close my eyes, listening to Randt's heart beat slower and slower and then stop.

He's dead, on his back, his eyes wide open and staring into the nothingness above our heads. His lips are bright red, as if he licked them with a bloody tongue. Flowers are already beginning to overtake his body, sprouting from between his arms and legs. Growing *out* of him. As if he were just part of the field.

I think I turned off his heart somehow. Is that what the source does? Lets you sense the heart, the very fundamentals of another person's life force, and then manipulate it—use it, heal it, extinguish it?

Sticking out of a pocket on Randt's chest is something black and box-shaped. I pick it up in disbelief. It's Rob's OtterBox. It's at 2 percent. I look at the map, the tiny shapes that seem to know me, that seem to speak to me. I see my father again, painted white. I see the spear. My instinct is to run, but instead I roll the phone around in my hand and try to focus. At the end of the map there is a Keeper—*maybe* a Keeper; I can't make that mistake again—and a stream flows through his torso, right into his heart. And then the screen goes black and the power's gone. I let the heavy phone slip through my fingers.

I close my eyes and feel a steady drumbeat on the edge of my consciousness, so faint it might as well be my own heart. Suddenly, four sounds, four beats come into focus. They're close, pounding, afraid. One's weak, sluggish. Somehow, I know whose it is.

Brayden.

I run, and my body moves faster than I know how to control. At the altar there are ten cups again, still a plain glass one but the blue and yellow cup, the one of topaz and sapphire, it's been replaced by a cup of deep emerald. I try not to think about it as I run by. The cyclone turns behind me, the source that gave me these strange powers. I don't look back, and instead sprint straight at the deadly waterfall. I don't stop, just jump, as far as I can go. I hit the waterfall and its weight pushes me down for only the briefest of moments before I'm through, landing in the pool. The water doesn't hurt me. It can't anymore.

I feel three strong heartbeats and see three faces, Jo's, Rob's,

Lisa's. Blond, black and blue. They're gathered around Brayden, who's curled up like a fetus, an old withering man, his eyes cloudy and white.

"Mia!" Jo shouts, and hurries to me, arms open for a hug.

I hold up my hand to stop her, happy she's alive and not wanting to kill her myself. "Don't touch me!"

She freezes.

"The water, Jo. It'll hurt you."

"Why isn't it hurting you?" Rob asks.

Lisa's watching, her eyes shrewd and knowing. "Because she has been to the source. The water will not hurt her." She pauses, grinning. "My father didn't stop you? He must not be happy. What a change of this world to have a Topsider be part of the Three."

I don't answer. My stomach is hit with shame and guilt, but now doesn't seem the time to tell her I killed her dad. I hurry to Brayden's side and kneel; he looks awful, his face screwed up in a thousand wrinkles, a wispy white beard hanging from his chin. His eyes are sealed in yellow gunk, like he has a bad infection. And he wheezes, a disgusting smell, like the inside of a garbage bin. Death itself, and then his heart skips. It's almost gone. With shaking fingers, I touch his lips. Lisa grabs my arm.

"You cannot give him the source."

"It doesn't work that way," I reply, not bothering to explain to her. I came here for the source, to get water for my dad, but after being stuck in the well again I realize that you can't just give it to someone else. You have to enter the source, and find it yourself.

I feel Jo's hand on my shoulder. Panicking, hand on Brayden's chest, I listen to his faint heartbeat. I try to focus on the feeling, on what a healthy heart might sound like, the rhythm and the noise. I'm getting the hang of whatever the source gave me. I'm a walking EKG. Great. But it *is* great because—and I don't fully understand how, yet—I give his heart a little nudge. It's like kicking a piece of coal in the fire. His body pulses with life, and I can feel the water I just gave him begin to circulate through his limbs. His eyes flutter, gunk stringing across his eyelids, and I wipe them clean with my shirt. Brayden groans, stretches, and as he does so his body seems to grow, to thicken and strengthen. He rubs his face, and pulls off a dead layer of skin, a wrinkled mask of himself. It smells like the locker room back at Westbrook and for a moment he stares at this skin dangling from his fingers like a newborn discovering his hands. He blinks, his scar gone, his gorgeous eyes alert.

"You're alive," I say, relief making me dizzy. I realize now that I have the ability to reverse—not just halt—the virus.

"Am I?" Brayden asks, his voice a croak.

"Apparently."

He smiles and reaches out to touch my forehead, and somehow, dizzyingly, I can see myself. I look pale, my lips nearly the same color as my skin. My hair's all over the place, covering my face, stuck to my sweat. I look feral. And terrified. I watch myself get more terrified. I watch myself through Brayden's eyes. *I watch myself through Brayden's eyes.*

"What the fuck is going on?" I whisper. It echoes through my ears. Through Brayden's ears.

Rob and Jo and Lisa watch me, their concern and fear flashing like beacons through their bodies. Etched in their faces. I close my eyes and can almost see the pounding. I can do more than sense their heartbeats. I can touch them.

"Jo," I whisper, holding out my hand, keeping my eyes closed. She reaches for it, and suddenly I can see myself again through her. Color drained from my face. I touch my cheeks and watch my fingers move. This is crazy.

"Mia, what's happening?" she says, not sure whether to be scared or relieved. I can feel what Jo's thinking, I can sense her confusion and rising alarm. I look at Rob *through Jo's eyes*. I can feel an ache in Jo's hip. Lisa's standing up now, and is watching me warily. She's looking at the waterfall, then back at me. Seeing her through Jo's eyes is disorienting and scary and I let go of Jo's hand and then there's only darkness because my eyes are closed.

"What is it?" Rob asks.

I breathe deeply, letting their heartbeats fade from my mind, and focus on what's in front of me, on the smell of the room and the warmth in the air.

"It's nothing," I say, looking at each of them. I don't want to even try to explain; would they want to know that I can see what they see?

"Friend Mia," Lisa says, her voice hesitant, staring at the waterfall. "Where is my father?"

She can see it in my face. She gives a small shake of her head. Rebellious or not, her eyes sheen with tears. She's trying hard not to cry, her pale chin quivering.

"He attacked me," I whisper. I don't want to hurt her, but I'm not going to lie.

"And you killed him?"

I clench my jaw. The others stare at their feet, shifting uneasily. "Lisa . . ." I pause, my stomach feeling queasy. "He hurt me, and I managed to stop him. I don't even fully get how I did it. It happened so fast."

"Go bring him back, then," she says. "Go restart his life like you just did Brayden."

I remember his body, the flowers growing through him. He'd be decomposed by now. "I can't," I say. "Brayden was still alive. Your father's . . . He's not even him anymore."

She comes so close her breath presses against my face. She raises a hand and I somehow don't flinch and then she lifts my hair, exactly where it had been ripped out. There's blood there still, I know. Her enormous eyes study me, calm and curious, but inside of her I feel the rage and hatred build. She presses a thumb to my cheek, right below the eye her father knocked in. It takes everything I have to let her do it.

"Lisa," Rob says, stepping forward.

"He hurt you?" she asks, watching me intently. I nod. Lisa swallows, pushes down her anger. "We have to stop the fighting," she says. I can't tell if she's trying to distance herself from her father's death, or whether she means it.

We're a pretty pathetic group, all of us covered in blood and grime. How can we stop a civil war?

"But Mia needs to bring the source," Jo says.

Lisa looks at her strangely. "Look at Brayden, Jo. Mia does not need to bring anything." She turns and begins to jog out of the tunnel, leaving the others looking at me. Rob shrugs apologetically, and follows Lisa, disappearing into the tunnel too.

"I'm glad she didn't just kill you," Brayden says. Physically, he's looking better, but his eyes are troubled, as if bearing a weight.

I think about Randt's body, the flowers, the source. We all have our weights to bear.

There are no more Keepers guarding the entrance to the tunnel. Whether that's good or bad is hard to tell, because there *are* Keepers strewn about, moaning or dying or dead on the ground. Others, thousands, still fight down the avenue. I see a blue and yellow Keeper go down with a cut to his chest and almost immediately another Keeper splashes water on his wound and helps him up. The Keepers can regenerate so quickly that the battle might be endless. The ones who are dead on the ground were hurt so badly the water couldn't help them. They have catastrophic injuries; I see many with heads cut off, some with a half dozen arrows embedded in their backs, others with two or three spears quivering from their chests.

As soon as I take a step from the tunnel, I'm hit hard by the insistent pulsing of all these hearts nearby. My knees wobble and I put my hands to my ears, but of course that doesn't help.

"Mia?" Brayden asks, holding me up.

Very slowly, deliberately, I try to push down the noise. I try to block it out, but I can't. It's like someone implanted headphones into my skull, and I can hear the beat internally. Like an alarm going off only for me.

"Where do we go?" Rob shouts, and I can barely hear him over the noise.

Lisa scans the crowd. "We find Arcos. He is the only Keeper left of the Three." I want to argue, to say we have to find Dad. I need to try to help him. I need to bring him back.

"No way," Jo says. "We need to go. We're done with this place."

On the edge of my vision I see a glimmer of light. The wall that circles this city is freaking *tall*, and I can make out the entrance to the city, the gates with their enormous columns shining. But there's something else there now, bright and moving.

A spark of light from the lip of the crater drifts lazily into the air and then seems to pick up speed, faster and faster until it strikes the side of one of the taller buildings. Arcos's building.

A flash, and I feel air get sucked from my lungs. The building explodes, the dome bursting apart and toppling down, crushing smaller buildings below in a flaming pile of wreckage. My mind can't process what I'm seeing.

Lisa cries out. All the Keepers stop and stare, their faces shining in the brightness of the explosion.

There're more noises now, small *cracks*, and gashes of light. I feel ill, remembering the sounds from Furbish Manor, the *buzz* of bullets whistling through the air. It's the sound of an attack.

"Sutton," Brayden says over my shoulder. I start so badly I lose my balance and slip, but he catches me. For a second I lose control and watch through his eyes, not mine. He puts his arms around me and we watch Capian on fire as if this was fireworks and not the end of this world.

24

JO TURNS TO BRAYDEN, HER FACE ETCHED WITH ANGER.

"You did this, didn't you? You did this again."

My stomach turns. I remember the moment he betrayed me back in the Cave. The moment he opened the back door for Sutton.

"What?" he says, raising his hands. "How could I? I'm here with you. I *told* you he sent me here to get the source. I've been with you the whole time."

"Who? For who?" Lisa asks. She's skittish, I feel it in her heartbeat and see it in her pale face; she's almost shivering. I don't blame her. Her entire world has changed in the blink of an eye.

"For Sutton," Rob says, trying to be helpful. "He's the one who replicated the effects of the waterfall water in a virus Topside. The guy who's responsible for the explosions."

The Keepers on the street stand side by side now, confused and distraught. Some are running to Arcos's tower to help. Others use the time to see to the injured. It's an opening in the fighting and I feel a little more in control of my body so I'm gonna take it.

I jog unsteadily to the mini-aqueduct in the center of the boulevard, toward where my father was, and the others follow.

Keepers run to and from the water, filling their little bags like firemen in a bucket brigade, rushing to help others. I find him there, his head bent over the edge by the weight of the spear. Blood pools around him, swirling in the water.

I touch his face, my shaking hands betraying me. His skin is clammy and cold, and I concentrate and try to *reach* out to him but am not sure it's working. It's hard to understand what you can't see, what you can only *feel,* and when I try to will his heart into beating nothing happens. I wait; the others give me a moment even though we have none to spare. But nothing happens. Maybe I can only heal the living, maybe I can't bring back the dead.

"Oh, Mia," Jo says, joining me. She hugs me from behind, but all I want is to make his heart start again. What's the point of this power if I can't bring back my dad?

There are more shots, many more, and it's clear that Sutton and his crew have made their way into the city proper. Another rocket launches, smashing another building, and the Keepers around us let up a moan. Their hearts flare up in my mind, the noise unbearable.

"We have to stop Sutton," Jo says, and I feel her rage through the warmth of her embrace.

"How?" Brayden asks. "He has guns. We have a spear."

"It does not matter. There is no choice," Lisa says, looking grim.

I move closer to Dad and put my hand on his chest. *Please,* I say to myself or to the source, the little bit of it that I have inside me.

"Come on, damn it," I grunt, pushing at him. He sloshes in the water. I push again, I reach out, I try to imagine his heart starting. I try. But I don't know what I'm doing. I don't understand or realize what the source has given me. The others watch me, and then Jo puts her hand on my shoulder and I stop, breathing hard.

I can't take him with me. I can't bury him. I can't do anything.

"What have you done?" a voice bellows, and we all startle up. Everyone near us is surprised. Hurrying our way, now armored in fine, shining red chain mail, is Arcos. He seems bigger than I remember, his bulk bulging from the armor. There's a gash on his forehead that's closing as he walks, and by the time he gets to us he's healed, and pissed.

"You brought them?" he shouts, pointing toward the gunfire. "Do you think I do not know of your metal pieces that rip open bodies? You think we do not understand how to make your gunpowder, that we do not have your charcoal or sulfur? You are unwanted, you usher in the death of Feileen, and now . . ." He stops, looks at me for the first time. His pupils dilate and I can feel something tugging at the edge of my conscious, like he's searching for something.

"What did you do?" he asks, his voice barely audible.

Lisa steps in front of me, hiding me in her shadow.

"She has taken Feileen's place."

"This is not possible. I cannot feel Keeper Randt. Where is he?" he asks, confused. He blinks rapidly, his face flustered, and I can almost see him reach out with his mind to find Randt's beating heart. I try to mimic him and extend my senses his way. Suddenly, the world around me flashes into color and heat, every person around me shining with energy and pulsing with light. Like little halos. Jo and Rob and Brayden, even, their skin tints gold and shivers with every movement. I'm getting tired, a headache growing on the spot, and I realize quickly that whatever I'm doing I can't do for long. Arcos, though, is unlike the others. He's a bonfire among twigs. He could turn into a phoenix and fly away and I wouldn't be surprised—the amount of energy pushing through his veins and out of his body is mind-boggling. Does he see the same from me, now that I've drunk the source?

"You abominate yourself," Arcos finally says, his lips flapping like bright butterfly wings. I pull back, let the brightness around everyone fade and take a tired gulp of air. "The Topside is dying, as are we. We keep and protect the source *from you.*" He pauses here, his eyes searching. The gunfire gets closer. Keepers nearby don't move. They're shaking, real fear of this new enemy swelling all around us. But I keep my gaze on him. He is, in some ways, the only one who's like me now. "And we failed," he says, almost to himself.

I gently touch my father's cold and lifeless hand. He has no aura around him, like a battery gone dead. "I didn't ask for this. For any of this. But it seems like now it's just you and me. And the real *danger* is them." I point down the street. "There's the man who's killing your people. Who's trying to get to the source. Who will use it in ways I can't even imagine." I stare him down. "You will help us leave. Stop this man, and I'll destroy the entrance to the well when we get back. No one will bother you again."

"But you drank of—"

"I'll leave, you'll be alone. The Seven are gone. You will choose Randt's successor and rule however you want to. Now help us."

He considers. The Keepers around look on eagerly. They don't want to be fighting one another. They're all cousins, they're all

Keepers, and just down the street is a threat that they probably used to whisper about in bed, the Topside, monsters from above coming down here to get them, to kill them. Trying to steal the source.

"You're Keepers. This is what you do. Keep it safe."

The big man takes on a shrewd look, and I can see I've got him. He buys my logic, or wants to. He can let me go and save face. Arcos turns to the Keepers near him and shouts an order. They let out a cheer and rush off, dispersing in all directions.

"They spread the news," Lisa says. "We are to keep together once more."

Many of the Keepers were dazed by the flames and the fires. But as Arcos's men run through their ranks, rallying everyone together, it's as if a spell is broken. For the briefest of moments there's a pause, and then the Keepers turn and run, straight to the sound of fighting, their bodies a blur of white and color, their sins forgotten. They run to do their duty, to protect the source.

Lisa makes to follow them, but Arcos takes her by the arm, his hand easily wrapping around her bicep.

"You are a clan leader now. You cannot be risked," he says, somewhat disdainful. She looks so small and young next to him. Her face frowns up in the rebellious way I've come to know, but she doesn't fight him.

"Girl," he says to me, "make their hearts stronger."

I don't get it, but then I feel him, pushing a flare of energy out of his body, and though I doubt the others can see it, I can. It zooms down the street, hitting Keepers in their backs, and I can feel their bodies surge faster, their colors glowing, their resolve strengthened.

He holds out a shining hand, and I take it, feeling him work through me, using my source of energy. I *see* how he does it now, how he pulls from me to feed the women and men who rush off to fight. It feels strange, but familiar, like the way my body drains during a good swim.

The Three weren't just leaders, they *made* things happen. Just as they took from Keepers, their thoughts and visions, they also gave part of themselves to their people to ensure health and good spirits and strength. They literally were the heart and soul of the Keepers. I gasp, exhausted, and Arcos breaks contact. He looks winded, his face sagging, and he stumbles. His honor guard, three Keepers and Palu, are here with us. They catch him, hold him up.

"We need to get him to safety," Palu says.

Arcos shakes his head. "No, we are the Keepers of the Source. I must be here."

They look dubious but stand down.

"I'm not staying here," Jo says. "I'm not going to just sit and wait. The Keepers have this under control—now's our chance to get back to the Cave without Sutton waiting for us."

"She's right," Brayden says softly in my ear.

Rob's watching me, waiting for orders. They've seen the change in me, and I wonder if they're afraid at all.

"We go. I should never have brought you here." I pause, a pain welling in my chest. I don't want to look at Dad; his body seems empty and unreal. I don't want to say good-bye.

"Little one, sister of mine," Arcos says, his deep voice genuinely worried, his pale face paler. I'm surprised at him, but then again, he just sucked my energy out of me to help his people. He was *in* me and my mind. Maybe he knows I'm not his enemy. "Stay. You can learn from me. I can teach you of your powers, of what you can or cannot do, of what life flows through you. You can keep. The others will go."

"I've got to keep my own people safe, Arcos. I'm sorry."

There's a loud explosion just up the road, and I see Keepers run for cover, white hands over their heads. I motion to my friends, and begin to jog down the boulevard toward the gates and the explosion.

"Mia," Lisa calls.

"We're not staying, Lisa," I say, my voice sharp.

She catches up to me. "I was not trying to stop you. Do not be impatient and a fool, running to the fires. I will guide you safely through the worst of this."

Down the road, there are thousands of Keepers charging into battle. I wish I'd told them that standing in tight clumps is the worst thing to do against machine guns.

"Yeah, okay, thanks Lisa. Lead the way."

"Come," she says, and turns sharply down a street and then into a tunnel. We follow, four Topsiders sprinting into the darkness.

We run underground into the tunnels and around for what seems like forever. I reach out with my senses and warn Lisa when I feel large groups nearby. Above us, tangled masses of Keepers push forward. Occasionally I sense a different feeling, a Topsider, but more than once the soldier's pulse is weak and dying. It sounds like we're winning. It *feels* like we're winning.

When we come out of the tunnel, there is smoke and wreckage everywhere. A building must have toppled onto the street. Lisa only hesitates briefly, then turns our way. "It is still the quickest path," she says, indicating the jumble of rock.

"Go," I say, nodding forward. Soon we're climbing over and through rubble, the dust almost suffocating. The fighting's closer, gunshots so near that we see muzzles flash.

Jo takes a step ahead of me and falls straight through a pile of debris, a scream escaping her lips.

My instincts are shiny and new, and I manage to catch her arm before she's under.

I feel it snap or tear or dislocate. She groans in pain, and I fall on my ass, trying to find purchase to keep myself from falling in after her.

Brayden grabs me around the waist, and Rob manages to get ahold of Jo's hand. We pull her up, slowly. She's covered with a fine dirt, her clothing brown and her hair sifting dust. She gratefully takes a sip from Lisa's water pouch and rotates her shoulder gently into place.

"I'm glad the water heals and all, but I wish I didn't have to use it," she says, in decent humor considering the circumstances. "You think everything's okay Topside?" she asks, suddenly serious.

For a moment, I try to figure out what exactly she's looking for. Does she want me to reassure her about her mom? About Fenton? Does she feel guilty for having stayed so long? I remember the argument we had when we first arrived, how she wanted to go back home. And I want to reassure her that the source that's in me now was worth it, is going to fix everything. But our dads are dead, the world we knew is gone. I can't just lie. I tug her hand, to let her know I'm here, to remind both of us that after all this, she has me and I have her. I need her. I have no one else.

I smile, and open my mouth to tell her that, but then I see the red dot appear on her chest.

"Jo," I whisper, quick and harsh.

"What?" She's oblivious.

"When I count to three, I want you to fall to the ground. Everyone. And then go back the way we came as fast as you can."

The red dot is connected to a red beam that swirls in the dust. Jo sees it now twitching on her chest and freezes. The others tense too, like deer in headlights.

"One," I say, reaching out with my mind to find the soldier with the gun, but I don't have a good handle on how to focus. Behind me I feel hearts beating, but I can't tell how many or who or where.

"Don't move," someone shouts over my shoulder.

"Two," I say, giving up trying to learn more about the soldiers. I can't try something I don't fully understand. Jo's staring at me, the dot still there. She's breathing hard but otherwise is calm, ready to dive, standing at the edge, trusting me.

"Three," shouts someone who's not me and then a *bang*, much closer and louder than I could ever have expected. Jo's knocked backward, right off her feet.

I don't even get a chance to scream, because a gun butt smashes into the back of my head and I go down to my knees, the pain making me gag for an intense moment. And then it fades. By the time Sutton and his four men have stepped into view on the mound of rubble, I'm feeling better. I scramble toward Jo's body, but a pair of hands grab my feet. I scream in desperation, my voice scratching against my throat. Jo's heart flutters and weakens. I'm turned over and find myself staring into the barrel of a machine gun, and when I make to get up the soldier presses the barrel into my forehead.

Soldiers move past me, covered in black gear, their guns raised. They glide like slow shadows among the ruins around us. Rob and even Lisa have their hands raised, but not Brayden.

"You didn't," I say to him, unable to even articulate the potential. I reach out for his mind but only see flashes of light, nothing coherent. I want to scream again. I just don't understand how to use the powers the source gave me. I can cast out a part of me, but I don't know what to do with what I find.

Sutton's boots *crunch* beside me.

"Brayden did," Sutton says, "sort of. Unknowingly, I'm sure."

Brayden charges at Sutton, but the Westbrook alum backhands him and sends Brayden to the ground. We're pathetic and weak and broken. Jo's not moving at all. Lisa's inching closer to her, and I feel a flair of hope. She has the water in her pouch. She can help! I reach out to make sure Jo's still got a pulse, and she does, but she doesn't have much time.

"He's lying, Mia."

I can barely hear him, I'm so focused on Jo. Brayden either betrayed us again or not, my best friend is dying.

"Brayden didn't tell us," Sutton says, assuring me. "The chip we planted in him did." He prods Brayden's arm. "What, that shot we gave you at Furbish? You think that was for the flu?"

"I have a chip in me?"

"Stopped working, you know, when you came down here. But as soon as we arrived here, the signal came through real clear."

Sutton approaches Lisa, taking her chin in his hand. So much for her sneaking over to Jo. She spits in his face. I want to adopt her.

"Interesting point this brings up," he says, wiping his face with his hand. "We're all made of water, but she's made of *healing* water. So why can't her spit heal me?"

"Why are you here?" Lisa asks, her voice hard. "Why are you doing this?"

Sutton manages to look semi-thoughtful. "A combination of Greg and my own dumb luck. Researching the water, creating the virus, it all leads here." Sutton's watching me now. Lisa doesn't know what he's talking about, but I do.

"Let me help her," I say, pointing to Jo.

"I'll let you help her when you give me the source. That stuff Greg always talked about's true, yeah?"

"I don't have it, it's on the far side of the city," I say, gritting my teeth at the mention of my dad. "Please, Sutton. Let me give her some water."

He shakes his head, his narrow face somehow believably regretful. "Don't believe you, little Kish. I know you came for it."

"We can't help you. You have to believe us," Rob says, his voice breaking. "If you studied the map, you'd know where the source is. Go get it yourself."

"I studied the map," Sutton confirms. My mental finger's on Jo's pulse, but she's almost gone and I'm becoming desperate. "I took copies of the high-def imaging. I broke it down like I broke down the water to create the virus. A map within a map, a world within the well. But even still, I wasn't sure. Not until you guys vanished into thin air.

"Oh, it took some guts to try it out. Had to really convince one of my men." He smiles, like he's recalling a happy time. "But once they made it here and back, we tied a line through to guide us, sent weapons down in the nifty plastic barrels your dad left for us and voila, I'm Christopher Columbus." His lips twitch, as if remembering something annoying. "The natives down here were still a bit of trouble."

"Leave us alone, Blake," Brayden says, getting to his feet. His face is covered with grime.

"Sure," Sutton says. "Where's my source water? Where is Greg anyway?"

He's asking me, so he sees me flinch. He has the decency to look taken aback.

"Well, that wasn't what I was hoping for. You know that, right? He brought it upon himself. Upon you for that matter. He never should have come here."

I'm so upset I can't speak. I get to my feet, the soldier's gun following my rise and settling on my chest. I look into his eyes, this soldier, this no one, and see that he's not happy. He's scared. He keeps glancing at Lisa, like she's an alien. His finger shivers on the trigger.

Sutton claps his hands together, scattering dust from his palms. "Okay, fine. None of this went the way we planned. But now I'm here, in this crazy place, and I'm going to get what I came for. Where's the source?" Around us, the fires still burn, the smoke making a thick fog. I can hear fighting. I can feel the heartbeats of everyone here, pumping fast and desperate.

We all look at one another. He catches that look.

"I *knew* you had it." he says to me, triumphant. "You are your father's daughter, huh? You actually went and got it yourself." He doesn't realize that the source isn't a physical thing, at least not like he's imagining it. I made the same mistake when I first arrived. But you don't just go and drink it. Sutton almost twitching he wants it so badly. I notice, for the first time, that he's got stubble, the makings of a beard. It looks like dirt all over his face and it reminds me that, like us, he's been going nonstop these past days. He'll never stop. All these years, all this obsession. He's like my dad. I can't deal with him anymore. I need to help Jo. "Fine," I say, "I have it. And if you want it, you have to let me help her."

"Doesn't work—"

"Fuck you, Sutton. I'm helping her."

He doesn't stop me, and I hurry to her side and roll her over. Her head lolls, and her chest is red and sticky. Her eyes are open, glazed. Her lips as full as ever. I touch her neck and can't feel a thing, I *reach* and can't feel a thing.

I motion to Lisa, who throws me her water pouch, and I drip the remains on Jo's wound and between her lips.

"So pale face here's got the source," Sutton's says, sure of himself. "And you're using it to bring back your friend."

"That's right, Sutton," I say over my shoulder, something I vaguely realize I shouldn't do. Of course he believes me. Why wouldn't he? "This is your precious stupid source."

"Wonderful. I knew you'd find it." He pulls a walkie-talkie off his belt and says into it, "Take it down. Fall back to the gate."

Yes sir, crackles the reply.

And almost immediately we see flashes around us, hear loud bursts of rocket fire. I tear my eyes from Jo to watch the bright swirls of light lob toward the wall above the tunnel entrance and then I lose them in the smoke.

"What just happened?" I ask, frantic.

Sutton holds up a finger, tips his ear to the sky, and then we hear it, explosion after explosion as his rockets smash into the wall, into the mountain. Into the source.

"You were right," he says. "I do know where the source is." He turns to his men. "Take them."

They come at us, but we're kids and they're soldiers.

Jo's not moving. She's broken and empty.

My body burns in anger and helplessness and I duck from the nearest soldier's black-gloved hand and leap, surprising him, knocking him to the ground. Around me I sense movement as my friends try to do the same. Lisa, especially, is a blur, her white skin and blue hair so easy to identify in my periphery.

The soldier outweighs me by a hundred pounds. He's trained and armed and wears protective padding on his chest and legs. But I realize something, something I learned from Randt's relentless beating back at the source: pain is temporary.

I scratch his face and feel his skin under my nails. He shouts. I go for every exposed surface. I'm a fury of untrained violence, and even still I realize that in a half second he's going to take control of the situation. *Pain is temporary,* I keep repeating in my mind. *Use it.* So I give him my left arm, just hand it over to him, which he takes and twists in some sort of jujitsu move so painful my eyes might pop out. I feel my tendons straining, but he has a knife in his belt and I need it so I accept the pain, swallow it, and reach for the blade. He twists harder, wrenching my shoulder from its socket. *Pain is temporary.* I scream, my throat scraping, pain now just a means to an end, and I manage to snag the knife. It's black-handled and serrated, and when I plunge it into his inner thigh, where I've been told an artery runs, it gives like a tomato: a little resistance then nothing.

His grip goes loose and I pull the knife. My arm pops into place on its own and begins to heal. The pain fades, temporary.

Lisa's done something devastating to her soldier and is helping Rob, who has no skills at all for this kind of thing and lies curled in a ball; she kicks out the back of his soldier's knee and I don't bother looking anymore. But Brayden needs me. I jump over a black-geared body and slide the knife into the soldier's back, trying to ignore how easily the blade slips through the padding and into his skin. He slumps onto Brayden, covering him like a fat sleeping child.

I don't have time to help him up. I need to get to Jo.

I whirl around, looking for her body in the dust, when suddenly I feel an ache in my bones, deep and unexplained. It freezes me, like what I might imagine a heart attack would feel like—a dark and helpless pain, and there he is, Sutton, a handgun trained on my chest.

"Where's the source water, Kish?" Sutton asks. His eyes dart around, seeing his men lost. "Give it over."

I don't reply, that unexpected pain still ramping through me.

"What does it do?" he goes on. "Did these albinos tell you?"

Sutton's ruined my life. It's that simple. He holds the cards now too, the gun steady in his hand. I know I heal quickly but I also know I'm not immortal. I doubt I could withstand a bullet to the head. But I'm not going to let him control anything anymore. *Pain is temporary.* I dodge left and hear/feel him fire, the bullet punching into my arm and spinning me. I dive for his legs and he shoots again, missing me, and we tumble to the ground together. I hear the satisfying *thud* of his gun falling to the rubble.

Lisa and Rob materialize beside me, then Brayden, and they hold Sutton down. He struggles, kicking up dust, shouting for his men, trying to buck me off. All the while, my arm shivers, pushes out the bullet, and stitches itself closed. I put my hand on Sutton's neck, as if to choke him, and I see myself through his eyes, my face fierce and my chin covered with flaking blood. My hair falls down around my head and I look terrifying. Good.

I feel for his pulse, and intuitively realize I can just sort of pinch his artery closed. Like I did to Randt, only this time I can do it on purpose. He's scared, his lips wet and brown eyes desperate.

Behind me, far away, Arcos sends out a pulse of warning and hurt. I can feel it—it's familiar, like his signature. He's incredibly upset. I try to focus, to gather his thoughts. Something's happened to the source.

"Why did you do it?" I ask through gritted teeth. Sutton doesn't understand what I'm asking. He did so many things, he doesn't know where to start. He's stopped moving and his chin's bent to chest, as if to protect his neck from me. He's sweating, panting, broken.

"Let me fix it. I'll fix whatever it is. I swear."

I shake my head, his voice barely registering. He's nothing now.

"The source," I whisper, finally understanding. "It's broken."

Lisa makes a noise. "The source is protected. It is *inside* the mountain for a reason."

There's no reason to argue with her. She doesn't get it. She doesn't feel Arcos in her mind. She doesn't know.

I let go of Sutton and move to Jo's body. Her eyes are lifeless. Gone. Her body's covered in a fine ash. From far away, she'd just be part of the rubble and dirt. I wipe my hand across her face, smudging the dust from her eyes and mouth. I know it won't work—she's as empty as Dad was—but I still try, *reaching* into her, pressing her heart to flare. But nothing. Her blood is cooling. Her mind is a black hole. For a moment the pain overwhelms me, and then I'm crying, my body shuddering uncontrollably, the tears dripping from my face. *My tears!* I tasted them in the well in the source. A flash of hope and I wipe my cheeks and wet Jo's lips and wait for her to wake up and smile and say let's go home. But nothing. She's still dead. Along with Dad and everyone else. The city around me is burning, its life draining away, and Jo's just one part of that. I wonder if Arcos feels my anguish, if he's looking our way and wondering what could be hurting me this much.

"Let's go," I say, because I have to. Because we can't stay here. I pick Jo up and drape her arm around my neck. She's heavier than me, but I try anyway and soon Rob's holding her other side, and we begin to shift through the rubble with her between us, like a drunk friend at Westbrook, only not at all.

"What about him?" Lisa yells, her voice pained. She and Brayden are still holding Sutton down. I reach out to his mind and feel confusion, hope and a tint of regret. It's strange, recognizing his emotions. They float like colors through his body. His mind feels like anyone else's I've touched so far, nothing special; he's pathetic and broken and desperate. Brayden's eyes bore into Sutton, and I can almost see the blazing hatred peel off of him into the air. I'm surprised I can't muster the energy. I'm tired of hating like that.

We could use him. If we bring him back Topside, he'll be able to control his men much better than I can.

"Pick him up," I say. "Bring him with us."

"You can't be serious," Brayden says. "He just had Jo killed. He's responsible for all of this. For your dad. For my parents."

Rob and I look at each other from across Jo's body. In some ways, he's all I have left. He shakes his head, just barely, his ashen face drawn and exhausted.

"We need him, Brayden. I'm done killing."

Brayden's about to protest, but he sees how serious I am. His lips thin, and I can feel him make up his mind. I can feel him take matters into his own hands. If I wasn't holding Jo, maybe I could have stopped him. If I knew how to control my powers, maybe I could have soothed him. But I don't make much of an effort to try.

"You might be done," Brayden says, "but I'm not." He slams a knife into Sutton's chest and holds it until Sutton's body stops jerking. Brayden shudders and appears to somehow relax, as if a weight just left him.

"I couldn't let him get away with it," he says, wiping Sutton's blood on his pants.

I'm too tired to answer. I know Dad wouldn't want me to kill, but I also know I'm not Dad. I chose not to kill Sutton. I don't have to be unhappy that he's gone.

25

THERE ARE NO MORE SOLDIERS. INSTEAD THERE ARE Keepers, swarms of them, chanting in unison. The streets are clogged, spears and swords and guns that were captured raised in the air. I don't feel cheered though. I'm empty and the weight of my friend on my shoulder is everything.

We're all quiet. And Brayden's hand on my arm does little to comfort me.

The Keepers let us through, Lisa calling in her tongue to clear the way. The streets are so crowded, the Keepers so tall, we can't see more than a few yards ahead.

Some of the Keepers we pass are injured, being fed water by their brothers and sisters. They seem to be congregating in clumps by clan, not mixing much. I see Keepers stare at their dead in disbelief. I see other on their knees, wailing. I don't doubt that there was a sore price paid for the guns that I notice some Keepers carrying. But then again, the Keepers had numbers, healing water, and a real insider's knowledge of the city.

The source flexes inside me, wounded but present, and for the first time I get a real chance to think about what it's doing to me, and what I can do with it. The people around me, these Keepers, the source takes each of their pulses as I walk by, and if I want to, if I pay attention, I can focus on the beating heart of any one person. Most of them feel relief, shock, overwhelming pride, and a searing, mounting pain.

Without warning, the group that we're wading through starts moving toward us, and it feels like we're fighting a riptide. Giant eyes stare at us as we go by. A couple Keepers stop and point at us; they even spit at us. Lisa talks them down, she yells them down. But I don't blame them.

The crowd thins, but even so, it takes a while to get to the steps at the edge of the city, the very steps that Straoc took us down. As we head up, making our way to a lookout landing, I can see the wreckage of Capian, the smoke and the fire, and a part of me can't help but feel a tug of guilt. On the landing, we find Keepers of all colors, and it isn't hard to figure out that these are clan leaders. They are better outfitted, their armor more decorative, their faces painted extravagantly in matching shades and accented by their loyalty to Arcos or Randt or Feileen—pearl earrings and a black necklace for one dressed in deep green trousers and vest, blue and yellow gloves on a sparkling purple dress for another. They stand in a semicircle and face Arcos, who sends them back to their people. At their feet, lined in a perfect row, are Topside soldiers. It's shocking, seeing the twenty or thirty men, their eyes closed, their black gear covering any bloody wounds they have. Next to them, a pile of guns and rocket launchers and a few things I don't even recognize. A Keeper, even now, is pouring what looks and smells like gas on the pile.

"I am sorry for your friend," Arcos says when he sees us. His face covered in sweat and grime, bobbing with each word. He touches Jo's cheek gently, genuinely sad, and I can *feel* that he's not lying.

"Me too," I say. "I'm glad you managed to stop them, though."

He tsks, indicating the city behind us, the smoking ruins of several buildings, the dead everywhere. "We did not win anything." He takes a step closer, close enough for me to feel the warmth and surprisingly sweet smell of his breath.

"You feel it, do you not?" he whispers in my ear.

I stare at him a moment. My friends and nearby Keepers gawk. Who am I, the Keepers must think, to get this attention from their leader? But I do feel it, I know what he's talking about.

"Something's happened to the source."

He nods, looking down at his hands. "The water's drying up. It has never been this way." It's hard to fully comprehend. I only just drank the source, so I don't have much experience in what powers the source actually does give me. But the dull throb of the heartbeats that I feel around me has changed; they aren't as linked to each other as before, as connected. I try to reach out for the source but there's an almost screeching sensation that runs across my mind as I do, like a scratched record.

"But I can still . . ." I pause, grappling with the words. "*Do things.*"

He sizes me up, most likely wondering what powers I've discovered so far. "Yes, me as well. The source must be damaged, off its axis and unable to spread through our aqueducts, but not destroyed."

"Can you fix it?" I ask.

"I do not know with honesty. And I am the last original Keeper of the source left. The tunnel has collapsed. I do not know, little Mia. My new sister. I do not know."

I'm quiet for a moment, imagining the source, the cyclone splintered and bent, broken into smaller offshoots. It pulls at me, and a part of me wants to help. But I can't. This isn't my world. I'm no Keeper. We have to get back and help our own.

"Will you be okay?" I ask.

"I do not know," he says, and I try to imagine him living here, feeling the ache of the source every moment. "I would hope you would stay and learn and be here. But I understand." His eyes go distant, and he looks up the stairs. "The water . . . You must hurry, you don't have much time," he says, louder, so everyone can hear.

"Wait," Brayden says, his voice as weary as I feel. "I thought we had, like, eight days or something before the gates closed."

Arcos shakes his massive head. "You do not understand. The source is damaged. The water does not flow correctly. We have to take as much of it as we can, at the very moment, or it may be gone forever."

Lisa slips into her own tongue, but I can still hear the alarm in her voice. Arcos is kind enough to answer in English.

"The gates open only because of the water, so without it, they are closing early, ending the cycle."

I share a look with my friends and we go, pushing past him up the steps. Arcos calls to us. "Remember, sister, you took of the source. It is in you."

I don't look back. We can't get stuck here. We can't.

"Push it, guys. Double-time!" I slip into coach-speak on instinct.

"Here," Lisa says. She hefts Jo up, fireman style, and begins to jog up the steps. I don't have time to gape. We run, not about to get stuck here for seventeen years or maybe for forever. I risk a glance out over the city and see the wreckage below, the true devastation Sutton wreaked with his men. The wall holding the tunnel is crumbled and distorted by dust, chipped away and calved like a glacier. The entire city, lit by gas lamps, is a combustible playground and there are fires and small explosions everywhere. It looks like what I'd think of hell. An underground city of fire and brimstone. But it's not. Not at all. Those are innocent people, hurting because of us, and we aren't staying to help. I try not to think of what they will do if the water runs out. How long they will survive. I try not to wonder if they should all be running with us.

We crest the rise out of breath and aching. My body quickly gets over the pain, and for that I'm grateful, but the others don't have it as easy. Even Lisa's hurting, doubled over and taking in huge hunks of air.

Arcos was right; the gates are closing. They're three, two feet apart, and I can hear the groan of the hinges pulling the massive weight together.

"Run run run," Brayden shouts, and we do, pulling the last reserves from our feet.

A smallish soldier's standing near the gate's entrance, most likely waiting for Sutton. The lone member of the rear guard. He raises his gun and shouts for us to stop, but we don't. We don't have any weapons, so I sprint harder and get in front of the others, ready to take a bullet, but the guy doesn't have it in him. He knows something's wrong. He also knows there's no time. So he lowers the gun and passes through the gates five steps before I do. The things are so big, so tall that I can't fathom *not* being able to squeak through their arms. But when I get there, the gold bars squeeze my shoulders. I turn and hold out my arms for Jo and Lisa passes her through, her body a weight I can barely hold. The soldier, a skinny young guy, no more than twenty and still pimpled, surprises me by helping out. We get her through and lay her on the ground. Brayden clears the gate, then Rob, who turns around and holds his hand through the bars for Lisa, beckoning.

She hesitates, then shakes her head, her blue hair a blur.

"I cannot leave them. Not as it happened today. My father would not want it."

Rob opens his mouth to speak, maybe to disagree, maybe to say what he really thinks about Randt, but he stops himself. Rob never stops himself from speaking. *We have to go,* I mouth to him.

Behind her there's the sound of another explosion. Some building falling. The gates pull closer. Lisa grimaces. She looks back over her shoulder at Capian, unsure. "But I have nothing here left. Not anymore." She hesitates, then her lips curve into the barest smile, a little of her former self cracking the surface, a little of her hope shining through. And she lunges forward, squeezing her tall body sideways through the gates. It's tight enough that Rob has to pull, that her shirt rips, that the side of the gate leaves a gash, that they fall together on the ground.

For a moment they laugh and rest against each other but we don't have time for more than that.

"Come on," I shout. "We have to get to the lake."

We struggle up, but the soldier hovers, watching the gap close to nothing.

"Where's the commander?" he asks. He's having a hard time not staring at Lisa, who's bound to be his first Keeper.

"He's dead," Brayden replies. And I realize that he's asking Brayden. He's probably seen Brayden before, knows that he's been helping Sutton. "So are the others. If you want to make it out of here, you gotta come with us." Brayden doesn't even wait for an answer, just runs past the soldier toward the lake. After a moment, the soldier follows, which I'm glad for. No need for anyone else to get hurt.

The lake is dark, the glowflowers fading. The water's receding from the edge rapidly, and at the shore we can make out a slow whirlpool, like a drain emptying, spinning loudly in the center of the water. Fish of all shapes and sizes twitch and flop on the mud. In the faint light of the forest edge I make out a half-dozen blue barrels, lying about. The ones Sutton used to bring the weapons, the same containers Dad created to store water.

"If we don't make it," Brayden says, "we'll be stuck between the gates and the well."

"Trapped," I murmur to myself. Then I turn to Lisa, who's still lugging Jo's body. "Give her to me," I say. "I'm the best swimmer."

Brayden puts an arm on my shoulder. "It's dangerous to take her with us through the well. Maybe we need to leave her."

I round on him. "I left my dad in there. I'm not leaving Jo too."

Brayden raises his arms, surrendering. "Okay, okay. They brought their guns, we can bring Jo."

"Guys," Rob says, pointing to the receding waterline, at the tree roots exposed along the bank. It's moving faster.

We trudge through the wet muck of the waterless lake bed, though the mud makes it hard going. But we get there, into the middle of the lake, where the water surrounds us, rewarding the others, relieving their pain and giving them energy. With the source in me, I don't need it. I lean back and put Jo's body against my chest and then swim, outpacing the others by far. Jo would have kept up. The water splashes her face as I swim, and I see her like I've done a thousand times—at the pool, coming up for air, her eyes closed. She never used to smile after a good dive. Not even after a perfect one. She won't be smiling anymore.

Somewhere in the middle of what's left of the lake, I turn and watch the others flail through the water, especially Lisa, who's had no real practice swimming. Brayden and Rob are pulling her along, her ashen body splattered in mud, but she's not afraid; this is her healing water. She knows she can't drown in this. Even the soldier plods steadily on, intent on the new mission.

The swirling in the center of the lake is near, and I feel it tugging on me. I feel something else too, the heartbeats of my friends, like little beacons in the water. I don't even have to look to know that they've caught up with me.

"Hey soldier," Rob asks, spitting water from his mouth. "Are there guys on the other side, ready to shoot our brains out?"

"I . . . I don't know. Maybe one or two." His teeth are chattering and he looks like he's about to cry. He's so small in all his huge black army gear. I almost feel sorry for him.

"Whatever happens, happens," Brayden says, slicking hair out of his eyes. "We know we can't stay here."

"We're going," Rob says, taking Lisa's hand.

Rob's thin face is serious and scared—swimming into a toilet bowl is a lot more daunting than jumping into still water. He looks at Lisa, her blue hair slathered across her white forehead, her eager fear. "Just keep swimming down. I'll hold your hand the whole time, okay?"

She nods. They push into the whirlpool spinning slowly around in the darkness of the water. They gulp air. And are gone.

I point at the soldier and to his credit, he goes, disappearing under the surface, his black boots flailing for a second before he's gone. I reach for him to follow his progress and hear a few unsteady beats, then nothing. He could be dead, he could have made it. I'm not sure.

"You ready?" Brayden asks me as we wade together.

I'm not, not really. I spin Jo around to face me, her skin as white as a Keeper's, her blond hair scattered around her in the water. I wish I could say that her closed eyes make her look peaceful, but they don't. She looks hollow, empty. She looks alien to me. Not at all Jo.

"Mia," Brayden says, softly but with real urgency.

I have to take her. I have to. Mrs. Banner already lost her husband and now her daughter, and I owe it to Jo.

I turn to Brayden, and notice something different about him. I can sense that he's scared, watching the dwindling water. But there's more. I don't fully understand what the source has given me, but I can feel an invisible piece of him trying to cover me, to envelop me. It's like I can feel his pulse louder now, closer. I can sense it reach out from him and touch me, warm and comforting, wrapping around my shoulders.

I take his hand and then, with Jo in my arms, I suck a deep breath and dive. She's like a weight at first, making it easier, and I swim down and down, feeling the water rush around me.

I can't see anything. I thought this would be easier the second time. But already my lungs feel empty and strain against my chest. Even with the source I can't not breathe. Something moves past me, quick and dark. *Brayden,* my mind screams, but he's gone. How did he pass me? How *could* he pass me?

For some reason, Jo's hard to move. She's weighing me down, as if she's sinking back toward where we came from. Did I get turned around? I shoot out a hand and hit stone. I look up and down and still can't see anything. Panicking, I reach out with my sense and feel something, a beat, very soft, very far away. I swim for it, frantically, but I'm not getting closer. She's pulling me back. She snags on something. I'm killing myself.

Before I even admit what I have to do, I do it. And she's just gone. Like she was never there.

I stare into the blackness below me. I hurt so badly I go numb. I drift, alone, and for a moment I want to stay that way. But then I feel the hearts above me, my friends and others, many many others. And I let go, leaving Jo and my father behind. I follow the sound of my home, beating for me.

EPILOGUE

He takes my hand and pulls me from the well, my clothing soaked, water splashing onto the railing. The water behind me makes a sucking noise and slips away to wherever it goes, maybe forever.

I hug Brayden fiercely. I hold him tight. If I stay like this I don't have to move on.

"This is Topside?" Lisa asks, her voice carrying a clear note of disappointment. "Looks a lot like my world." She's right. The well is situated in the midst of a giant cavern, filled with the same trees she had in her home tower and gear set up to extract the liquid. Those trees will slowly start to die, now that the water's gone. A long wide orange hose dangles over the railing and leads to a pump that's still on, its engine grinding loudly now that there's no water left to pull.

"Yeah," Rob says, "but don't worry, it gets better."

Brayden doesn't ask me about Jo. No one does. I'm grateful for that.

The soldier shivers on the floor, his hands locked tight around his gun. Water streams down his chin and drips on the floor, and he sucks snot into his nose, on the verge of crying. Brayden lets go of me and steps to him, his hand outstretched.

"Where is everyone? What is happening?" the soldier asks. "Drummond and Winter were supposed to be here."

"I need for you to be quiet," Brayden says, and then points to Lisa. "And I need that gun, or I'll sic her on you."

The soldier doesn't need much convincing. This is beyond the pay grade of a gun for hire. He hands over the rifle and slides backward on the ground until he hits the railing. I see, now, that he has a name tag stitched into his shirt. Shoemaker.

"Looks like they still pumped plenty," Rob says, scanning the room. I follow his eyes, and see the giant blue containers sweating with water. Good. At least Sutton wasn't dumb enough to use all the barrels to transport weapons below.

Rob sways a little in place, clearly exhausted. So is Brayden. We haven't slept in forever. The source is keeping me going fine, but it looks like the water isn't enough to stave off exhaustion from my friends forever.

A ringing *thud* comes from the elevator, and we all jump. I crouch, as if we could actually hide down here. The elevator door's jammed open already, probably forced by Sutton's men, but I can't see anything inside from this angle. I look back at the well; it's a gaping black abyss, no longer a place to run to.

"Not after all this," I murmur. Brayden takes my arm, positions himself in front of me with the rifle raised. I wonder if he even knows how to work the thing.

I hear footsteps like someone's stomping in place, and I reach out with my mind and feel a pulse. Just one. I'm relieved; just one means we have a chance.

A pause, and then a middle aged man with a semiautomatic steps from the belly of the elevator. He's big, and wears the same gear Shoemaker has on, though he unstraps a helmet and throws it to the floor. He has a huge smile on his face, like he's our best friend.

"I thought I'd never see you again," he shouts, and then lets out a laugh of disbelief.

"Jimmy?" I say. It *is* Jimmy. His adult self never really seared into my mind. He looks buff and awesome, with hefty facial hair, kinda like a modern Hercules.

"Didn't recognize old man Jimmy?" he says, walking toward us in big strides.

He slows on seeing Brayden, his expression troubled. "Mia, you need to be careful of—"

"I know," I say, stepping in front of Brayden, as if to shield him from suspicion.

Jimmy shakes his head stubbornly, tightens his grip on his gun. "No, we saw Sutton send him in. They were on the same side."

Jimmy doesn't know what we've been through, so I can't blame him for trying to protect me. "He's fine. Trust me. What's happened here?"

Jimmy huffs, but then sees Lisa for the first time. He squints, as if to get a better look, but beyond that he manages to hold it together remarkably well.

"Long story," Rob says. "This is Lisa. She's with us."

"All right then," Jimmy says. He picks up Rob in a giant bear hug and spins him around. He laughs. We all do.

"Where's Odessa?" Rob asks, when Jimmy puts him down.

"Where's Jo?" Jimmy replies, noticing the absence for the first time.

I shake my head, and he doesn't press further, understanding immediately. His face falls.

"Jimmy," Rob says again, "where's Odessa? What happened here?"

Jimmy rubs his head, his big brows furrowing.

"Oh no, did the virus come back?" I ask, my stomach sinking. "Is she okay?"

"Odessa's fine," he says darkly. "She's out delivering water."

"Then what?" I ask.

"The virus spread."

"To Fenton?" Rob asks. His parents are there. I feel a shiver up my spine. So are Jimmy's.

Jimmy shakes his head, staring at his feet.

"Not just to Fenton. It's gotten to Denver, to New York. It's all over the place now," he says, his body racked with sudden sobs. He falls to his knees. As if making a confession. As if *he* were responsible. "It's everywhere."

I try to push away the news, to deny it. But when I reach out with my newfound talent, I can feel Jimmy's heart, and the ache there. Beyond him there's the rock face that the map had been dug out from, a perfectly cut square of rock pulled out of the wall and taken to be mounted in the Map Room. Randt wanted the map because of the others. He thought it a guide, but I know better. It's a prophecy. It tells of Dad's death, speaks about everything that's happened. But if I was meant to go below, then I was meant to have found the source. And I was meant to return here.

I close my eyes and I move my sense beyond the room. But there's almost nothing. A beat here. A pulse there. A pocket of people aging together. I reach farther and farther into the world and find it dying, crumbling into itself, afraid and alone.

But there's something more. An insistent buzzing, a vitality I haven't felt since I stood in the center of the source. And it's coming from me. I touch my hand to my chest. I'm aware my friends are watching me. That all conversation has stopped. I'm aware they're confused and growing alarmed. They shouldn't be. Inside me the water is flowing, thick and loud, pounding like a second heart. Maybe Dad was right. Maybe I carry a sapling inside me, a sprig of the source.

I squat and touch the cold stone of the Cave. A part of me wants to move, wants to drip from my mouth or tears into the ground and take hold. It's as if the source is begging me to let it go, to release it right here so that it can begin again, Topside.

"Mia?" Brayden asks, at my shoulder.

I don't answer. I can't. Instead I spend all of my energy holding myself back, forcing the source to retreat inside, to stay there just a little longer. I smile to myself, and feel the others relax around me. I'm not sure exactly what I can do. I'm not sure what it means to release the source, or whether I can release it more than once. But I feel it, this life stirring inside of me, ready to take root and grow and grow and grow.

ACKNOWLEDGMENTS

A second novel is much harder than a first, for some obvious and some surprising reasons. To everyone who helped me get through the many drafts, I am very much in your debt.

Stacey Barney, I'm not even sure how many times you read this. I know how hard it is to maintain enthusiasm and editorial consistency but you did, and I am entirely grateful for all the support and guidance during the process.

Kirby Kim, my agent in crime, I'll follow you anywhere.

Kate Meltzer, for your last minute encouragement around the clock.

Brenna English-Loeb and the team at Janklow & Nesbitt.

I want to prethank Emily Pan, Tara Shanahan, Bri Lockhart, and Mia Garcia, my brilliant and creative publicity, marketing, and con team.

To my incredibly diligent, helpful and wise copyeditor team: Ana Deboo, Cindy Howle, Rob Farren, and of course Chandra Wohleber—thank you (I hope the punctuation inthis paragruph isnt two problem-atic!?!).

To Zarren Kuzma and Dana Bergman, my paperback editors, I couldn't be happier to have (or have had) you on the team.

And big thanks to Jennifer Besser, Richard Amari, Vanessa Han, Eileen Kreit, Erin Dempsey, and all the incredible Penguin evangelists who hit the road around the country and are such advocates for *The Well's End* and *The Dark Water*.

Extreme gratitude to everyone else who's played a role in these books, the bloggers and mountaintop shouters, family and friends, but most especially the readers who came back to find out where the hell Mia went when she fell down that well.

To Michelle Kroes, for my west coast translator.

And to my clients, for their incredible and generous enthusiasm.

Finally, my wife Marget. Your support, your kind words, your patience; I couldn't have done this without you, especially not this year, when our lives changed forever.